Unbreakable

An Alessi Brother Series

Sonia Stanizzo

Contents

Chapter One

PENNY

As I stand backstage at Madison Square Garden, my heart is beating hard and fast. I place a hand on my chest, take a deep breath, and will myself to relax.

Relax! How can I relax with fifteen thousand people out there waiting for me?

They have come to watch me cook, decorate, plan a party, and learn to organize their homes. Who would have thought when I started my little YouTube channel eight years ago it would blow up to this scale? Not me, that's for sure. I used the platform as a creative outlet. Shy and introverted, I was happy pretending no one was watching.

My mother, Elizabeth, who is also my manager, sidles beside me. Her blonde hair is styled in a neat chignon and pearls decorate her neckline. She's wearing a blue and white floral dress that flares to the knee, and a white cardigan is draped over her shoulders. She radiates true southern elegance.

"Sweetheart. How are you feeling?" she asks. We moved to New York City from South Carolina eleven years ago, and we have both lost the southern accent.

I swallow hard. "Like I'm going to throw up." You'd think I'd be used to this by now. I've been thrown in the public eye and have done multiple presentations and shows—just not to this scale. I've filmed a TV series on Netflix, and yet, I'm still that shy and introverted girl.

She fluffs out my hair and brushes the locks off my shoulders. "They are here to see you. Keep it together."

If that's a pep talk, it sucks. Although I'm used to it. She's not one for showing an abundance of loving encouragement. She's all business and making sure I do it well and don't screw it up.

"I'll try," I say.

Positioning herself in front of me, she adjusts the collar of my navy blouse. Her gaze travels the length of me. If her forehead could crease, it would, because I can see distaste in her expression. "Why aren't you wearing the Gucci skirt I bought you to go with this top?" she asks. "It's much more flattering than what you have on."

By *flattering*, she means the skirt she bought makes me look thinner. Will she ever accept that I'll never be a size two like she is?

"I didn't think wearing an eight-hundred-dollar skirt to the show was appropriate when I'm teaching an audience how to decorate on a budget," I reply.

My mother rolls her eyes. "You are successful. There is no shame in showing how hard you've worked to get where you are. If anything, wearing expensive clothing tells people they too can be in the position you're in if they try."

I don't have time to argue with her, the MC is revving up the crowd and listing off all my achievements. When she calls my name, my body grows cold, and my feet don't budge. *I can't do this. What was I thinking? Madison Square Garden is for rock stars, not little nobodies like me!*

Before I can turn and run from the building, my mother nudges me from behind. Breaking my frozen state, I stumble forward.

"Good luck. Don't forget to..." My mother's voice gets drowned out in the applause.

As I step onto the stage, the vibrations of thousands of people blast into me. Like I'm being hit by the pressure from a wave. The golden light following me is blinding. I have to stop myself from shielding my eyes. I've never been in front of so many people.

An adrenaline hit shoots through me, and I walk to the table set up in the middle of the stage for the demonstration without tripping over my feet. Waving, I smile and pretend I'm the most confident person in the room. Inside, I'm a shaking, scared mess.

Standing at the table, I wait for the audience to sit. I use the moment to take a deep breath to steady my racing heart. I look over the sea of faces, and my chest swells with joy. I've done a lot of great things with my career, but a live show at Madison Square Garden tops it all. My career is skyrocketing. I'm getting married tomorrow. My life is perfect. My life can't get any better than this.

I start the show and talk to the crowd. My body begins to relax. Once the nerves settle, I feel more in control. *I've got this. I know what I'm doing.*

Behind me, the big screen that's set up to show everyone a close-up of what I'm going to make, flicks on. First up is a cooking demonstration. All the ingredients to make garlic and tarragon butter beef skewers are set up in transparent glass bowls. It's a recipe that is simple and easy, yet delicious. A dish I'll be including in my cookbook.

Step by step, I tell the audience what I'm doing. Then something seems to happen to the speakers, because I can no longer hear my voice. There's a muffling noise. Then a second later, gasps ring out through the arena. Confused with what's happening, it takes me a moment to understand what's coming from the speakers. Sounds that have nothing to do with cooking echo through the room. My brain isn't comprehending how it's possible. I glance into the wings. My mother is covering her mouth with her hand. Her eyes, as wide as dinner plates, are staring at the screen behind me.

A producer comes rushing to me, grabs my arm, and pulls me toward backstage. "Don't look at the screen," she demands.

Of course, when she says that, it only makes me want to look. Tugging my arm free, I turn and stare up at the screen. The nausea I felt earlier before walking onto the stage is nothing compared to the waves rolling in my stomach and clogging up my throat. The sounds I'm hearing now make sense. A video is playing of a man jackhammering into a woman bent over a desk. A desk I know well because it's in my home office. And the man having sex with the woman is my fiancé Darren.

I thought my life couldn't get better.

I've just discovered it can get a hell of a lot worse.

⸺◆⸺

Sitting on the king-sized bed in the penthouse suite of The Plaza Hotel, I flick the red rose petals off the plush bedspread onto the floor and drop onto the mattress, bouncing slightly. My best friend, Claudia Lockwood, sits on a chair next to the bed with a sympathetic look.

"How could Darren do this to me?" I wail into my champagne flute. Almost done with this bottle, I eye the Dom Perignon chilling in the ice bucket. *Don't worry, I'll get to you soon. I need you to make me forget the chaos happening in my life.* With Darren's affair broadcasted in the news and social media, I might need more than two bottles.

I scan the room and wince. After the news broke, I didn't expect to find the room decorated with romantic honeymoon aesthetics. Another reminder of my humiliation. Well, I got what I paid for even though the wedding is dust. "Th-this should be my wedding n-night." I hiccup.

"It's doing you no good staying here and getting drunk. It's upsetting you. Just because you booked the room and had your luggage delivered here doesn't mean you should have left my apartment," Claudia says with a comforting tone.

I had spent last night at Claudia's house. When I woke up, I asked her to bring me to the hotel. There was no way I'd go home. What if Darren was still there? I walked out on him while he was groveling and spewing excuses about his behavior. There was nothing he said that I wanted to hear, and I never want to see him again.

My spine stiffens. "And let Darren and his new girlfriend use it? Because he probably wants to shack up with her here too. No way! This-s i-is my room." I point my glass toward Claudia. Alcohol splashes onto my hand, and I suck it off my skin. "I hosted a party for her. I taught her how to make swans out of table napkins!"

"Penny, give me your glass before you spill champagne everywhere." Claudia reaches for the glass. I hold it up over my head so she can't take it. A few drops land in my hair.

"It's mine." I quickly lower it to my mouth and gulp the rest down before she can stop me.

Claudia shakes her head.

I slide off the bed, stumble on wobbly legs to the ice bucket, and pluck out the Dom Perignon. Popping off the cork, I don't bother with a glass this time, just drink straight from the bottle. I hold it out to Claudia. "Want sum?" I hiccup and sit back on the bed.

Claudia frowns. "Don't you think you've had enough?" I can see the concern on her face, but my life is too much of a shitshow to care right now.

"Nup. I'm drinking until I forget about Darren and Karen." I slap my hand over my mouth and giggle. "*Darren* and *Karen*. Their names rhyme! Oh, they are so meant for one another." A second later, my laughter turns to sobs. "They've ruined my life. How am I ever going to face everyone again? My followers think we had the perfect relationship. We were filming a Netflix series about our wedding. They were getting set up to film the finale—our wedding day. I'm such a fraud."

As I start to lift the bottle to my lips, Claudia leans forward in her chair and snatches the champagne from my hand.

"Hey, when did you become a ninja?" I ask. She had moved so fast she blurred.

"The alcohol has slowed your reflexes. Another reason you need to stop."

"I need it to numb the pain." I shoot out my hand to grab the bottle.

With her ninja-like moves, she hides it behind her back. "What you need is to get out of this depressing hotel suite and sober up. Let's book another room."

Flopping onto my back, I splay my arms out wide and stare at the spinning ceiling. "She's a supermodel. Of course he'd screw someone who is in his league."

The mattress dips next to me as Claudia sits on the bed. "What are you talking about?"

The spinning ceiling is making me feel sick, so I close my eyes. "I always wondered what he saw in me. I'm not what big, muscular, popular, sexy football players usually date." In the past, he was known for dating models. All tall, slender, and beautiful; not five foot five, curvy women like me. Early in our relationship, the media made it clear they were surprised he'd chosen a woman like me too.

"He saw a beautiful, sexy woman. A woman he loves," Claudia says.

I snort and turn my head to look at her. "If I were those things, he would have never had sex with another woman. God, how many times has he been with her? And in my house!" Nausea rolls around in my stomach.

"This could be a one-time thing. A mistake."

I throw Claudia what I hope is a dirty look and not some drunken, cross-eyed grimace. "It doesn't matter if it's one time or one hundred times. He screwed up. Big time. He went to the trouble to star in his own porno. This isn't some 'I was drunk and my penis accidently fell into her vagina' excuse. Who got hold of the video? Why did they air it at my show? Who hates me that much to do such a thing? Was it Darren?"

Claudia gives me another sympathetic look. "Will you talk to him about it?"

My body stiffens. "No way."

"You might get the answers to your questions."

I shake my head; pain shoots through my skull and I regret it immediately. "I'd rather get hit by a bus."

Claudia grins. "A little dramatic. It's probably for the best you don't speak to him. He'll only lie about it."

I agree. I'll believe nothing he says again.

Claudia's shoulders sag on a heavy sigh. "I wish I knew how to help you or make this better."

Nothing can make this better. He's ruined everything.

I lift into a sitting position, hold my arms out for a moment to steady myself, and wait for the room to stop spinning. "You can give me back the champagne. That might help."

Claudia's lips tighten. "Not happening."

I blow out a frustrated breath. "Party pooper."

Giving me a sympathetic smile, she says, "What are you going to do?"

I scrub my hands over my face. "That's something I need to think about when I don't have two lumberjacks chopping wood in my brain."

"Then let's sober you up." Claudia jumps from the bed, takes me by the hand, and tugs. "You need a cold shower, and Tylenol."

My body loosely jerks as she yanks at my arm. "Leave me alone," I complain.

"No. What kind of friend would I be if I left you in this state?"

"A good one."

She raises an eyebrow. "Penny, I know you've been through a lot. It's understandable that you want to drink your feelings away, but alcohol is only a band-aid. It will give you a hell of a hangover—nothing more. What you need to do is go out there and show the world you are strong and fierce, and fuckwit Darren can't bring you down."

My back stiffens and I sit up straight. Claudia is right. After what Darren has done to me, there's no way I want to look like the pitiful, heartbroken victim. "He's the one who should look pathetic. Not me. I'm going to show everyone this will not drag me down." I slide off the bed. With steel in my spine, I stomp barefoot to the door.

Before I open it, Claudia calls after me, "Where are you going?"

I turn around. "To show them how fierce and strong I am." Isn't that what she said I should do?

"Your clothes are disheveled, and you smell like a brewery. Maybe you should shower first."

Looking down at myself, I see there are creases in my top and a few suspicious-looking water stains in the fabric. Then I cup a hand over my mouth, breathe into my palm, and sniff. I wince. Oh geez, I could knock a cowboy off his horse. I change direction and head for the bathroom. "I'll be out in a minute."

In the bathroom, I fill a glass with water and swallow it with two Tylenol I find on the counter, which I assume were provided by Claudia. Then I strip out of my clothes and turn on the water. Once it's at a temperature to my liking, I step under the spray.

If only a shower could wash away the past twenty-four hours. I wish Darren wasn't a cheating bastard. I wish my life wasn't in such turmoil. Unfortunately, I can make as many wishes as I want, and unless I find a magic Genie in a bottle who can turn back time, nothing will change my situation.

Leaning my back against the tile wall, I slide to the floor. I wrap my arms around my bent legs and drop my head onto my knees, letting the tears fall. Being tough is easier said than done.

After a few minutes, Claudia knocks on the door. "Penny, are you okay? Do you need help with anything?"

Carefully getting to my feet, I grab the bodywash and scrub my body. "I'm fine. Nearly done," I call out.

What would I have done without Claudia? As soon as the video was leaked at my show, she was by my side, whisking me away from frenzied journalist circling for a great story to sell. The honeymoon suite wasn't where she wanted to take me. For some dumb reason, I'd insisted.

When I'm done, I step from the shower, put on a bathrobe, and wrap my wet hair in a towel. I walk back into the room, and Claudia's gaze trails me from head to toe. "You look... fresher."

I crack the first genuine smile in hours. "Is that your way of saying I still look like shit but cleaner and smelling better?"

"You never looked like shit. Just sad."

I tighten the belt of my robe. "I can't face anyone yet." The bravado I had earlier washed down the drain of the shower with the water and soap.

"There's no rush. Whenever you're ready." Claudia's phone chimes, and she picks it up. Biting her lip, she reads the message.

"Who is it?" I ask. "If it's my mother, tell her I'm fine. I'll call her later." Much later. The only person more devastated about the affair is her. She loved Darren. Couldn't wait for the wedding. Probably because she believed no one like him would want to marry me. I don't have the energy for a conversation with her tonight.

"It's your mom. She's been trying to call you. You haven't answered, so she texted me. She's suggesting we get a statement out quickly as the news is exploding with different stories."

I sigh and drop onto the nearest chair. Why can't this disaster just disappear? "My brain is too muddled to deal with a statement right now."

Pulling a chair up next to me, she says, "Well, as your PR manager, it's my job to take care of it and handle the press. I should have done it by now, but I didn't want to leave you."

"I'm fine on my own. You should go to the office. I'd be grateful if you sort it out." I trust Claudia will say the right thing. I don't have the energy to think let alone write a statement about my cheating ex-fiancé.

"Are you sure? It can wait until morning." Claudia looks undecisive. Like she's not sure whether to leave me.

"I've already waited long enough. I'm fine," I reassure her. "I'm going straight to bed." And pray I wake up from this nightmare.

"Okay. Call if you need me. I'll be here in a flash. Actually, I can work from here and stay the night."

I shake my head. "It's getting late. Go home. I'll only be asleep. I'll call you in the morning."

Claudia nibbles her bottom lip. "I hate leaving you like this."

"I'm fine. The shower and Tylenol have sobered me up. I'm exhausted. All I want to do is sleep." Most of what I said is true. I am exhausted and need sleep. I'm not exactly sober. The room is still slightly spinning.

She narrows her eyes. "Don't call room service for more champagne."

Like she doesn't trust me, she takes the bottle I was eyeing and hoping to finish off, and goes into the bathroom. I'm assuming to pour the liquid down the sink. My suspicions are confirmed when she comes back with an empty bottle.

She won't know if I order more. "I won't," I lie. What she doesn't know won't hurt. Except the thought of drinking more champagne makes my stomach churn.

Claudia picks her phone up from the bed. I stand and give her a hug. "I'll email you the statement for you to finalize," she says.

"I trust you. Just publish it." It's only going to be something vague about needing time away and privacy.

"Okay. Well, I'll see you tomorrow morning. I'll pick you up and we can go on that honeymoon to Bora Bora you paid for."

There's no way I'd let Darren take the vacation. "Can't wait." A secluded tropical island is what I need. A place where I can get away from everyone.

I walk Claudia to the door and say goodbye. When the door closes behind her, I sigh with relief. As much as I love her and am grateful for her help and support, it's nice to have some time to myself. I don't want to talk. Or think. Or pretend I'll get my shit together. All I want to do is sleep for about five days.

Before I can face-plant onto the bed and fall into what I'm hoping is a dreamless sleep, I spot Claudia's purse on the table. "She forgot it," I mumble.

I sprint for the door and out into the corridor to catch up with her. The elevator doors are closing before I can call out her name to stop her. Oh well, she'll come back for it if she needs it, or I'll give it to her in the morning.

Something bangs behind me. A surge of dread fills me. I slowly turn around. The door to my room is closed. Crap! I don't have the keycard. I grab the door handle and jerk it up and down in case it miraculously opens. It doesn't budge. In frustration, I kick the timber with my bare foot. "Ouch," I whimper.

What am I going to do now? I don't have my phone to call reception. And I don't want to go down there wearing a bathrobe and a towel wrapped around my head. What if paparazzi know I'm staying at this hotel and are camped in the lobby? They can't see me like this.

What other choice do I have? I can't spend the night in the corridor.

As I'm deciding what to do next, the elevators chime to announce they've reached my floor. My shoulders sag with relief. Oh, thank God. Hopefully, Claudia has come back for her purse, or it's someone I can send to reception for me. Spinning around, I race to the elevator then skid to a stop. Four men step out, and when they spot me, they rush toward me, pointing cameras in my face. Bright lights blur my vision, and I hold my hand up to shield my eyes.

"Penelope Aldin," a man with a black, bushy beard shouts. "How do you feel about the video of Darren Ellis and Karen Featherstone having sex?"

Another says, "Did you know about the affair?"

A guy with a potbelly and balding head asks, "Will you still marry him?"

The fourth man wearing a Hawaiian shirt snickers. "Does Darren have sex tapes of you too?"

Fear and embarrassment grip me. My arms flail around as I yell, "Leave me alone."

My outburst only makes them more trigger-happy, and they press in closer, snapping more pictures.

"Come on, Penelope. Give us the details," the photographer with the bushy beard says with a cajoling tone.

In my frazzled state, trying to get away, the towel slips off my head and falls onto the floor, causing my hair to fall in tangled, wet clumps around my shoulders. Again, the clicking noise of the cameras go wild.

Since I can't get back into my room, I have no choice but to run to the elevators and somehow keep them from following me inside and hope the concierge can help me. The photographers have circled around me and are practically glued to my body. There's zero chance of getting away without them following me in. Still, I have to try. I can't stay out here so exposed.

Before I can find a gap and sprint, the elevator doors ping open and a couple steps into the corridor. The man's arm is flung over the woman's shoulder, and she's pressed against his side. Their faces are buried in each other's necks, and they appear to be unaware of the commotion going on.

I rush to them and plead, "Can you help me please? I'm locked out of my room, and these men are bothering me."

They pause from their amorous embrace to stare at me. I suck in a startled breath. It's Lucas Alessi. One of the owners of one of the most famous fashion houses in the world, Alessi Fashion, and the boy who ruined my senior year. Our brief encounters lately—due to me being good friends with his sisters-in-law, Harper and Alyssa—have been nothing but hostile. Normally, he'd be the last person I'd ask for help, but with the paparazzi hounding me, I'm desperate.

The men are too busy taking photos of me and yelling out questions to notice Lucas and don't pay him any attention.

Without letting go of the woman, Lucas takes in the scene. A huge grin spreads across his face. He knows I'm in trouble, and he's enjoying it. "I'm sorry, I'm busy."

He pulls a keycard out of his pocket and taps it on the lock of a door. He steps into the room, and the woman follows him. She's no help either.

Lucas turns around and grins. "Good luck out there." Then the door closes in my face.

Bastard! How can he leave me like this? Tears sting the backs of my eyes and burst free. I cover my face with my hands. Backing away from the paparazzi until I feel the wall pressed against my back, I slide to the floor and drop my head on my knees.

If watching a video of Darren having sex wasn't humiliating enough, this tops it all.

I've reached rock bottom.

Chapter Two

LUCAS

The grin on my face drops as soon as the door closes on Penelope's distraught face. What the hell has happened to have the paparazzi out for her blood? Whatever it is, she can handle it herself. If she thinks I'm coming to her rescue, she can think again. She doesn't deserve my help; not after what she put me through in high school.

"Was that Penelope Aldin out there?" Angel asks. Is that the name she was born with or her stripper name? Who even cares? I brought the raven-haired beauty to my hotel room to fuck, not to get to know her.

"Yeah, it is." My jaw clenches like it does every time our paths cross. Now that she's become close friends with my sisters-in-law, I've seen her more lately at family events than I want to. I banished her from my mind years ago. With her getting involved with the family, it's only making me relive the past. And the pain she caused.

"Should we help her? She looked upset. Do you know her fian—"

I hook a hand around Angel's waist and pull her toward me, interrupting whatever she was going to say. The last thing I want to do is talk about Penelope Aldin.

"You can go out there and help her. What I want to do is fuck. So, what's it gonna be?" I ask.

Angel bites her bottom lip with indecision. To help her decide, I cup her ass and trail my tongue along her neck.

"I want to fuck," she says breathlessly.

"Good answer," I mumble against her neck.

Spinning her around, I pin her against the door. I lift her arms above her head. Her ass wiggles in front of me, and I grind my cock against her, pulling a moan from her. Just as I'm about to remove the tiny piece of glittery, gold fabric wrapped around Angel's body, the muffled sounds of Penelope's name being called repeatedly can be heard from the hallway. For fuck's sake! With Angel pinned against the door and ready for me, Penelope's name is the last name I want to hear.

Trying to block the commotion outside, my hands roam along Angel's hips and up her torso until I reach her breasts. I pull down the top of her dress, and her large, firm tits fall into my hands. She cries out when I massage them and tweak her nipples.

"Penelope! Penelope! Give us the story!"

"Penelope! Will you take him back?" The muffled voices continue to interrupt me.

Blowing out a frustrated breath, I lean over Angel's shoulder and look through the peephole into the hallway. Penelope is curled up on the floor with four men surrounding her taking pictures. My stomach twists into a tight knot. As much as I hate her, I hate the paparazzi more. What they're doing is fucking disgusting.

Why the hell isn't she getting away from them? She said she got locked out of her room. Surely she can get another key at reception. Or are those fuckwits stopping her from leaving? If that's the case, this is fucked up. No one should feel trapped.

"Excuse me." I move Angel to the side and open the door. "Penelope," I call. She doesn't respond. Probably can't hear me over the noise the assholes are making. "Penelope," I yell.

At the sound of my voice, her head snaps up. Tears are sliding down her flushed cheeks. Her eyes are red-rimmed and wide with fright. I nod my head for her to come to me. Without hesitation, she scrambles to her feet and takes a step toward my room only to have her path blocked.

I propel from the doorway and barge my way through the assholes. "Get out of the fucking way!"

When I reach her, I throw my arm around her shoulders. Turning toward me, she buries her face in my chest. Her body is shaking in my arms. I nudge the men out of my way to get back to my room.

"Hey! You're Lucas Alessi," one of the photographers states.

Crap. I was hoping I wouldn't be recognized. I don't want my name involved with whatever shit Penelope has gotten herself into.

"Is this why Darren Ellis cheated on you with Karen Featherstone?" another says.

"Are you two dating?" The vultures keep firing questions at us.

When I rushed from the room, the door had closed behind me, and I have to pull the keycard from my pocket to unlock it again. The men follow close behind, still yelling out questions. Once the door opens, I usher her inside the room, slamming the door on the assholes' faces.

Pulling away from me, Penelope swipes the tears from her cheeks. "Th-thank you f-for helping m-me," she says, her voice shaking. "Th-they wouldn't leave m-me alone."

"What the hell was all that about?" Whenever photographers are that frenzied, something major has happened.

"You don't know?"

"Know what?"

"About…about…" She fiddles with the belt on her robe. "The video?"

"What video?"

She gives me a dubious expression. "It's all over the internet."

Did she burn a cake or paint the wrong color in someone's living room? Isn't that what all her videos are about? Not that I've watched any. Harper and Alyssa are obsessed with her show. They're constantly talking about how Penelope's given them the motivation to redecorate their homes.

"Tell me about it," I say.

She wraps her arms around her waist when her gaze lands on Angel. The top of Angel's dress is back in place. As soon as I can get rid of Penelope, I'll get back to removing it again.

"Oh, sorry," Penelope says. "I'm disturbing you. I'll just—"

"What?" I nod toward the door. "Go back out there? You said you locked yourself out of your room. How did you manage that?"

"I ran out to stop a friend before she got into the elevator, but I missed her. The door to the room closed behind me, and I didn't have the key. Before I could decide what I was going to do, those men—" She shivers. "—surrounded me." Then her eyes narrow. "They couldn't have gotten onto my floor without a key. Did *you* let them up? Did you find out I was staying here and sic them onto me?"

My jaw tightens. There is a reason I never want to see this woman. She's a cold, heartless bitch. "I just saved your ass out there and you're accusing me of creating that circus. What was I thinking helping you? I should have left you in the hallway." I stomp toward the door and grab the handle. "Good luck out there."

She holds her hand out like a stop sign. "No! Please don't open it." Her expression turns contrite. "I'm sorry. I can't make sense of anything at the moment."

I drop my arm by my side. "You need to tell me what's going on."

"You really don't know?"

I shake my head. "I just got back from a photoshoot in Brazil. I haven't touched my phone or been online." After working five long days all I wanted to do was unwind in bed with a naked woman. Now Angel is sitting on the edge of the bed, swinging her leg from the knee, looking impatient. I have a feeling this night will not end the way I planned.

"Darren got caught cheating. Somone broadcasted a video of him having sex with Karen Featherstone at my show last night."

"*Darren* and *Karen*? Those names are a joke, right?" I'd laugh out loud if she wasn't looking so serious.

"With rhyming names like that, they're a match made in heaven," she says, her voice dripping with sarcasm.

The paparazzi's questions now make sense. They also asked if we are dating. I'll have to shut that rumor down fast. No way in hell do I want to be connected with Penelope Aldin.

"Who leaked the video?" I ask. "Was it Darren? He's always been an attention whore." Before he hooked up with Penelope, he was constantly tipping off the paparazzi as to where he was and who he was with. But his relationship with Penelope was his golden ticket, so would he risk losing it all?

She scratches her chin. "Who else could it have been? It had to have been Darren. I don't know who hates me that much."

I can think of one person who hates her—me. Although, I'd never stoop to such a low level to hurt her. It would be a waste of my time. Time I don't want to spend on her.

"If it was him, why do it? Doing such a thing could ruin everything for him," she says. "You're right, he does like the limelight. But would he risk ruining his reputation?"

"Maybe he thought a good sex tape would boost it? Celebrities have done it before."

She shuffles to the minibar and grabs a tiny bottle of whisky and twists off the cap.

"Help yourself," I say with sarcasm.

"Don't worry, I'll pay for it," she says then drinks it. "You might be right. He could have done it for the attention."

I'm not worried about the money. I don't want her passing out drunk in my room. The quicker I can figure out how to get her out of here, the better.

"Weren't you and Darren getting married soon?" I ask.

She cocks a questioning eyebrow, her eyes looking a little glassy. "How do you know that?"

I lean my shoulder against the wall. "I've heard Harper and Alyssa talking about it." Not that I care what's happening in her life. It's hard not to overhear their excited chatter.

"Tonight would have been our wedding night," she says.

She drops on the edge of the bed next to Angel. Two contrasting women, each beautiful in their own way. Angel with her black hair, enhanced breasts, and olive skin looks like she can grace the covers of a swimsuit magazine. Penelope's robe gaps slightly open, and I get a sneak peek of the tops of her creamy, full breasts. Her long, wavy, auburn hair hangs in wet strands over her shoulders. Even in her disheveled state, her natural beauty outshines Angel. Back in school I always thought Penelope stood out among the girls. Now she's more beautiful as she's gotten older.

"Oh, that is so sad," Angel says, the comment pulling my gaze and thoughts away from Penelope. Why the hell am I looking? I hate everything about her.

"What's sadder, or rather more pathetic, is I'm spending the night in our honeymoon suite." She rubs her fingers along her forehead.

Angel massages soothing circles on Penelope's back. "I saw the video. Darren Ellis is disgusting. Men are such dogs." She gives me an apologetic look. "Except for you, Lucas."

Penelope gives Angel a ghost of a smile.

Don't sound so sure about that, Angel. I like to fuck hard and often, with rarely the same woman. I may not cheat, but that's because I'm never in a relationship. And never want to be.

"You need to plan a payback. Maybe make your own video, only spice it up. A threesome would do the trick." Angel glances at me like she's running the production in her head.

I push away from the wall. "Keep me out of this. I'm not starring in your porno." Although, with two beautiful women on my bed, my cock hardens at the thought. Then I quickly remember that one of those women is Penelope and I turn as soft as a cooked marshmallow.

Angel pouts her full, red lips. "Well, we'll think of something else."

For fuck's sake, this isn't a slumber party where girls sit around and gossip. What will they do next? Start a pillow fight? Actually, that thought has stirred my dick back to life. Shit! I have to get Penelope out of here.

"Can we save the girl talk for another time?" I say. "We need to figure out how to get Penelope back to her room without the paparazzi surrounding her."

"Thanks again for coming to my rescue. I know I'm the last person you want to help." The sincerity in her tone and expression makes me uncomfortable. Normally, whenever we see each other, we're throwing death stares and insults at one another.

"You're welcome." I walk to the door and look through the peephole. "The fuckers are still out there."

"What should I do?"

Dropping my hands on my hips, I blow out a frustrated breath. "I'll see what the hotel staff can do."

Walking to the bed, I pick up the phone on the nightstand and dial the reception desk. Asking to be put through to the manager, I explain the situation.

When I end the call, I pull a chair out from the table in the corner of the room and straddle it. "So, the fuckers out there have rented a room for the night. That explains how they got onto the floor. I'm surprised they paid that kind of money. Your photos must be worth a lot for them to go to so much trouble."

"Unbelievable!" Penelope scoffs. "How did they know what floor I'm on? Would a staff member have told them?"

I shrug. I don't have the answers to her questions. But my guess is that they slipped someone some money to find out.

"I hope the manager is asking them to leave."

"All she can do is tell them to stop harassing you. If they don't listen, then they'll kick them out."

"Great. They'll probably watch me through the peephole and spring into action as soon as they see me leave your room. They won't care if they get kicked out. As long as they take all the photos they can."

"There's not much more we can do," I say.

"Thanks for trying. How do I get back into my room?"

"Someone will come up as soon as possible to give you a replacement keycard."

She shuffles back on the mattress until her back is pressed against the headboard, making herself comfortable. Tilting her face to the ceiling, she gives a heavy sigh. "I just want to disappear."

There's nothing I want more too, yet I'm stuck with her. Well, only until she gets a key to her room.

Her eyes flutter closed as she mumbles, "To a place no one knows who I am. Where no one can find me." A few seconds later, her head tilts to the side and she's making soft breathing sounds.

"Did she fall asleep?" Angel asks.

"I think so."

"What do we do now?"

"I don't know." Tonight has turned to shit. The woman in my bed was not meant to be Penelope Aldin.

Angel slaps her palms on her thighs and rises to her feet. "Well, we should try this again another time." She walks over to me, cups my cheeks with her hands, and kisses me long and deep. "Call me." And then she struts from the room.

I could stop her and tell her we can continue what we had started as soon as Penelope leaves, but I don't. And I won't be calling her either. That kiss didn't stir an ounce of interest. It's like the events of the evening has caused my body to malfunction. All thanks to Penelope.

Yet, when I look at her with her robe scrunched around her upper thighs and the top gapping open, there's nothing wrong with the way my body is responding. Christ! I rake my fingers through my hair. I can't be perving on a sleeping woman.

Turning away, I walk to the door and look through the peephole. I see a hotel staff member talking to the men. With disgruntled expressions, they make their way down the hallway and disappear from my line of sight.

A moment later, there's a soft knock at the door. Answering it, I take the keycard, thank the man, and give him a tip for his assistance with the paparazzi. Now I can get Penelope back into her room and salvage what's left of the evening.

Maybe I can go back to the club and find another woman to hookup with. I immediately shake the thought away. I've lost all desire.

Exhaustion is catching up with me, and I just want this night to be over.

Ready to give her the keycard and get her out of my room, I walk to the bed. My shoulders slump. She's fast asleep. Well, she's not staying here a moment longer; I'm going to have to wake her up. I stare down at her. With her makeup-free face soft in sleep, her mouth slightly open, she doesn't look like the cold, heartless bitch I know she is. Instead, she looks sweet and innocent. My spine stiffens. I can't let her fool me.

"Penelope." I shake her shoulder. "Wake up."

No response.

"Penelope." I nudge her harder. "You can go to your room now."

She grabs my hand and hugs it under her chin. "Just five more minutes, Mom," she mumbles.

Mom? She's obviously dreaming and talking in her sleep, and has taken my hand prisoner. I try to pull it free, but she grips it harder.

"Don't tell Lucas," she mumbles again.

Hmm. I could get some information from her. Maybe even hold it against her. "Don't tell Lucas what?"

A smile spreads across her face. "Don't tell him I think he is hot."

Now I know she's dreaming. There's no way she'd confess something like that fully conscious. I smirk. "You think he's hot?"

She nods. "Mmm-hmm."

"How hot?" Asking the question gives me a moment of amusement.

Little creases form between her brows. "Too hot for me."

Okay, time to stop playing games. When I tug my hand again, this time she lets go. Instead of waking up, she slides onto her back and rolls on her side. Snuggling a pillow to her chest, she breathes heavily with a slight snore.

Unless I throw a glass of water over her head—which sounds like a great idea—she's not moving. Shit! I should have left her in the hallway. But no, I had to stick my nose in her business. Now I'm stuck with her.

There's no chance I'm sleeping on the floor or the uncomfortable-looking sofa. This is my room. My bed. I could leave her here and go to her suite or book another room, but I'm too exhausted. Jetlag is settling in, and doing anything else feels like too much trouble.

Kicking off my shoes, I then strip out of my jeans and t-shirt and toss them onto a nearby chair. My fingers hesitate at the waistband of my briefs. Should I take them off? I always sleep naked. If I'm sharing a bed with Penelope, I should leave them on. I wouldn't want her accusing me of indecency or some shit.

Sliding into bed, I prop my head on the palm of my hand and stare at the ceiling. Not in a million years did I think I'd end up in bed with Penelope Aldin. Ten years ago, I never would have helped her with the paparazzi. I would have walked past her without giving her another thought. She got me expelled from high school, which completely change my life. I lost my chance of getting into college and playing football. A career path I was working toward. Luckily, I'm doing something I love more than football, and that's being the head photographer and part owner of Alessi Fashion.

I look at Penelope and the old rage still simmers underneath the surface. I've switched my passion for football to photography, but that doesn't mean I'll ever forgive her.

Not only for my career, but for the death of my best friend.

The next morning, I wake to the sound of my cell phone vibrating on the nightstand. I scrub my hands over my face and prop myself into a sitting position. It's then I remember Penelope. How could I have forgotten? Twice during the night I woke up with her arm flung around my waist and her leg wrapped around mine. Feeling her warm, soft body pressed against mine made for a difficult night's sleep and a painful hard-on. Any woman draped over me like a second skin would pull out that reaction from me.

Grabbing the phone, I walk into the bathroom to take the call. I know what it's about. I get this call from either Hayden or Finn on this day every year. My big brothers want to check up on me. Make sure I'm not going to drown myself in alcohol and do something stupid. I know they care, but after nine years, I'm getting sick of telling them I'm okay and they don't need to bother.

I guess I'm not convincing them, because I haven't convinced myself yet either. When I leave the hotel and head to the cabin, I plan to drink until the memories stop flooding my mind.

Not wanting to wake Penelope and have her overhear the conversation, I close the door behind me. I glance at the caller ID before I answer. "Hayden," I say. It's his turn this year.

"Hey, Lucas. How are you?" He doesn't mask the concern in his voice.

"Like every other year, I'm good. I will not crack. Make sure you tell Finn too." In the past, they've seen me broken. Picked me up from the floor. It's no wonder they call on the anniversary of Garrett's death.

"Just making sure."

I lean my hip against the vanity. I know they mean well. The three of us are as close as brothers can be. If one of us is going through something, we all are.

"I'm fine. Really," I say as convincingly as I can. "I'm heading to the cabin as soon as I get Pen—" I stop myself from saying Penelope. That's a conversation I don't have the energy for. I've never told them why I hate her so much. All they know is that something happened between us in high school.

"So you do have Penny Aldin in your hotel room. They're saying you're a couple. What the hell is going on? If you're using her while she's vulnerable after her public humiliation, I'm going to chop your balls off and shove them down your throat."

"But if this is fuck-you revenge sex to get back at her ex, then well done to Penny," Alyssa's voice in the background cuts into the conversation.

"How do you know about Penelope?" I ask.

"It's all over social media," Hayden explains. "I thought you hated her."

I pinch the bridge of my nose. *I do one good deed, and now I'm paying for it.* These assholes work fast.

"Nothing happened between us. I was helping her get away from the paparazzi. Ask Raymond to shut it down. Get a statement out saying I was helping her and that we are only...friends." The word clogs my throat. We are anything *but* friends. Hopefully, our PR manager will write something to shut the rumors down.

"The photos they took look like you're more than friends," Hayden says.

Shit! "*Nothing* happened," I reiterate. "Fix it. I'm spending the next few days at the cabin. I don't have the time for this."

"I'll see what I can do. I can't promise we can make it go away." He clears his throat. "If you need us while you're away, just call, and we'll be at the cabin as soon as we can."

"I know. Thanks. I'll be fine. I want to take some photos for my exhibition."

"How's that coming along?"

For years I photographed beautiful women wearing beautiful clothes, which I love. Then one photoshoot in Italy pulled my attention into the direction of the culture, history, architecture, and people living in small villages with their lives etched on their faces. It was photographic heaven, and I was hooked.

With so many photos of fascinating subjects from all over the world, Hayden and Finn encouraged me to get a collection together and show them in a gallery. This was a creative outlet, something fun with no pressure. But now, with the exhibition only a couple of weeks away, I'm wondering if this hobby should stay that way. Are my photographs good enough? It's too late to back out now. Everything is booked. Invitations have been sent. I have to see this through.

"Putting the finishing touches on a few things. If I take some good shots at the cabin, maybe I'll have more to add."

"Good luck with it. I'll talk to you when you get back."

We say goodbye and I end the call.

Hayden said the photos on the internet look like me and Penelope are more than just friends and they're calling us a couple. What the hell did they publish? Though I'm hesitant to check, I go online and look.

My stomach twists into a knot. Multiple photos show Penelope's hand resting on my chest with her face trustfully pressed against me. My arm is thrown over her shoulders in a protective way. The fierce expression on my face says *this woman is mine; back off or I'll fuck you over*. None of the photos show we are in fact enemies.

Hopefully Raymond will shut it down. If not, give it a few days and the paparazzi will hunt down the next scandal. As long as we're not seen together again, there's nothing to gossip about. It's time to get her out of my room.

While I'm in the bathroom I shower. When I'm done, I wrap a towel around my waist, and I walk back into the bedroom to get my clothes. Instead, I pull up short. Penelope is still sleeping. The sheet covering her is pushed down to her feet, leaving her sprawled on the bed in her robe, which is doing nothing to cover her creamy-colored thighs. The belt has come loose, and an open gap runs from her collarbone to her naval. Her breasts are precariously close to spilling out. One slight move and the robe will part to show me if she's wearing panties or not.

Swallowing hard, I turn away, willing my dick to die down. I can't be attracted to Penelope Aldin. I'd rather poke my eyes out with a blunt stick. To distract myself from the view, I call room service and order breakfast and strong, black coffee.

When I turn back, Penelope is sitting up against the headboard, the robe secured tightly around her body and her fingers combing through her hair. Something so shapeless as the fluffy hotel robe and disheveled hair shouldn't look as sexy as it does. I scrub my hands over my face. God, I need to stop looking at her.

Then her gaze travels the length of my body. I'm not the only one appreciating what they're seeing. Like she realizes what she's doing, her eyes snap away from the towel to my face. "Good morning," she says, her voice hoarse from sleep. "Thank you for letting me stay the night."

"Had no choice. You fell asleep. The keycard for your room is on the table." If I sound abrupt, it's because I'm pissed at myself for having any kind of attraction toward her.

She frowns. "You could have woken me up."

"I tried. You were out cold—not even a bomb would have made you stir. I seriously considered throwing water on your face."

"I'm glad you didn't." She glances around the room. "Where's your date?"

Calling Angel a date is a bit of a stretch. "You cockblocked me. Thanks a lot for that."

"Oh, I'm so sorry." Mirth shines from her eyes. Yeah, she's not sorry at all. Then her face turns serious. "Arhhh, you slept on the couch, right?"

"No, in the bed."

"Next to me?"

"Do you see any other bed? Yes, next to you. Don't you remember clinging to me last night?"

Her eyebrows shoot into her hairline. "I did not!"

I cross my arms over my chest and grin. "You did. And pinned me down with your legs. I had to put a stop to your wandering hands."

"I would never do that."

I shrug a shoulder. "You even talk in your sleep. Told me how hot you think I am."

"Now I know you're joking." She rolls her eyes. "I'd never touch you. Or say that you're hot."

If only she knew I was telling the truth. "Whether or not you believe me, it's time for you to leave. I'm going into the bathroom to get dressed. I want you gone by the time I come back out."

Chapter Three

PENNY

When Lucas goes into the bathroom, I grab my hotel room keycard from the table, and I head to the door. Looking through the peephole, I'm thankful to see the hallway empty. Quickly and quietly, I leave Lucas' room and dash across the hallway and into mine. I breathe a sigh of relief when no one catches me. Last night was a nightmare. I know the paparazzi can be brutal, but I've never experienced anything like it, and I never want to again.

And then there was Lucas Alessi—my rescuer. The devil himself. That was the biggest surprise of the night. I had expected him to leave me in the hallway to fend for myself. What I didn't see was him coming to my aid. It was probably his date that had him changing his mind. Whatever the reason, I'm grateful for his help. It doesn't mean I dislike him any less. Although, unfortunately, I still think he's the most gorgeous man I've ever seen.

When I woke up to see him wet from a shower with only a towel around his waist, displaying his tanned skin and corrugated abs, I nearly swallowed my tongue. I'm not attracted to him at all, but I'm not blind. The man is gorgeous.

Did I really lie all over him and tell him he's hot? I walk to the bed and sit on the edge. I shake my head. No, surely I wouldn't do that. He was teasing me. Playing with my mind. My punishment for taking his bed. The man is evil with a cold heart. Except for when he helped me at my most vulnerable state; even if it was his date's idea, he could have said no. That was far from cold. Then he let me sleep in his bed. If he really wanted me out, I'm sure he could have woken me up. The alcohol had knocked me unconscious, but I wasn't dead.

Whatever his reasons, I don't have time to worry about that now. I need to catch a plane, and I have to get ready fast to make it to the airport on time. And I need to figure out how I'm going to get out of the hotel without the paparazzi noticing. If I could wait a little longer, maybe they'd get bored of spying on me and leave. However, my flight leaves for Bora Bora in three hours, and I need to get to the airport right away.

Picking up my phone from the nightstand, I check my text messages. There are five from Darren, which I delete without reading. There's nothing more he can say to me that I want to hear. Seven from my mother. I don't have the energy to talk to her just yet. I'll call her before I board the plane. And there are two from Claudia. I open those.

The first one says: *The statement is out. Fingers crossed it takes the spotlight off you. I'll talk to you in the morning. Hope you get some sleep xx*

The second one, which was sent ten minutes ago, reads: *If you don't reply to my message in twenty minutes, I'll assume you're still sleeping or dead and will call to wake you up.*

I text back: *Hey, I'm alive! Terrible hangover but ready to sit on a beach and do nothing. Are you picking me up or am I meeting you at the airport?*

Claudia: *Glad to hear you're alive. I'm running late, so I'll meet you at the airport. I've arranged for the hotel to have a security guard meet you at your room in half an hour and take you to the garage where a driver will be waiting for you.*

What would I do without her?

I reply: *You're the best! See you soon xx*

After a quick shower, I swallow down two Tylenol to help with the jackhammering in my brain and dress for the airport. I wish I had time for coffee, but the security guard will be here soon. It will have to wait until I get to the airport. Once I'm there, I plan to forget about the past two horrible days and switch onto vacation mode. Seven days on a tropical island with my best friend sounds like heaven. There's nothing on my itinerary except soaking up the sun and trying every cocktail on the menu.

Right on time, there's a knock on my door. I collect my things and look through the peephole to see the security guard.

"Good morning, Ms. Aldin," he says when I open the door. "I have a private elevator ready. It will take you straight to the basement parking deck where a car will be waiting."

"Great, thank you."

"You're welcome. Here, let me take your bags." He takes my luggage and rolls it down the hallway.

I hold my breath, waiting for the paparazzi to spring from a room and shout at me. When I step into the elevator without incident, I breathe a sigh of relief. Then I pause. Lucas is leaning casually against the mirrored panel wall. He's dressed in faded jeans and a light sage colored t-shirt that draws out the green in his eyes. His dark brown hair looks finger-combed off his face. With a disgruntled expression, he appears just as annoyed at seeing me as I am at seeing him.

"I hope you don't mind Mr. Alessi sharing the elevator. I thought the quicker I can get you both out of the hotel, the better," the security guard explains.

"It's not a problem," I say through a fake smile.

I step further inside and turn my back toward Lucas. When the doors close, his image is reflected on the elevator doors. I focus my attention on the illuminated descending numbers. Why is Lucas sneaking out? It's not like he has the paparazzi hounding him.

"She loves my company. Don't you, Penelope?" I hear the sarcasm in his tone.

I throw him a dirty look over my shoulder. I want to wipe the smug grin off his face. "Oh yes. You are such a delight." I don't hide my distaste.

"After the amazing night we spent together, I thought you'd be a little more friendly toward me."

I gasp, take a quick look at the security guard, who is inspecting the cuff of his sleeve like he's taking no notice of our conversation, then swing toward Lucas. "All we did was *sleep*." All I need is for the security guard to think there's something going on between us. Who knows what rumors he might start?

"What about your wandering hands?" Lucas winks.

I turn my back on him again. "In your dreams."

He chuckles, which makes my blood boil, because I really don't know what I did in my sleep. Surely, even in my alcohol-induced coma, I would never go that far. Not with Lucas Alessi.

Thankfully, the elevator arrives at basement level, and we step out into the garage.

"See you later, sunshine. Actually, hopefully see you never," Lucas says before he walks away, disappearing among the rows of cars.

Jerk! I want to scream at him. Instead, I take a deep breath and keep my composure.

After a moment, I notice there's no car waiting. I turn to the security guard. "How long will my ride be?"

He flicks out his wrist and checks the time on his watch. "Should have been here by now. Let me check and see what's happening."

As he's on the phone, a black jeep drives toward us. It must be my car.

Then the elevator chimes, indicating it's reached the basement. Seconds later, voices shout behind me. "Penelope! Penelope!"

Spinning around, I'm faced with the same men from last night. Darn it, how did they find me? Why won't they just leave me alone? Don't they have enough humiliating pictures of me? I need the car to get to me *fast*.

Before the men get too close, the security guard lifts his arms out wide and steps in front of me to block their view of me. "Get back now or I'll get the police involved!" he warns.

Ignoring the guard's threat, one asks, "Did you spend the night with Lucas Alessi?"

Another asks, "How long have you been together?"

One by one, they fire questions at me. Trying to hide behind the guard isn't keeping them away.

The jeep approaches and slows down. Thank God my ride is here and this will be over with soon. But the car doesn't stop. Instead, it picks up speed and drives past me. My mouth drops open as it continues on. If that's not my driver, where are they? I need to get out of here.

Once again, I'm surrounded with cameras pointed in my face and men asking inappropriate questions. I search around the garage for any quick exits I can run to and hopefully lose them. Because even though the security guard is on the phone talking to what I'm assuming is the police, these men aren't going to stop pestering me until the authorities arrive. I can't stay here a moment longer.

Just as I'm about to hatch a plan to get out of here, the screeching of tires echoes through the garage. Up ahead, the black jeep has stopped suddenly, its brake lights illuminating in the dim garage. Then it reverses toward us and stops in front of me.

The passenger side door flings open. "Get in," Lucas demands.

For a moment, I'm stunned to see him, and I don't move.

"Are you going to just stand there, or do you want to get away from those fuckers?"

That breaks me from my frozen state. Once again, Lucas is coming to my rescue. I'd rather it be someone else, but I don't have the luxury of being picky.

Opening the passenger side door, I hop into the car. Realizing what's happening, the security guard opens the back passenger door and tosses my suitcase onto the backseat. I slam the door in the paparazzi's faces, and the wheels of the jeep squeal as Lucas floors it out of the garage and onto the busy street. Without saying a word, he zigzags and cuts through the morning traffic.

"Are they following us?" I twist in my seat to look behind us.

"By the time they get to their cars, there will be no chance of them catching up."

I turn back around and slump into the seat with a relieved breath. "They're vultures. Don't they have anything better to do than harassing people and making their lives miserable?"

"You're the hot topic of the day. It's how they make their money."

I lean my elbow on the door and drop my head on my hand. "I wish I wasn't. Thank you for helping me again. I know how you feel about me. I'm surprised you didn't leave me behind."

"The thought crossed my mind," he says dryly. "I'm not gonna lie, I'm not sure why I did it." His face is expressionless as he drives. The clenching of his fingers around the steering wheel is the only indication that he's not happy with his decision. I'm not happy being stuck in a car with him either.

"Well, I'm grateful you got me out of there."

While I waited for my driver to show, the paparazzi would have bombarded me. I'd hate to see what they've posted about me. That's why I've avoided opening social media on my phone. After what happened last night in my disheveled state while sitting on the floor in a bathrobe, I'm sure the photos will be anything but flattering.

But I don't have the energy to worry about that now. Better to avoid it and deal with it later. I need to focus on what's important. Right now it's getting to the airport to meet Claudia. All I want to do is disappear and forget what a disaster my life has become.

"Where am I taking you?" Lucas asks.

"Do you mind dropping me off at JFK, please?"

He pulls his attention off the road to glance at me for a beat. "Are you running away?"

"Yes." No point denying it. "Hopefully to someplace no one will find me."

He doesn't respond to that, and we fall into uncomfortable silence. I'm grateful for the music coming from the speakers that fill the car with noise.

During the ride, my thoughts bounce all over the place. From needing to call my mother—she'll be so worried I haven't spoken to her yet—to hoping Claudia is waiting at the airport, ready to whisk me onto the plane. My thoughts are also drifting to whether Darren has moved Karen into *my* apartment now that I'm gone.

Lucas takes the ramp to the departure terminal. A bunch of people are standing at the entrance of the building. When they spot the car, they lift cameras to their faces and aim them in our direction.

My heart drops to my stomach. The paparazzi found us.

"Those slimy fuckers." Lucas slams a palm on the steering wheel.

"How did they know I'd be here?" I hold my hand up to conceal my face.

"They're snakes. They find these things out." He pulls the car over to the curb and stops. "I hope you can run fast and get to your gate," he says with no sympathy.

Panic pinches my skin. "You're not leaving me here, are you?"

"Don't you have a plane to catch?"

"Well, yes, but—"

"Then you better hurry," he suggests.

I look out the window at the people surrounding the car and then back at Lucas. "If I go in there, they'll know where I'm heading. I won't have any privacy on my vacation."

He gives a nonchalant shrug. "Not my problem."

My heart races. My breathing grows choppy. I've used up all my lifelines. Lucas isn't helping me anymore.

Oh God. This is it. I have to walk out there.

Lenses press against the windows. Flashes of light blind me. With a shaky hand, I try to unlatch my seatbelt. I keep missing the button with my fumbling fingers. After multiple attempts, a large, warm hand covers mine. I glance at Lucas' frowning face.

"Leave it. I'm getting you out of here. Okay?"

I nod, my throat too clogged with unshed tears to speak.

Claudia is probably worried where I am, so I send her a quick text.

Me: *Don't wait for me. I've left the airport. The paparazzi found me.*

A moment later she replies: *Are you okay? I'm heading back to my apartment. I'll meet you there.*

Me: *I'm fine, don't worry. I'll call with details of where I'm staying as soon as I can. Talk soon x*

I send another text to my mother so she doesn't worry.

Lucas quickly pulls out onto the street. "I should hit these fuckers for getting so close to my car," he grumbles. As the car veers away, the paparazzi jump out of his way.

He pulls into the traffic. Cars honk at him for cutting them off. I clutch white-knuckle tight to the edge of the seat, praying we don't get into an accident.

"Where do you want to go?" he asks.

Darren is probably still in my apartment. I can't go back there. The thought of seeing him makes me sick. I wonder if he's getting this much attention. He's the captain of the New York Dragons; surely they're hounding him too. Hopefully, they're showing what a dirty, cheating worm he is. I could stay with my mother or Claudia, but if the paparazzi know my every move, I'm sure it won't take them long to find me there too.

I sigh. "There's no place I can go where they won't find me," I say with defeat. I want to curl into a ball and fall into a dark hole. Maybe then I'll get some peace.

Lucas gets back onto the freeway. He's going faster than the speed limit, frequently changing lanes and glancing in the rearview mirror. After a couple of minutes, he slows down. He must know no one is following us.

"Where were you headed?" he asks.

"Bora Bora."

"Nice."

"I was going on my honeymoon with my best friend."

He scoffs. "That's so pathetic."

I swing my head toward him to glare at him. "No, it's not."

"No? This is how it would have gone. You'd arrive at a fancy hotel room overlooking the crystal blue water. Rose petals are spread over your bed. A bubble bath is waiting with more rose petals floating on top of the water with a bottle of Dom Perignon chilling in an ice bucket next to it. A beautiful welcome basket filled with chocolates and strawberries addressed to Mr. and Mrs. Ellis is displayed on a table for you to enjoy. All that romantic stuff will smack you in the face, reminding you of getting cheated on, and you'll spend the entire vacation crying into your pillow while your best friend hand-feeds you the complimentary chocolate." He shakes his head. "Like I said, pathetic."

I cross my arms over my chest. "Oh? What would you have done?"

"Never gotten engaged," he says like it's a no-brainer.

If I knew what a lying, cheating, scumbag Darren was, I never would have said yes to his proposal.

"Instead of taking your best friend, you should have traveled alone, found your rebound guy at a bar, and taken him back to your room to fuck the asshole fiancé out of your system. And to top it off, I'd make sure he found out about it."

I cough out a shocked laugh. "You're not serious."

"Totally."

"Well, I don't work that way."

He glances at me with a cocked eyebrow. "Really? Because I thought getting revenge was your thing."

A guilty shiver trickles down my spine. Of course he'd think that; I've given him every reason to. But I'll never forget the humiliation he put me through that caused me to strike out the way I did.

I don't want to poke at old wounds, so I don't reply to his comment. Instead, as I notice we've left the city, I ask, "Where are we going?"

"Someplace no one will find you. Isn't that what you want?" he says with an ominous tone.

"Are you taking me someplace where no one will find my body?" I joke to lighten the mood.

"There's too much evidence showing I'm the last person you've been seen with. I'd be the number one suspect. Don't worry. You're safe."

"If you're not burying me in a shallow grave, where are you taking me?"

"I have a cabin in the woods a few hours away from the city."

"A cabin in the woods! Are you sure you're not going to kill me?"

"The thought crossed my mind," he grumbles under his breath, but not low enough for me not to hear. Letting go of the steering wheel for a second, he says, "Do these hands look like the hands of a killer?"

They are large and strong and look like they could easily wrap around my throat. "I don't want you going out of your way. If you could just drop me off at the nearest hotel, that would be great." And I'll hope no one finds me there.

"I'm on my way there anyway."

"You're going to the cabin too?"

He frowns. "Would I drive for hours just to take you there?"

"Are you staying the night?"

His frown deepens. "I'm planning to stay a few days."

I nibble my bottom lip. "I can't stay there with you." How can I spend days alone with Lucas when we hate each other? This car ride is uncomfortable enough. We'd probably kill one another.

"Didn't you want to go someplace where no one will find you?"

"I do." More than anything.

"If that's what you really want, the cabin it is. If not, I'll drop you off on the side of the road and you can find your own way to a hotel. I've wasted enough time already."

Well, what kind of reaction did I expect? I have dragged him into my problems.

The cabin is far from lying on a white, sandy beach with a mojito in my hand. Although, it is a place where no one can find me and I can take the time to nurse my wounds. Sort my feelings out and heal my broken heart. Except, at the moment, I feel more furious than heartbroken. Darren embarrassed me in front of millions of people. How could he do that? So, if sharing a cabin with Lucas is what I need to do to sort out the emotions swirling through me, then so be it.

"I'll stay at the cabin." The Alessis are rich. It's probably more a mansion than a cabin. If I stay in my own room and keep to myself, we won't have to be in each other's space much. Right?

Chapter Four

LUCAS

After six hours of driving, which included Penelope needing three bathroom breaks and a stop for snacks, we finally arrive at the cabin. Thankfully, for the last two hours, she's been sleeping, and I could try to pretend she wasn't in the car. Except the soft rose and vanilla scent of her perfume drifting toward me wouldn't allow me to.

What have I done? Last night's events have snowballed into something I never thought possible. Helping Penelope and taking her to my cabin is the last thing I'd ever imagine doing. Years of resentment toward her is coiled in my gut. Yet I've pushed it aside to get her out of the shit she's fallen into. What the fuck?

Pulling up in front of the cabin, I turn off the engine and nudge Penelope's shoulder. "Wake up."

She doesn't move. This woman really can sleep, even without alcohol.

I try again. "Wake up. We're here."

Her eyes blink open, and she stretches her arms out wide. I dodge a fist that is heading toward my face. Wouldn't surprise me if she did that on purpose.

After rubbing her eyes, she glances out of the windshield, looking confused. "Where are we?"

"The cabin."

"This is your cabin?"

"Yes."

"It's so...small and...*old*."

"What were you expecting, the Taj Mahal?"

"No. Something...else." Worry lines crease her forehead.

If she's changed her mind, she can find her own way back. I'm not spending another six hours trapped in a car with her again. Once is enough.

"Well, this is it," I say. "Sorry it doesn't meet your standards. Are you coming inside or staying here?"

She nibbles on her bottom lip with indecision. As she decides, I get out and head around to the trunk to take out my bag.

What was I thinking bringing her to the cabin? Obviously I wasn't thinking. The place isn't big enough for the two of us. The last thing I need is to be cramped with her in a tiny room.

Penelope must have decided, because she gets out of the car and takes her luggage from the backseat and follows me.

"Careful of the top step. It wobbles," I warn her.

The cabin needs a few repairs. It's never bothered me before; I spent my time hiking or fishing. Now with Penelope here, and the way she's cautiously scanning the cabin, those necessary repairs to the log shack are glaringly obvious. The porch sags, and the timber stairs are rotting—it's only a matter of time until my foot breaks through one. The support beams holding up the awning look like they can keel over with a puff of wind. And I know there are shingles missing from the roof. There are buckets inside in case it rains.

Maybe I should have warned her about the cabin's condition before I offered her a place to stay. Oh well, it's too late now.

As I open the door, her eyes widen with surprise. "It's not locked?"

"Don't need them. I'm the only one who comes here."

Penelope is standing on the rickety porch like she's too scared to go any further. "What if someone does?"

"They won't."

"What if they do?"

I sigh with frustration and drop my bag onto the floor. Dust particles bounce in the afternoon sun. "I have a gun if I need it. It's mainly to scare off bears, but I'll use if for intruders if I have to."

Her face pales. "There are bears here?"

"Yes."

She fiddles with the strap of her purse on her shoulder. I bet she's regretting her decision to come here. "Oh..."

"Don't worry. They rarely come to the cabin."

"So, we will be safe here?"

"Don't annoy me and you will be."

She pulls a face.

I hold my arm in a way to gesture her inside. "In or out."

Lifting her luggage, she steps inside then gasps, "This is it?" Her mouth falls open as she slowly spins on the spot to take in the small space.

The interior isn't much better than the exterior. The one room functions as bedroom, dining room, and kitchen. The bathroom is outside. An old, blackened fireplace needs missing stones replaced, and the chimney needs cleaning. Timber floors have gaps between the planks, letting in cool air, and the log walls do little to keep the draft out either.

Feeling defensive of my home away from home, I cross my arms over my chest. "It's not a five-star hotel, but it's comfortable."

Her nose screws up. "If you say so."

"You don't have to stay." I point toward the door. "Follow the track until you get to the main road. Maybe you can hitch a ride back. You better hope some psychopath doesn't pick you up. And oh...watch out for bears."

She dips her head. "I'm sorry. I'm acting like an ungrateful bitch. All I've done is complain when you have gone above and beyond for me."

Giving the room another scan, her gaze lands on the double bed up against the wall. I've never brought a woman here before, and therefore, needed nothing bigger or cleaner.

"There's only one bed," she says, stating the obvious. "Umm...We're not going to...arhhh... Where will we sleep?"

Now she has a problem sharing a bed with me? She seemed quite comfortable last night.

I pull the dust sheet off it. "The bed is mine. You can sleep on the recliner."

She stares at the old chair with disgust. The brown faux leather is peeling off the seat, and if you sit on a certain spot, a spring pokes you in the ass. Garrett hated it and opted to sleep on the floor in a sleeping bag.

"This is my only option?" she asks.

Is she hinting for an invitation for me to give up the bed? Not going to happen.

"Your options are the chair or the car." I fold the sheet and place it inside a cupboard.

Her shoulders sag on a sigh. She looks so miserable I think she might cry.

"While you're sorting out your sleeping arrangements, I need to head into town to get supplies."

"There's a town?" Hope sparks in her eyes.

"A small one. There's a convenience store with a post office, a diner, and a bar. That's about it."

"Do the locals know you?"

I frown. "Yes, why?"

"Do they know you're Lucas Alessi from Alessi Fashion House?"

I shrug. "Not sure. It's never come up in conversation with anyone. Why are you asking?"

"If anyone recognizes you as 'Lucas Alessi', someone might realize I'm here with you." She gnaws at her fingernail with worry.

I chuckle. She has no clue about this give-no-fucks town. "No one will care."

"Really?"

"Yes, really," I reply.

"That sounds like heaven."

She smiles, the gesture lighting up her face and drawing my attention to her full lips. Kissable lips. I quickly glance away. Why am I looking at her mouth? And why the fuck am I tempted to kiss it? Nothing good comes out of that mouth.

Oblivious to where my mind has wandered to, she says, "If there's a town, do you think they have accommodation?"

"Ready to leave so soon?" It's a great idea. Two minutes alone in the cabin and I'm wondering what her mouth tastes like.

"It feels a little crowded in here," she says.

Is she too polite to tell me the cabin is a run-down piece of shit? It's mine and I love it. I've had many great memories here. Mostly with my best friend Garrett. He never complained about where he had to sleep.

If Penelope wants to find accommodation elsewhere, it's probably for the best.

"Last I heard, they were renting rooms at the bar. If one's available, I'm sure Allie, the owner, will rent it to you."

"That would be amazing," Penelope says with exhilaration.

I cock an eyebrow. "Sick of me already?"

"Oh...no...I didn't mean..."

"Yeah...well, I like the idea of you not being here too." The sooner she's out of my life, the better.

She huffs. "I know you don't like me, but you can at least pretend you don't hate me so much. I'm no fan of yours either, yet I'm not nasty."

"Why would I do that? I don't hide my feelings."

"So I've noticed," she says dryly.

"I didn't promise you a trip to Disneyland."

She grabs the handle of her luggage and rolls it toward the door. "Nor did you mention you were taking me to hell."

Chapter Five

PENNY

Maybe *hell* was too strong of a word. But when I took in the cabin, it surely wasn't the mansion I'd imagine. Not even a quaint cottage with gingham curtains, plush rugs, and comfortable furniture. More like a dilapidated shack that might fall down with the breeze. And the recliner he said I could use to sleep on looked like it had been picked up off the side of the road after a semi-trailer had run over it.

There I go again sounding like an ungrateful bitch. He could have dropped me at a hotel where I'd be hounded again by the media. Yet he offered me a safe haven. A place where no one will find me.

When did I become such a snob? After my dad left when I was fifteen—never to be seen again—my mother was drowning in debt, and we had to move into a dump of a house. If it weren't for my Uncle Gerry, my mother's brother, moving us to New York two years later and taking us in after things got so bad we got evicted, who knows where I'd be today. Not only did he give us some place to live, but he also sent me to an upscale high school—where I met Lucas—and set me up for college. I'll always be grateful to him. My teenage years left no room for snobbery, so what happened between then and now?

Nothing that I was aware of, but yet... Has becoming a success and having money turned me into one?

On the drive into town, I place my elbow on the door and stare at my surroundings. Because I'd fallen asleep on the way to the cabin, I missed out on seeing the beautiful scenery. The sun is dappling through the thick leaves of the tall oak trees lining the road, guiding us like a tunnel. The greenery covering the ground looks like a lush carpet. The area gives the feel of being secluded and hidden away from the rest of the world. Exactly what I need. Not a sunny seaside vacation, but just as beautiful. Claudia would love it here.

Oh darn. Claudia! I told her I'd let her know where I was staying as soon as I could. It's been hours since I sent her a message. She must be worried. I pull my cell phone from my purse. There's no signal. I hold the phone up toward the windshield. Still nothing.

"What are you doing?" Lucas asks.

"Trying to get a signal to make a call."

"There's no reception out here."

My arm drops to my side. "Are you serious?"

"Yep." He slows down to avoid a deer scurrying across the road.

"What about in town?"

"The reception is sketchy. Calls drop in and out at the best of times."

My mouth falls open. Have we traveled back in time? "How do people communicate? Shop online?"

Lucas shrugs. "Not everyone's lives revolve around the internet. They like to do things face to face. Now's your time to try it. You might like it."

"Not having to deal with any calls for a few days does sound appealing."

"Then you're in the best place, Penelope."

"Why do you call me Penelope?"

"It's your name," he says like I've asked a silly question.

"No one calls me by my full name unless it's for work. All my friends call me Penny."

He takes his eyes off the road and his gaze bores into me. "We are not friends, are we, *Penelope*?"

A heavy weight lands on my chest. "No, I guess we're not." How stupid of me to forget how we really feel about each other.

A few minutes later, we pass a *Welcome to Oaks Valley* sign and drive into the town. Lucas was right, there isn't much here. There's a small strip of red and brown brick shops with arched windows, and rows of planter boxes filled with colorful flowers decorate the sidewalk. It looks like something from a movie.

Lucas pulls into a parking space in front of the This 'n That convenience store. I get out of the car and follow Lucas inside. Maybe I can get service to call Claudia and my mother. A bell chimes as we enter. By the looks of the empty aisles, we are the only customers. How do people survive financially out here? They are so remote and cut off from any major city.

We both pick up a basket. I may need some snacks; who knows what food the bar offers. I keep it simple with muffins, fruit, and bottled water. I'll get more later when I know how the accommodation is set up for cooking. Lucas fills his basket with whatever it is he needs.

When we have everything, we take our groceries to the counter. An older woman with flaming red hair, wearing tight, skinny jeans and a blue flannel shirt, greets us with a cigarette dangling from her lips. Taking a long drag, she puts it out in an ashtray filled with butts. She gives Lucas a beaming, yellow-toothed smile. "Lucas, darlin'. I was beginnin' to wonder if you were ever comin' back." Her voice is deep and raspy, probably from smoking.

"I could never stay away from you, Flo. You're the light of my life," Lucas flirts.

Flo pats her short curls and blushes like a young schoolgirl. "You're always so charmin'." Then her gaze travels over to me. "And who have you brought with you?" She scans me from head to toe. It's been a long day traveling. My cream-colored linen pants and shirt are wrinkled from the car ride. I must look a mess.

"Flo, this is Penelope. She's my...arhh...she is..." Lucas stumbles with the introduction. As we are not friends, like he pointed out earlier, what are we? Will he introduce me as his enemy?

Flo smacks her hand on the counter, causing a cigarette to fall from the ashtray. "You've gone and gotten yourself a girlfriend." She chuckles. It comes out more as a hack. "I never thought I'd see the day. Don't let Alison find out."

"Penelope is *not* my girlfriend. I'm just helping her out with something," Lucas explains.

"Mmm-hmm." Flo grins, looking unconvinced.

I place my hand on Lucas' forearm and pout. "Honeybee, you told me I was the love of your life." I sniff and dab at my eye. "I thought we had something special." That's payback for looking so appalled over Flo mistaking us for a couple.

Lucas' head swings toward me. Anger pinches his face. I smirk with glee, not caring that I pissed him off. I have to entertain myself somehow. I need something to help me crawl out of the cave of misery I'm living in.

Through gritted teeth, he says, "You are *not* my girlfriend."

I drop my bottom lip and make it tremble. "How can you say such a thing? You told me last night how much you loved me."

"Penelope, stop talking crap," he warns.

I dab my eyes again, ignoring him. "I have to tell my momma to cancel the wedding. She'll be so disappointed. The swan ice sculptures have already been ordered."

Lucas' mouth opens and closes with exasperation.

Flo laughs/hacks. "Oh boy. You've got your hands full with this one, Lucas. I like her. It's about time you find a woman who's gonna tame you."

A vein ticks at the side of his jaw. "She's not...we're not..." He shakes his head with defeat. "Just ring these up please so I can get the hell out of here."

I silently snicker under my breath. It's funny seeing Lucas so flustered. Although, I'm sure I'm going to hear about it when we get out of the store.

After Flo bags our groceries, we head back to the car. He opens the passenger side door and tosses his bags onto the backseat. He slams the door and spins around. "What was that about in there?"

Here it comes. The anger is vibrating from him.

Oh, he's mad, yet I can't bite back my smile. "I was just teasing you."

He throws me a disgusted look. "Don't. People around here talk and will get the wrong idea about us. That's the last thing I want."

With him looking so irritated, I'm not offended by his comment. It makes me giggle. "You should have seen your face. When Flo said it was about time you found a woman to tame you, your eyes bugged so far out of their sockets I thought they were going to drop to the floor."

Taking a step closer to me, his face is inches away from mine. His expression darkens. My breath catches in my lungs from the intense look on his face. All hilarity is dropped. Not from fear; from something else I can't explain. For a second, his gaze lands on my lips. I swallow hard, waiting for what may come.

When he looks back at me, coldness flashes in his eyes. "No one will ever tame me."

Wow. "Touchy subject, is it?" I need a moment to figure out what just happened. Was Lucas about to kiss me then changed his mind? Surely not.

When he'd looked at my lips, my heart stopped with anticipation. Goodness, there is something seriously wrong with me if the thought of Lucas kissing me isn't so bad.

It must have something to do with how messed up my life is at the moment. I have feelings and emotions getting jumbled around inside me. I don't have time to stew on it, because instead of answering my question—not that I thought he would—he points to a small building across the street with motorcycles and a couple of cars parked out front.

"That's the bar. Ask for Alison. She'll let you know if she has a room available." He moves around to the driver's side of the car.

When he opens the door and starts to slide in, I realize he's leaving me here. "Wait! Are you not coming in?" Suddenly, I'm feeling vulnerable, not knowing what I'll be walking into. For the first time since learning about Darren's affair, I'll be alone with my thoughts of my failed relationship and where I go from here.

"Why would I?" He frowns.

"What if they have nothing available?"

"You'll work it out." Again, he starts to get into the car.

"Wait!" I stop him again.

He drops his head and blows out a frustrated breath. "What now?"

"I need my luggage."

I know this is what I wanted, yet anxiety at being left alone in a small town is tightening my chest. What if something happens? I'm in the middle of nowhere with dodgy cell reception. Lucas isn't exactly a friend—he made that perfectly clear—but he's no stranger. I'm clinging to him for support.

Lucas pulls my luggage from the back of the jeep and places it at my feet. "Can I go now?"

I shift my shopping bag from one hand to the other, secure the strap of my purse over my shoulder, and hold onto the luggage's handle. I have no reason to keep him here, yet I say, "Can you help me with my stuff please? I'm struggling to carry it all." I make a show of adjusting the bags I'm holding like it's all so heavy.

What is wrong with me? I'm acting like some damsel in distress. This is not me. I always take care of myself. I'll blame it on a temporary brain malfunction due to my life-changing experience. When I get my act together, I'll make sure I'm never this vulnerable again.

Lucas raises an eyebrow like he's not sure whether to believe me, but he doesn't comment on it. "Sure." He closes the car door and takes the luggage handle out of my hand and rolls it across the street. I quickly follow behind him.

Lucas pushes through the solid timber doors. Immediately, I'm met with the smell of stale tobacco and old beer. The log-lined walls are covered in battered street signs, old license plates, and longhorn skulls. Scarred wooden tables and red stools are scattered haphazardly around the room. Shania Twain is blasting how she feels like a woman from the speakers. This bar looks like it belongs in Texas, not six hours from New York City.

A woman behind the bar stops drying a glass, smacks the dishcloth on the counter, and saunters her way to us. Her hips swing from side to side in tight, faded jeans that look painted on. A black leather vest is working hard holding in her full breasts. Tanned tassel cowboy boots click on the hardwood floor. She pauses in front of Lucas, tosses her long, straight, silky black hair over her shoulder, and slaps him across the face.

Lucas' head snaps over his shoulder, and he holds a hand over his red cheek. Looking at her with shock, he rubs his face. "What was that for?"

"That's for slinking out in the middle of the night. Do I mean nothing to you?"

He straightens. "Allie, I'm sorry. Of course you do. I...I...thought we were having fun. We agreed it was only a one-time thing."

She pokes a finger in his chest, the force hard enough for him to stumble back a step.

"What the hell, Allie?"

Is this Alison who Flo mentioned earlier? Looks like she's paying Lucas back for being a dirty dog. Probably promising her things he had no intention of giving her. I have to admit, seeing Lucas getting pushed around by a woman half his size is entertaining.

As I scan the room, men with leather vests and big, bushy beards—who I'm assuming belong to the motorcycles outside—are staring at Alison and Lucas and are grinning at the show. I'm not the only one finding Lucas' discomfort amusing.

"And why has it been months since I've seen you?" She crosses her arms over her chest.

"Allie, I've been busy and—"

In mid-sentence, Alison grabs Lucas' face with her hands. "Shut the fuck up and kiss me." Pulling him to her, she plants her lips on his mouth.

The bar erupts in a chorus of whistles and cheers. Alison presses her body against him and deepens the kiss. The cheers turn into lewd suggestions.

When they don't pull away and Lucas' hands slide down her back to palm her butt, something hot clutches in my stomach. Heat rises across my chest and up my neck. My reaction feels something like jealousy. How can that be? I don't even like Lucas. Barely know him. Plus, a couple of days ago, I had a fiancé whom I loved and was going to marry.

This feeling must be something else. Annoyance? Yes, that's it, because I'm tired, frustrated, heartbroken, and I'm trying to find a room to rent. While all I want is to lock myself away and be alone, he's hooking up with the woman I need to speak to.

Clearing my throat to distract them, I wait for them to stop. When they don't hear me or are ignoring me, I do it again, only louder.

Nothing.

I roll my eyes and tap Lucas on the shoulder. He breaks away with a disgruntled expression on his face at being interrupted. Too bad. I have things I need to do.

"I'm sorry to interrupt this joyful reunion—"

"Then don't." Lucas starts to turn away to go back in for another kiss.

I put my hand on his shoulder to stop him. "I've come here to get a room, remember? After we've settled that, then you can get back to playing tonsil hockey."

Alison juts out her hip and rests a hand on her waist. Her gaze travels over me from head to toe. With an air of indifference, she says, "Who are you?"

"I'm Penny," I don't give her my last name just in case she recognizes it. "Lucas said you might have a room to rent for a few nights."

"There are no vacancies." She hooks her arm through Lucas' and places a hand on his chest like she's staking her claim.

Well, you can have him. There's no competition from me.

"Oh," I sigh with regret. "That's too bad. Is there anywhere else in town I can stay?" If not, then I'm going back to Lucas' cabin. Although, with such tight accommodation and unappealing sleeping arrangements, I'd rather not.

"The bar is the only place that rents rooms," she says without looking at me. She's too preoccupied with running her finger along Lucas' jaw.

Blowing out a breath, I look around the bar like a solution is going to jump out at me. All I'm met with is deer heads hooked on walls, staring down at me with unblinking, glassy eyes.

"That means you're stuck with me for a few days, Lucas," I say. What other choice do I have? Besides, that was the original plan. Surely it won't be so bad.

Alison's head swings toward me. "You're staying with Lucas? In his cabin?"

Oh, now you want to look at me. Feeling threatened, are you?

"Lucas was kind enough to let me stay with him because—" I can't give her the real reason. The less people know around here, the better. I want no chance of the media finding me here. "Because I'm such a nature lover and his cabin is perfect for bird watching."

Alison narrows her gaze. Lucas pinches the bridge of his nose and shakes his head. It was the only thing I could come up with. By the way Alison is pinning me with a baleful glare, I don't think she believes me. If she only knew I'm no threat to her. Lucas is all hers.

"Is she your girlfriend?" she fires the question at Lucas.

If I was, would I let her have her hands all over him?

With a warning glare aimed at me, he says, "Don't even think about pulling the same shit you did in the store."

Now would be the perfect time to mess things up between him and Alison, but I keep quiet. I have no intention of causing trouble between the two.

To Alison, he says, "Allie, would I be kissing you in front of her if she was? And why would she be looking for a place to stay?"

So he calls her Allie, not Alison. Oh, that's because they're *friends*—and we are not. Although, from the way she stuck her tongue down his throat, they're more than friends.

She purses her lips. "Good point."

With another head-to-toe sweep over me, she nods to a door at the back of the bar next to the restrooms. "There is one room. I don't normally rent it out. It's not much. Could use a clean. There is a single bed, small stove—which doesn't work—and a kettle. You'll have to share the communal bathroom upstairs. The hot water lasts for about two minutes. If you're not showering first, it takes a few hours for the water to warm up again, or you can take a cold one. The bar gets noisy and rowdy and closes at two in the morning. You may not get much sleep. It's twenty dollars a night."

As bad as it sounds, I'll take staying in a dingy room at a noisy bar over spending the next few days with Lucas confined in a tiny cabin. "I'll take it."

Lucas raises an eyebrow. "After hearing what the accommodation is like, you still want to stay here? Do you think you can handle it?"

"Of course I can."

He shrugs a shoulder. "Doesn't sound like your kind of scene, city girl." He smirks.

There's no way I'm going to admit to him that the room is far from what I'm used to. And at twenty dollars a night, I'm a little scared to find out what it looks like. "And how do you know what my scene is?" I don't wait for him to answer. "Thanks for your concern. I'll be fine."

Before I find out what kind of room I've booked—or more like putting it off for as long as possible—I set my luggage by a booth and slide onto the cracked, vinyl seat.

"What are you doing?" Lucas asks.

Picking up the plastic menu, I scan the food selections. "Ordering food."

He doesn't respond, but I sense his hard presence getting closer. I glance up and am met with an annoyed expression on his face.

"Is there a problem?" I ask.

He crosses his arms over his chest. "Yes, there's a problem. I'm having dinner here with Allie."

Alison caresses her hand up and down Lucas' arm with sultry eyes. "And after dinner, I'll have you for dessert."

I roll my eyes, forcing myself not to gag. "I'm not stopping your dinner plans," I say to Lucas. Then I pass Alison the menu and order the buffalo wings, fries, and a diet coke.

Pulling a face like the last thing she wants to do is serve me, she tucks the menu under her arm. "I'll be right back." She plants a kiss on Lucas' lips before she leaves.

Walking away, she sways her hips, grabbing the attention of every man in the room. Except for Lucas. His eyes bore into me.

"What are you doing?" he asks.

"Waiting for dinner."

He rubs the tips of his fingers across his forehead then slides into the seat opposite me. "You wanted to stay hidden in case you get recognized. Now you're sitting in a bar packed with people. Are you doing this to piss me off?"

"First, the bar is far from packed." I scan the room. The motorcycle gang has just left, there's a couple having drinks in the booth next to mine, and two men are playing pool on the other side of the room.

No one is paying any attention to me. Except for Alison. She's wiping down the bar, throwing heat-seeking missiles with her eyes in my direction. I hope she doesn't spit in my food.

"And second, I didn't know you were staying. You bought food. I assumed you'd eat at the cabin."

"I changed my mind."

"Not my problem. If you don't like that I'm here, leave." I point at the door. I'm staying here now; he can't kick me out. "Or do you want to stay so you can continue to suck face with Alison?"

He smirks and casually relaxes in the seat. "*Suck face*? Are you in high school? Or just jealous?"

I scoff. "Jealous? Oh please. There's nothing to be jealous of. If you were listening, Alison said the stove in the room doesn't work, so I need to eat. That's why I'm staying."

Leaning forward, he sets his forearms on the table. The smirk drops from his face. "The sooner you're back in the city, the better."

I mirror his posture, our faces only inches apart. "You could have left me there. But you didn't. That's on you."

His gaze drops to my lips, lingering long enough for my heart to stop and my breath to quicken.

The thud of plates hitting the wooden table jerks me back. "Your wings and fries," Alison says tightly.

I busy myself picking out silverware from a basket on the table. "Smells delicious. Thank you," I say a little too enthusiastically.

Why did my stomach flutter when Lucas looked at my mouth like that? Maybe I should get out of here before I want him to do something stupid like kiss me. I inwardly shake myself. Kissing Lucas is the last thing I want to do. Obviously, if I was in my right mind, the thought of kissing him would make me ill.

"Let's get dinner over with so we can go back to my house. I have a table ready."

I glance at where Alison points to a corner. She's picked the darkest spot in the room. I have a feeling she'll get dessert started before their main meal arrives.

"Enjoy your dinner." Lucas rises to his feet.

"You too." I give him a tight smile.

He nods. Then he turns and follows Alison to their table.

My shoulders sag on a heavy sigh. Now that I'm on my own, I don't know what to do next. I should probably call Claudia and my mother; they'd know where to start. Plucking my cell phone from my purse, I swipe the screen. It doesn't turn on. *Great. The battery has died.* I'll charge it when I get to my room and call later.

The smell of tangy wings causes my stomach to grumble. All I had to eat today was gas station snacks. Now I'm starving. Devouring the food, I lick the spicy sauce from my fingers. Like I sense someone watching me, my gaze drifts over to Lucas' table. Even in the dim light, our eyes lock. Heat flushes my skin, making me want to fan my face. And it's not caused from the hot chicken wings. It's the way Lucas is staring at me like I'm his next meal.

How can that be? I'm seriously seeing things, or I'm delusional. I need to get out of here and away from Lucas. As much as I hate to go over there and interrupt their romantic meal, I need the key to my room.

Just as I'm about to make my way over to Lucas' table, a man walks into the bar and stops in front of me. A big smile spreads across his face, causing dimples to form on each cheek. A dark blond lock of his hair falls over his sparkling blue eyes, and he combs it back with his fingers where it stays perfectly in place. He's gorgeous, and judging by the way he swaggered into the room, he knows it.

His head tilts to the side as he takes me in. Oh no! Does he recognize me?

"I've never seen you in here before. I'd remember someone so beautiful," he says.

I sigh with relief. He doesn't know who I am. Was that a pickup line? Men don't usually approach me unless it's to get an autograph for their wives.

"Can I buy you a drink?" The track on the jukebox changes to a Luke Combs song; something slow and romantic. "Or would you like to dance?"

The man oozes confidence, yet he doesn't come across as sleezy. I can sense a cheekiness about him. Someone who'd be a lot of fun. Although I'm not sure I can trust my judgment. Look who I nearly married. Under Darren's charming personality was a dirty dog.

"I don't want a drink. Thank you. And there's no one dancing."

He shrugs. "So? We'll start a trend." He grins. Oh, those dimples. I'm sure they can make most women do just about anything. He holds out his hand. "What do you say? Want to have some fun?"

Fun does sound wonderful. It's something I haven't had in a long time. Do I know how to anymore?

"Hey buddy, she's not available," Lucas interrupts.

My mouth drops open. What is he doing?

The man takes a step back and holds his arms up by his sides like it's a stickup. "Sorry. Didn't know she was taken." He gives me an apologetic smile and walks to the bar.

I drop my fists on my hips. "Why did you do that?"

"Pretty Boy over there was getting a little too friendly."

"So?"

Lucas slides his hands into his pockets. "Just thought you didn't need any attention—you know, in case he recognized you."

"He didn't recognize me. Your interruption wasn't necessary. Or did you have another reason?"

"What other reason could I have?"

I shrug a shoulder. "You tell me."

He's the one who zeroed in on my lips and was staring at me from across the room. Could he be jealous? I mentally shake myself. Surely not.

He averts his gaze for a second. "There's no other reason."

"If you say so."

"I do say so." Then he swings out his arm in the man's direction and says, "He's all yours."

He turns to leave, and I stop him by placing a hand on his arm. He turns back, glances at where I'm touching—the muscles hardening under my palm—and he looks at me with a raised eyebrow.

"I don't have the energy to deal with another man right now. All I want to do is get the key to my room and go to bed."

He calls out to Alison. When she approaches us with a pissed-off expression aimed at me, Lucas tells her I want to go to my room.

"I'll show her the room, and I'll be right back. Then we can head over to my place." Alison fiddles with the collar of Lucas' t-shirt.

"Allie, as much as I'd love to come over, I'm beat. All I'm good for is sleep. I'm going to head back to the cabin."

Alison pouts her bottom lip. "Are you sure? I promise when you're home with me, you won't want to sleep."

Oh please! Alison makes me want to gag. Doesn't she care that I'm standing right next to her overhearing everything she's saying? Obviously not.

He removes her hand from him. "Not tonight."

Her face hardens. I bet she's not used to rejection.

Well, this is it. It's time to finally part ways with Lucas. I hold out my hand to him. "Thank you for all your help. I know it hasn't been easy for you. So I really appreciate it."

When he takes my hand to shake it, the connection sends a shock of electricity through my arm and sizzles into my chest. My gaze snaps up to meet Lucas' eyes, and they lock on mine. Did he feel the current too? Is his chest warming up like mine? My heart is beating rapidly, so I pull my hand out of his grip, and I take a step back. Like putting distance between us will break the connection. It didn't work. A slight sizzle is still charging my body.

Lucas clears his throat. "You're welcome. Good luck with everything." Turning to Alison, he says, "Bye, Allie."

There's no mention of seeing her again. Or arranging another night to meet. That doesn't mean that they won't. He said he's in Oaks Valley for a few days, so there's plenty of time.

I watch Lucas leave. I'm not as happy as I thought I'd be to see him go. Probably because he was there for me during my time of need. As much as I hate to admit it, it's hard letting him go.

"Get your bags," Alison demands as she walks toward the room.

I hurry to the booth and take the handle of my luggage and fling the strap of my purse over my shoulder and quickly follow her. She unlocks and opens the door to the room. Stepping inside, the air is thick with dust, and it clogs my throat. The light turns on above me, bathing the ugly, dingy room with brown, peeling wallpaper in a dim, flickering, yellow glow.

"How many days are you staying?" Alison asks. "Because payment is upfront."

"Arrh..." I'm not sure I can stay one night. "Maybe four or five days."

Alison holds her hand out, waiting for payment. I dig my wallet from my purse and count out money for five days. She folds the bills in half and tucks them behind her vest.

My attention lands on the bare mattress. "Is linen in the closet?" I ask, pointing to a crooked faux timber wardrobe.

"There's no linen provided."

I wish she'd mentioned that before I handed over my money. "Where can I get some?"

"You can buy sheets and towels in Flo's store across the street."

"Right, I better get over there then."

Alison examines her pink, manicured fingernails. "She closed ten minutes ago."

My shoulders sag. "What am I supposed to do without linen?"

Alison shrugs. "It's a warm night. You'll be fine."

I throw a dubious glance at the stained mattress and yellow pillow. My stomach rolls with disgust. "People actually stay here?"

"If you don't want it, just say so. It didn't look like Lucas wanted you at his cabin, so you don't have any other option." She smirks. I bet she's happy I'm not staying with him.

Unfortunately, she's right. It's my only option. This is it. This is home for the next few days. Or until I can arrange something else. Is there another in-the-middle-of-nowhere town that I can hide in? Can I risk it? I'm too tired to think about that now.

I just need to make it through one night.

Chapter Six

LUCAS

Letting myself into the cabin, I put the groceries away and get my bed ready. It's been a long and mentally challenging day with Penelope. Man, that woman has been a pain in my ass. I finally get the peace and quiet I came here for.

I put a kettle on the stove to boil water for tea. I wonder how Penelope is doing without a working stove? Shaking myself out of the thought, I pull a mug from the top cupboard. Why is she on my mind? She's no longer my problem.

Except ever since leaving the bar, she's all I've been thinking about. Even in the bar my eyes were drawn to her. Her body, her lips. The way she licked sauce from her fingers made my balls tighten with the thought of her sucking my dick into her mouth. And when that douchebag guy approached her, I sprang from my seat so fast to get him away from her.

I place my hands on the counter and hang my head. What the fuck is wrong with me? When I look at her, I'm supposed to feel disgust—want her the hell away from me. Yet it's the opposite. Lust burns through my veins, and I have to control myself to keep my hands off her.

I should have gone back to Allie's place and fucked all thoughts of Penelope from my mind. It's so messed up that I'm even thinking that way. Except my dick didn't even stir when Allie touched me. Besides, when we hooked up the last time I was in Oaks Valley, she knew we were only having fun—no commitment. A one-time thing. That's all I can offer. Today felt different. There was a possessiveness about her. Like I was her man.

I don't belong to anyone.

Never will.

When the water boils, I pour it into the mug and take it out on the porch. I breathe in the warm air pungent with forest scents. Dense darkness surrounds the cabin. I gaze up at the bright stars, and they seem close enough to touch. You don't get a sky like this in the city.

This time every year I come to the cabin for the anniversary of Garrett's death. He loved this place. It was our escape from the drama in our lives. It's never been the same without him. In two days it will be eight years since the car accident that killed him. The heaviness of that night and the years leading up to it sit heavy on my shoulders. I doubt I'll ever feel light again.

Finishing my tea, I head inside and put the mug in the sink. I kick off my boots and strip out of my clothes. Dropping naked on the bed, I stare up at the ceiling. It's not long until my eyes drift closed from the exhaustion of the day. A moment later—or it could be hours after I've fallen asleep—a noise outside wakes me.

Groggy with sleep, I sit and listen to my surroundings. Was that a car I heard? No one ever comes to the cabin, especially at night. Then the sound of shuffling feet hit the porch, and all dredges of sleep instantly vanish, and I bound to my feet. There's someone out there.

I don't have time to grab the gun from the closet and load it, so I snatch a knife from the butcher block next to the sink. With light footsteps, I slink to the door. Just as I reach it, the hinges creak as it slowly swings open. A dark figure steps into the room. Before they can move any further, I push my forearm against the intruder's chest, backing them against the wall and holding the knife to their neck.

"What the fuck do you want?" I thunder into their ear.

"Lucas...it's me...Penny. Don't...hurt me." Penelope's voice is whisper quiet, like she's too scared to speak too loud in case I slice her throat open. It's then that the scent of her floral perfume and the softness of her body—her breasts under my arm—registers. Fuck! I drop my arms and step away.

"Jesus, Penelope. Why are you creeping around the cabin?"

"I didn't want to wake you." Her voice is louder and stronger now that the threat of a sharp blade at her throat has been taken away.

I rake my fingers through my hair. "I could have killed you."

She gives a sheepish smile I can just make out from the dim light of the moon shining through the open door. "I'm grateful you didn't."

Tossing the knife onto the counter, I stomp to the side of the bed and flick on the lamp.

Penelope's gaze drops to my crotch, and her eyes widen. With a loud gasp, she spins around. I'd forgotten I was naked. In my rush to get to the intruder, I had no time to dress.

Finding my jeans on the recliner, I pull them on. "You can turn around."

She peeks over her shoulder like she's checking to make sure I'm telling the truth. When she seems satisfied, she faces me. I haven't put a shirt on, and her gaze scans my chest. Is that an appreciative expression on her face? No, my mind can't go there. Not when I'm trying damned hard to stop thinking of her without *her* clothes on.

"What happened to your room at the bar?" With her bags sitting on the porch in front of the door, I'm guessing she's here to stay. And just when I thought I'd gotten rid of her.

She fiddles with a button on her blouse. "It was horrible. The place was filthy. There was no linen, and the bed was so stained it looked like someone had died on it and hadn't been found in days." She shudders.

"It's rumored that old Mr. Duffy drank himself to death in that room." Penelope's mouth drops open, and I add, "No one has ever confirmed it though."

"I'm not surprised. It was disgusting. I'm sure the mattress is rid-dled with bedbugs and other bodily fluids." She scratches at her arms like insects are biting.

"So you thought you could come back here?" There goes my peace and quiet.

She shuffles her feet. "You did originally offer to let me stay. I didn't think it would be a problem?" She says it as a question, like she's wondering if I'm retracting the invitation.

I scratch the back of my head. After the reaction I had in the bar, having her here might be a problem.

When I say nothing, she quickly adds, "It's only for a few days. You won't even know I'm here."

I doubt that. "You're still sleeping on the recliner."

She smiles with relief. And damn if it doesn't shoot into my chest. Then a thought hits me. "How did you get back here?"

Pulling her luggage inside from the porch, she closes the door. "Mitch from the bar gave me a ride."

"Who's Mitch?"

"The guy you threatened to leave me alone." She pushes her palms on the cushions of the recliner like she's testing it for comfort.

My body stiffens. "You got into a car with a stranger?" A stranger who wanted to jump her bones. "He could have been a serial killer for all you know." Is she nuts?

She nibbles at her bottom lip. "He seemed nice enough. Plus, Alison assured me I was in excellent hands. Mitch has even offered to take me hiking. Apparently there's a natural hot spring around here."

My jaw clenches. "You didn't accept his offer, did you? Just because Allie has given Mitch the thumbs-up doesn't mean he won't dispose of your body off the nearest cliff."

She rolls her eyes. "I thought that would make you happy. Then I'd be out of your life permanently."

"Normally, I'd be ecstatic. But as I've said before—since I'm the last person you've been seen with, that will make me the number one suspect."

Shaking her head, she says, "You're so dramatic."

Lifting the luggage onto the bed, she opens it. A bunch of multi-colored, lacy bras and panties get tossed around among skimpy bikinis and silky clothing.

"What the hell have you packed?" I swallow hard at the thought of her wearing any of those scraps of material.

She looks at me and back at the luggage. Understanding at my question springs to her face. "Oh, I was supposed to be in Bora Bora. I never expected to be staying in a cabin in the woods."

"Weren't you going with a friend?"

"Yes. Why?"

"You packed all that kinky stuff for a girlfriend?"

She picks up a long, white, silky negligée. "This was the bag I was taking on my honeymoon. I never got the chance to repack it." She lays the garment over her arm. "Where's the bathroom so I can change?"

Holy fuck! She's wearing that? Tonight? While my dick is getting harder by the second? Oh hell no. "As you can see, the cabin is only one room. It doesn't have a bathroom. There's only an outhouse."

Her lip curls. "An outhouse? Like *outside*?"

"That's where you find them."

She hugs her arms around her waist and glances out the window. Without a flashlight she won't be able to see two feet in front of her if she goes out there. "I guess I'll have to get changed here."

"You're not wearing that, are you?" I point to the negligée on her arm.

"I have nothing else."

"I have a t-shirt you can use...you know, so you're more comfortable." And to cover up as much of her body as possible.

"That would be great. Thanks."

At the dresser, I take out the first t-shirt I find and hand it to her. She looks at me and doesn't move. "Is there something else you need?" I ask.

"Can you turn around please?"

"Sure." I turn. The rustling sounds of her removing her clothes has me itching to take a peek.

After a moment, she says, "I'm decent. You can turn around."

When I do, my tongue gets stuck to the roof of my mouth. She is anything but decent. I thought seeing her in a t-shirt would be better than the sexy negligée. Man was I wrong. There's nothing sexier than a woman wearing a man's t-shirt. Why didn't I remember that? The neck of the white top slips off her shoulder, exposing her creamy skin. The hem falls mid-thigh, showing off a decent amount of leg. Holy shit! I can't drag my eyes away from her.

She adjusts the neck of the top so it covers her shoulder. "Thanks for this."

I clear my throat. "No problem."

Pointing to the recliner, she says, "I should get some sleep. Do you have a blanket?"

I nod toward the small closet in the corner of the room. "You'll find them in there."

She gives the closet a dubious glance. "Nothing furry and creepy is going to jump out at me, right?"

"Last I checked it was safe."

As Penelope walks to the closet, I get the back view of her in my t-shirt and my gaze lands on her ass. The fabric rises with each step she takes, threatening to expose what panties she's wearing. It makes me want to tell her to forget the recliner and join me in my bed so I can take it off her and explore her body.

This is *Penelope Aldin*. Why am I thinking of her this way? It's the last thing I want to do.

Except once there was a time I did.

Then everything turned to shit. Instantly, my dick deflates. My back stiffens. I move away and get into bed. Turning my back toward her, I flick off the light. Let her manage to get back to the recliner in the dark.

There's a bump and a hiss like she's hit something. Then a moment of silence before she says, "Goodnight."

I don't answer. If she hadn't gotten me expelled from high school, my life would have taken a different route. I wouldn't have fucked around for months with no purpose.

I wouldn't have called Garrett one drunken night.

And Garrett would still be alive.

Chapter Seven

PENNY

The soft glow of the morning sun filters through the windows. Yawning, I stretch my arms over my head. My neck is stiff from sleeping in an awkward position, and I tilt it from side to side to smooth out the kinks. The recliner was less than comfortable. I'd tossed and turned most of the night trying to avoid the springs poking into my butt. When I rise from the chair, my body protests like I'm a ninety-year-old woman.

I dread spending another night in that torture chair, but what other choice do I have? Sharing Lucas' bed is not an option—not that he'd have me—and there's no way I'm going back to that disgusting room at the bar. Maybe he'll be kind enough to swap tonight. Yeah, right. I have a better chance of being a backup dancer for Beyoncé.

Lucas' bed is empty, and he isn't in the cabin. A noise draws me out onto the porch where I find him sitting on the top step putting water, supplies, and a camera into a backpack.

"Are you going somewhere?"

Lucas turns his head over his shoulder, gives me a quick glance, then continues packing. "I'm going on a hike."

"That sounds fun. Give me a second to change and I'll come with you."

Standing, he flings the bag onto his back and slides his arms through the straps. "You're not coming." Without looking my way, he treks toward a footpath among the trees.

"Are you seriously going to leave me here on my own?" I call out to him. Anything can be lurking around the forest. Man or beast. I cross my arms over my chest and shiver. Scanning the area, I search for any predators.

"Yep," he yells.

"What am I supposed to do?"

"Go find the hot spring with Mitch for all I care." Then he disappears among the green foliage.

That's not a bad idea. I'd love to go exploring. Working in the city doesn't give me much of a chance to enjoy the great outdoors. But even if I had a way of contacting Mitch, he's not the one I want to go hiking with. My mind drifts to Lucas and I immediately shake the image away. Nor do I want to go anywhere with Lucas. What was I thinking asking if I can tag along? The more time we spend apart, the better.

Back inside the cabin, I open my luggage to change. I pluck through the clothes I packed for my honeymoon. The only outfits I have are suitable for the beach and fancy restaurants. Nothing appropriate for trekking through the woods. So I choose floral shorts with an oversized, white linen shirt. I tie the shirt into a knot at my waist and slip my feet into sandals.

Unable to put off using the outhouse any longer, I head outside. I find it nestled among shrubs, and I hesitate for a second before tentatively opening the door. I search for a light switch, but there isn't one. The only light is coming from the open door. Once I see that it's free from any creatures, I quickly do my business—with the door open, there's no way I'm closing it with no light—and head back inside.

I get my first proper look at the small space. Lined along one wall is a stone fireplace blackened with use. An old log is used as a mantel with a set of antlers hanging above. The wooden floors are scuffed from what looks like frequent use, and the limited furniture is mismatched. A small, dark blue kitchen with a pale timber counter and stove fill out a corner. The place is dusty, a little grimy, but cozy.

With Lucas gone, I sink onto the bed and look around. What am I supposed to do now? He said he's gone hiking. That could take hours...or days! No, he only had a backpack. He had no camping equipment. He'll be back today.

My gaze drifts to the window, and I spot his car. Maybe I can go into town, and then I can make calls. Claudia and my mother must be worried sick about me. Getting to my feet, I search the cabin for the keys. When I come up empty, I check his car in case he left them in there. It's locked. I drop my hands on my hips and blow out a breath. Why would he take them? Did he think I'd leave him here? I giggle. He'd deserve it.

Looking around the cabin, I contemplate going for a walk. But I don't know the area or have the right gear. Knowing my luck lately, I'd probably get lost, or worse, eaten by a bear.

Patches of tiny, white and purple wildflowers spreading along the forest floor catch my eye. I pick a bunch and bring them into the cabin. The space could do with a pop of color. I search for something to put them in. I'd be shocked if I found a vase. But I find the next best thing—mason jars. I fill three up with water, arrange the flowers, and place them around the room.

Next, I find cleaning supplies under the sink and get to work sprucing up the cabin. I feel like Snow White waiting for the forest creatures to help me for when the seven dwarfs arrive. Unfortunately, the only one coming home will be Grumpy. When I sing *Whistle While You Work* I know I must have something seriously wrong with me. Yet I feel the best I have in two days.

With everything going on, I haven't had the chance to unpack what's happened in my life. Darren cheated. Publicly. Humiliated me the worst way possible right before our wedding. I scrub the counter with vigorous strokes. When he told me he loved me, was it all a joke to him? I pause in my scrubbing and stand straight. When *was* the last time he told me he loved me or *I* to him? It wasn't a word we threw around daily for the heck of it, but we did say it often enough...didn't we?

Once the sink and kitchen counter are clean, I tackle the stove. It needs a bit more elbow grease than the counter. As I work, I try to remember the last time Darren and I did the simple things like snuggle on the couch while watching a movie. Kiss until we were breathless. Make love for hours. Quick pecks when leaving the house every morning was the most affection we've shared in months. Were we always so cold? Even if our relationship wasn't filled with hearts and flowers, shouldn't I at least feel heartbroken? Maybe I'm still numb with shock. I'm sure once it wears off it will all hit me.

I spend the rest of the day cleaning and scrubbing floors. For such a small space it's taken me hours. I wish I had fabric and sewing equipment to whip up curtains. Not much I can do about the cracked fabric on the recliner. It needs to be tossed out. I don't think Lucas would appreciate that, so I find another blanket in the closet, fold it into a padded square, and place it over the offending springs. Hopefully that will help me sleep better.

Exhaustion hits, and because Lucas isn't here, I lay on his bed, curl into a ball, and I drift off to sleep. When I wake and glance out of the window the sun is dipping behind the trees. Getting up, I stretch and walk to the door. Still no sign of Lucas. It will be dark soon; shouldn't he be back by now? Worry niggles. Is he okay?

While I wait for him to return, I pull out ingredients from the fridge to start dinner. Apart from fruit and a few crackers, I haven't eaten much all day, and my stomach is grumbling with hunger. Lucas stocked up on steak and vegetables, and I use it to make a meal.

I prepare carrots, potatoes, and pumpkin in a dish and slide it into the oven. When they're almost done, I fry the steaks in a wonky pan. Just as I'm plating everything up, heavy footsteps hit the porch. A moment later Lucas walks into the cabin. He nods a greeting and hangs his backpack on a hook by the door.

"You're back," I state the obvious and inwardly cringe.

"Yep."

His mood is dark. Closed off. After taking a walk in nature, you'd think he'd come back looking refreshed. Maybe it was a hard or treacherous trail and he's tired.

Stepping further into the room, he pauses and glances around. "You cleaned up."

"Since you left me here with nothing to do, I had to entertain myself somehow."

He doesn't apologize for leaving me. Not that I thought he would. "Thanks."

"You're welcome."

"Something smells good." He sits at the rickety—what I'm assuming is the dining table—and kicks off his boots then places them neatly next to his chair.

"I made dinner. I didn't know how you like your steak cooked."

"I'm sure it's fine."

He gets to his feet, pulls out silverware from a drawer, and takes two beers from the fridge and sets them on the table. I carry over our meal, and we sit down to eat.

"Where did you hike to?" I ask as I slice into the steak.

"Thomas Ridge."

"What's there?"

He takes a swig of beer. "Trees."

Wow. Lucas is in a mood. He's normally not the most pleasant man to be around, but this is next level. Did something happen on his hike? The only reason I'm trying to make conversation is because he's letting me stay with him. Otherwise I'm happy to ignore him. If he doesn't want to talk, I won't push him.

We finish our dinner in silence.

Lucas collects the dishes and takes them to the sink. "That was delicious. Thanks."

"I cooked, you clean," I say. Although I thought I was happy for no conversation, I'm not used to so much quiet.

"Of course." When the dishes are washed, dried, and put back into cupboards, he walks over to the bed. "I'm beat. I'm going to bed."

He turns his back to me and lifts his t-shirt over his head and tosses it on a nearby chair. The muscles in his back ripple. His shoulders are broad, his waist narrow. Next he takes off his pants, folds them, and places them with the t-shirt.

I swallow hard. This man is built. I got a brief glance of the total package last night, but it was so fast, and I was so shocked, I never got to appreciate what I was looking at. Now, with his back toward me, I can take my time.

His fingers slip into the waistband of his underwear like he's about to slide them down. I hold my breath. Is he going to get naked again? He stops—darn it.

He pulls the blankets back and gets into bed. Then places the blankets over his waist. It leaves his chest exposed, and I'm struggling to keep my eyes off his corrugated abs.

"Try not to snore tonight," he says.

I suck in an offended gasp, which snaps my attention away from his body. "I don't snore."

Placing a hand under his head, he turns to look at me. "Yeah, you do."

"I do not!" I bristle.

"I almost smothered you with a pillow."

Getting up from the table, I sit on the recliner. It's a little more comfortable with the extra padding on the seat. "Why didn't you?"

"As tempting as it was, I'd have a body to dispose of, so I decided against it. Too much trouble."

"How considerate."

He chuckles. At first I thought I might be hearing things. Lucas hasn't laughed once since he plucked me from the hotel's hallway. It's deep and sexy, and it makes my stomach quiver.

"The cabin looks great. Thanks again for cleaning it."

"You're welcome."

"The flowers are little much."

I smile. "Too feminine for such a masculine cabin?"

"Something like that." He grins. Then he rolls to his side, giving me his back. "Goodnight, Penelope."

"Goodnight."

I contemplate whether to stay up for a while. I packed a book in my luggage I could read. Yawning, I'm surprised to find I'm still tired even after taking a nap this afternoon. *Must be all that fresh mountain air.*

I pick up the t-shirt Lucas gave me to sleep in. There's no way I'm going into the outhouse to change. Can I risk Lucas not turning around? He's breathing heavily, but surely he's not asleep yet? I turn off the light. It's safer. In the cover of darkness, I dress in the t-shirt, sit back on the recliner, and place the blanket over my body.

As I'm drifting off to sleep, a flittering thought enters my mind. *Maybe Lucas isn't as bad as I thought.*

Chapter Eight

◆─◆─◆

PENNY

The next morning starts the same way. I wake up to discover I'm alone in the cabin, and I find Lucas sitting on the top porch step packing supplies into a backpack.

"Are you going hiking again?"

He turns to look at me over his shoulder. "Yes."

"Any chance you'll let me join you this time?"

"No."

I didn't expect any other answer, but I thought I'd ask anyway. I sigh with disappointment. "Have fun."

"There's nothing fun about it," I think I hear him mumble as he walks away.

If that's true, why is he going hiking if he doesn't like it? I watch him disappear among the trees.

There's no way I'm spending another day at the cabin with nothing to do. Racing inside, I rummage through my luggage, looking for something appropriate to wear. But it's not like the forest fairies repacked my bag with hiking gear. There's no time to search through Lucas' closet; he'll be long gone and I'll never find him if I take up too much time. I'm going to have to make do with what I have.

I pull out a sundress. Forgoing a bra, I quickly dress then slide my feet into strappy sandals. Tossing my hair into a messy bun, I secure it with a clip and run out the door. Hopefully he's not too far and I can catch up to him.

Pausing at the trail, I hesitate. He doesn't want company. Will he get mad if I join him? Probably. I pull my shoulders back. This forest doesn't belong to him. I'm free to wander wherever I want. He can't stop me. But I'll keep my distance, so he doesn't see me. With my mind made up, I scurry through the shrubs.

The sunlight dapples over the leaf-covered path. Birdsong and insect sounds float in the air. The smell of damp vegetation is strong. Being surrounded by the beauty and music of nature immediately sends a sense of peace through my mind and body. Like all the stress and drama of my life have flittered away.

Up ahead, I spot Lucas. His stride is long and determined, like he's not taking the time to soak up his surroundings. Like he's on a mission to get somewhere.

I follow him, taking care to not make noise as I avoid stepping on twigs. The bottom of my dress gets snagged on a fallen branch, and I yank it free, tearing a large hole in the soft fabric. The ripping sound, to me, seems to ricochet through the forest, and I freeze. Did Lucas hear? Looking up ahead, I see that he's still trudging along, unaware of me following him.

Breathing a sigh of relief, I continue on. If I keep following, eventually I'm going to make myself known. I can't keep creeping after him like some stalker. For now, I'll see how far he goes. If I get too tired, I'll turn back, and he'll never know I was here.

As time passes, the path inclines, and my legs grow heavier with each step. My breathing is labored. Sweat trickles between my breasts, and fallen strands of hair sticks to my neck. My feet are covered with dirt. My sandals definitely belong on the beach, not in the woods.

Why did I follow Lucas? I could have used the time alone in the cabin deciding how to move forward with my life when I get back to the city. I still don't know what damage the paparazzi have caused with the photos they took of me. When we get back from the hike, I have to ask Lucas to take me into town. I can't put off calling my mother and Claudia.

The path gets steeper and steeper. I'm now climbing over boulders and fallen trees. My dress is sticking to my body. I'd give anything to have a drink of water. I'm not built for anything athletic. This is why I should stop putting off going to the gym. Maybe if I did, I wouldn't feel like every muscle in my body is screaming in pain.

Just as I'm about to turn around and head back, Lucas stops, tugs the backpack off his shoulders, and drops it at his feet. Sitting on a flat rock, he unzips the bag and pulls out two beers. Did he go on a hike to drink? I move closer to get a better look and find a large boulder to hide behind. Squatting down, I peek around the rock and watch him. I should tell him I'm here. I don't feel right hiding. Yet something tells me in my gut I might be interrupting a private moment, so I stay hidden.

Lucas twists the bottle top off a beer and holds it up in the air in a toast. His mouth is moving like he's saying something. But the sound of his voice gets whisked away by the breeze, and I can't hear him. Then he takes a swig of beer, turns the bottle upside down and pours the liquid onto the ground. Why is he doing that? When it's empty, he sets it on the ground and picks up the other bottle. Again, he toasts toward the sky. This time he doesn't pour the beer out. He sips at it and stares out into the distance with a look of sadness on his face.

Folding his legs up, he rests his wrist on his knee, the bottle dangling from his fingers as he squeezes his eyes shut. A moment later, he swipes at his cheeks and tilts his head back to stare at the sky.

I shouldn't be here. Lucas is obviously going through something. Something private. I'm the last person he'd want witnessing his sorrow.

After squatting for so long, my legs stiffen and a sharp pain shoots into my thighs. Slowly getting to my feet, my sandal slides out over loose dirt, and I fall. Something sharp pokes into my butt.

"Ouch!" I cry out in pain. Immediately, I cover my mouth and scurry back behind the rock, praying Lucas didn't hear or see me.

"Penelope. Is that you?"

Crap! Busted.

The crunch of his footsteps on leaves and rubble gets closer. There's no way I can hide anywhere before he reaches me. I squeeze my eyes shut. If I can't see him, he can't see me, right?

"What are you doing?" His voice booms above me.

I open my eyes and glance up. His jaw is tight and his nostrils flare. There's no doubt by his expression that he's not happy to see me.

Getting to my feet, I dust dirt off my butt and give a nervous laugh. "I was out for a walk. What are the chances we would end up on the same hiking trail?" I lie.

A frown deepens on his face. "Are you following me?"

"No...I was just...I—"

"Unbelievable." He throws his hands up in the air. "Not only do I have to share a cabin with you, you're also following me on a hike after I asked you not to come. Can't I have a moment to myself?"

"I didn't want to stay at the cabin alone again. There's nothing to do." I don't even try to keep lying.

"Not my problem." He pushes his hair back off his forehead. "I keep telling myself I should have left you at that hotel."

"It was your idea to take me to the cabin. I'm here because of you. It's not my fault."

Lucas' face hardens, and a vein ticks on the side of his cheek. "Not your fault? *Everything* is your fucking fault. If it wasn't for you, Garrett would be—" He slams his lips shut and rakes his fingers through his hair.

What has Garrett got to do with anything? I remember Lucas and Garrett were best friends in high school. Wherever one went, the other followed. There was nothing they didn't do together. Why is Lucas bringing him up now?

"Garrett would be what?" I ask.

He shakes his head. "Forget I said anything."

"No. You brought Garrett up for a reason. What were you going to say? What does he have to do with me?"

He narrows his eyes and points a finger at me. "It's your fault Garrett is dead."

I suck in a shocked breath. "You're blaming me for his accident?" His accident had been a shock to all who knew him. Death is always hard, but dying so young is incomprehensible. How am I involved with what happened?

With a sneer, he says, "Yeah, I am."

Why is he saying this? "How is his death my fault? I wasn't in the car with the two of you. After the humiliation you put me through in senior year, I hardly stepped out of the house, let alone hung out with old high school students. After what you did to me, I had nothing to do with you."

"After what I did?" Tossing his head back, he gives a mirthless laugh. "I did nothing to you!" I open my mouth to protest, but he cuts me off. "*You* planted drugs in my locker and tattled to the principal. *You* got me expelled from school. Because of that, I couldn't get into any of the colleges I applied to. *You* did all that."

I hang my head with shame and stare at my feet. Yes, I put drugs in his locker. I was so upset and humiliated by what had happened, it was the only way to get back at him. But as much as he hurt me, it was a terrible thing to do. Had I known he would have lost so much, I never would have done it. It doesn't explain why he's blaming me for the accident though.

"Lucas, I'm sorry about what I did—"

His face darkens. "You're sorry? Tell that to Garrett's parents. He was their only child."

"Garrett's death was tragic. But I'm still confused as to how you believe I'm to blame. You need to explain how it's my fault."

Lucas links his fingers and puts his hands at the back of his neck, spreading his elbows wide. "You know what? I don't want to talk about this with you."

"Oh, no, no, no. You're accusing me of a person's death. You can't drop a bomb like that and not explain."

He stares long and hard at me. Just when I think he won't respond, he drops his arms by his sides and says, "When I got kicked out of school and couldn't get into any colleges, I fucking lost it. Thought my life would be over. If I couldn't study law, I didn't know what the hell I'd do."

"What about your family's fashion house? Isn't that where you were going to work?"

He shakes his head. "No. I never wanted to work for the business. I was planning on breaking out on my own. But after what happened, I had no choice but to join the family business. Thankfully, my hobby of photography turned into my passion and things worked out."

Dropping his head, he scuffs the toe of his boot into the dirt. "I drank and partied hard. Garrett deferred going to college because he didn't want to leave me in the state I was in. He was trying to pull me out of the hole you pushed me in."

Tears sting the backs of my eyes. My chest tightens. One stupid mistake turned Lucas' life upside down.

"The night of the accident, I was drunk, and I called him to pick me up from a party. He didn't hesitate. Never did. On the drive home, a storm hit, he lost control of the car going around a sharp bend and crashed into a tree. I walked away with only a few scratches and a broken arm. Garrett..." His voice cracks on his name, "You know the rest." He digs his fingers into his eye sockets like he's trying to wipe away the image.

How hard it must have been to watch his friend die. This is something that will affect him for the rest of his life. "It was a terrible accident. I still don't understand why you're blaming me."

He pins me with a hard stare. "If you hadn't pulled that stunt with the drugs, Garrett and I would have been in college. I wouldn't have been drunk and calling him to pick me up. He'd be safe with his nose buried in books. Not fucking buried in the ground. *You* did that."

Blood drains from my body, leaving an icy trail. He's right. It is my fault. It was a stupid thing to do. I shouldn't have listened to Claudia. She'd given me the idea and the cocaine. But she's not the one who went through with it. I did.

"Lucas, I'm sorry. Never did I imagine things going so far."

Anger pinches his features. "Why did you hate me so much? Why did you set me up? I thought we were friends. I would never believe you'd do such a thing if I hadn't overheard you talking to Claudia about it."

My legs shake and I sit on the nearest boulder. I had wanted to be more than friends with Lucas. That was until I learned that his 'friendship' was only a joke. A guy like Lucas Alessi—the hottest guy in school, rich, smart, and athletic—doesn't fall for the overweight, poor girl. None of the popular kids looked twice at me or ever dated me. I always wondered why Lucas talked to me. Until I learned his attention was all a sham. A fun game for him and his buddies.

"You humiliated me in front of the entire school," I say. "Pretended to be my friend when I was only entertainment for you. You took naked photos of me at the beach party and spread them around to your friends until everyone in school saw them. Do you know how traumatic that was? Knowing everyone had seen me naked? I wanted revenge."

Lucas' eyes grow wide, and his mouth drops open. "You think I took those photos?"

"You took photography classes and owned a fancy camera with a super-zoom lens. You texted me to tell me about the party at the beach. The one you never showed up to."

"Just because I owned a camera you think I took naked photos of you?"

"Your friend Travis told me you did it. He said you both laughed at how gullible I was." My face burns with embarrassment. It's something I'll never forget.

It should have been a night of fun; taking risks and being young. Claudia dared me to go skinny-dipping with her. Being so self-conscious about my body, it's something I never thought I'd ever do. But I wanted to break free from my shell. Live a little. If Lucas saw how fun I could be, he'd look at me differently. Not just as the girl he sat next to in math class.

"I never took those photos," Lucas says. "And Travis wasn't my friend. He was a jerk. I only tolerated him because his parents were friends with mine. Did you ever think he might be lying? Why didn't you ask me for the truth?"

I never thought to ask him because I had proof. "Travis showed me your camera with my photos on it."

Lucas blows out a frustrated breath. "I used to lend my camera out to people all the time. Travis used it often. It's possible he took the photos and shared them around. He probably deleted them before he gave it back to me, because I never saw them on it."

"Why would he want to hurt me? I hardly knew him."

Lucas scratches the back of his neck. "Who knows? He enjoyed causing trouble and playing pranks. Believe me when I tell you I never took those photos." His shoulders sag and he sits on the boulder next to me.

"It really wasn't you." It's not a question. I know the truth. I can see the sincerity on his face. If only I had asked him when it happened, things would have turned out a lot differently. And like Lucas said, Garrett would be alive.

Lucas scrubs his hands over his face. "I didn't take the photos, but I sent the text. I never made it to the party because—" He stops speaking and frowns like he's remembering something. "Travis called me because he was stranded at a party and couldn't get back. He said he'd been drinking and didn't want to call his parents to get him."

"Did you pick him up?"

"I went to the house, but he wasn't there. When I called him, he didn't answer. I assumed he'd gotten a lift and forgotten to tell me. Then the shitstorm happened with your photos and the drugs, and I never asked him about it." He slaps a hand on the rock. "He set us up!"

"Why would he do that? I rarely spoke to Travis. We weren't in any classes together. What did he have against me?"

"Good question. And I'm going to find out the answer. That motherfucker is going to pay for what he did." He springs off the boulder and marches toward the hiking trail.

I scurry after him as fast as I can on the uneven ground in my slippery sandals. "What are you going to do?"

"Find out where he is and beat the shit out of him."

Grabbing his arm, I pull him to a stop. "You need to calm down. Beating him up won't change what happened."

"It will make me feel a lot fucking better," he says as he starts to turn away.

Stepping closer, I reach up and place my hands on his shoulders. "No, it won't. Whatever you do to Travis, it won't bring Garrett back. It's not going to erase the photos. What if you take things too far? You'll never forgive yourself. Hopefully, karma will give him what he deserves."

He blows out a long breath. "It kills me knowing he's gotten away with this."

I rub his shoulders to comfort him. They're firm and strong, and I like having my hands on him more than I should. "I hate that he's gotten away with it too. And I'm so sorry for my part. I'll never forgive myself."

For a beat, he stares at me with an unreadable expression. I guess that's better than the hate he's been throwing my way. "I liked you. You weren't a joke to me or entertainment. I thought you knew I liked you more than just as a friend. I can't believe you'd think I'd do something like that." A fleeting look of hurt crosses his features.

What? He liked me? No way! "You were the most popular guy in school, with girls falling at your feet. Why would I think you liked me when you had your pick of gorgeous girls?"

"Those girls were all fluff and airheads. They couldn't hold a conversation if their lives depended on it. All they cared about was being seen with the popular crowd. You never cared about shit like that. I could talk to you for hours and never get bored. We talked about real shit, like your dad leaving. My goals in life."

When Travis told me Lucas' attention was all a joke, it had crushed me. Because the boy who I thought was kind, caring, and sweet, and took time to talk to me, turned out to be a creep. God, I'd gotten it wrong.

"I'm sorry. I know it's not enough. My insecurities got the better of me, and I believed Travis. I never thought I had a chance with you when you had so many other girls to choose from."

"Those girls never interested me, because you were the most beautiful. All I wanted was you."

My heart races as I suck in a startled breath. "I didn't know...You never told me."

"Yeah, I was building up the courage to say something at the beach party. Was planning to make a move."

He's saying all the things I wished he would have said in high school. And he would have, if life hadn't taken an unfortunate turn.

I'm not sure when it happened, but Lucas' hands are resting on my hips. Our chests a hairsbreadth from touching. We're standing so close I can see flecks of gold in his hazel eyes. My heart is beating so hard. His gaze drops to my lips and desire smolders from his eyes.

Whoa! What is going on? This is a man who has hated me for years. A man who *I've* hated for years. Now he's looking at me differently. Not like I'm dirt under his shoe. More like a woman he wants to devour in one bite. And gosh, I'm ready to serve myself up on a silver platter. In all the time I spent with Darren, he never looked at me like that.

His gaze drops to my mouth, and his tongue darts out to lick his bottom lip. Oh, my legs have turned to water as I imagine him kissing me. During high school it was something I constantly dreamed of. Is my teenage wish about to come true?

A second later, he dips his head and our lips meet. The kiss is soft at first, with a lingering taste of alcohol on his tongue. It doesn't take long until he clasps onto my waist and pulls me closer. Our chests touch and I can feel the steady thud of his heartbeat. The kiss deepens, and I throw my arms around his neck, anchoring onto him like he's a lifeline.

On this mountain top, time seems to stop. Pasts forgotten, we lose ourselves in the moment.

Breaking away, his mouth trails down my neck, licking over my racing pulse. I tilt my head to the side, and my eyes flutter shut. He takes it further and places kisses along my collarbone and the tops of my heaving breasts. Sighing with pleasure, my nipples harden, and I arch my back, giving him permission to take things further.

Like he can read my mind, his hands resting on my hips skim up my sides. His thumbs brush underneath my breasts as he sucks a nipple through the thin fabric into his mouth.

"Oh God," I moan. His touch feels so good. The loose-fitting clothing I'm wearing suddenly feels tight and restrictive, and I want to strip out of them and have him kiss me everywhere.

Fusing our mouths together, he pushes the straps of my dress off my shoulders and down my arms. Without breaking the kiss, he scoops my breasts up in his hands and massages them in gentle circles. With his thumbs brushing over my peaked nipples, the sensation travels down south and I'm wet with wanting.

He backs me toward the boulder, and my butt leans against the rough surface. Spreading my legs, he steps between my thighs. The firmness of his erection presses against my sex, and my pelvis automatically thrusts against him, wanting more. Needing him inside me.

Without breaking the kiss, he reaches between our bodies, hikes up the bottom of my dress so it's around my waist, and slides his hand behind my panties until he reaches my most sensitive spot. I hiss and bite my lip when he presses against my clit. I lean my elbows on the rock and my head falls back, and I let him take liberties with my body. He slides a finger between my folds and pumps into me. My body bucks and I press harder into his hand. I've lost all feeling in my elbows, and I fall back onto the boulder, not caring about the hard surface scraping at my back.

"This is perfect," he says with a devilish grin.

Perfect for what? I don't get a chance to ask because he drops to his knees, spreads my legs wide, and dives forward, kissing my sex with an open mouth.

"Yes," I moan. It's the only coherent word I can form. With his mouth doing wicked things, my brain has turned to mush.

Then he pulls my underwear to the side. If I thought his mouth was doing wicked things, his tongue takes over, and it's positively sinful: twirling, sucking, and licking with thoroughness. Everything inside me is humming and tightening, ready for a release. But before this ends, I need to touch him too.

As much as I hate for him to stop, I sit up, pulling him back onto his feet. My hands roam over his body as my mouth places wet kisses on his neck. With frenzied fingers, I pull his pants down and wrap my hand around his huge, hot erection.

On a long groan, Lucas grinds into my hand. "That feels fucking amazing. Don't stop."

I have no intention of stopping. In fact, I want to take it one step further. Shuffling off the rock, I drop to my knees. I cup his balls with one hand, and with the other, I guide him to my mouth, taking him in.

"Fuck me!" he cries. His hands tunnel into my hair as he pumps into my mouth. "I fucking wanted to do this to you for years. My imagination wasn't half as good as the real thing."

A giddy feeling swirls in my chest. I wasn't the only one who imagined the two of us doing wonderful things to each other. For months I dreamed of having a moment like this. Pulling away, I say, "I always wanted this too. I wish things had turned out differently."

Lucas stops moving, and I look up. A fierce expression is on his face. He takes two steps back. "We shouldn't be doing this." It sounds as if it pains him to say the words.

I slowly blink as the desire burning through my body is screaming at being interrupted. "Why not?"

"You just broke up with your fiancé. You must be heartbroken. This isn't what you need right now. I'd be taking advantage of your vulnerable state." He pulls his jeans up and zips them.

What he's saying should be true, yet I don't feel heartbroken or vulnerable. All I want is for Lucas to keep kissing me—touching me. Do all the things I yearned for him to do to me years ago. Making my body burn like it's never done before.

I get to my feet and dust dirt off my knees. "It's exactly what I need. In the six years I was with Darren, he never once looked at me with such desire. Never touched me with so much wanting. What I need is a man who wants me like he can't get enough of me."

"We can't do this. We hate each other, remember?"

My heart squeezes. Even after he learned it was Travis who set us up, he hasn't forgiven me for what I did to him. He suffered a tremendous loss. That's something that will take time to forgive—if he ever does.

After what Darren put me through, I need this. I want nothing but Lucas' hands on my body. Think about nothing but the pleasure we can give one another. I rest my hand on his chest. "Is that still true? Now that we know what really happened have things changed?" He still might not like me very much for the trouble I'd caused, but since learning the truth, my hostility toward him has vanished.

As he stares at me like he's contemplating how to answer, the sky darkens and thunder rumbles in the distance. He pulls away and turns his back on me. "We better head to the cabin before we get caught in the storm."

My shoulders sag with disappointment. This is new information he needs to digest. It may take time, or he may never forgive me at all. Maybe him stopping was for the best. It has only been four days since I learned of Darren's affair. What if taking things further with Lucas was a mistake I'd regret? I guess I'll never know. And that feels like a bigger disappointment.

Fixing my clothing, I stand next to him. "I'm ready to go."

Without saying a word, he nods. His expression is shuttered, giving nothing away. Just when I thought we'd made a breakthrough, he's gone back to being sullen.

We begin the trek back to the cabin. Wind whips through the trees, plastering my dress to my body and wrapping the fabric around my legs. Taking a step, I stub my toe on a tree root and stumble forward. Lucas catches my arm, stopping me from falling. Once I'm steady on my feet, he drops his hand so fast, like he doesn't want to touch me.

"We need to go into town and buy you appropriate clothing. What you're wearing is ridiculous and can get you killed."

Chapter Nine

LUCAS

We drive into town in silence, although I'm super-aware of every breath, sound, and move Penelope makes. The taste of her is still on my tongue. Her scent is on my skin. And I want to kick myself for stopping what we started. But how could I have taken what I so desperately wanted? She's just come out of a serious relationship. The last thing I want to do is take advantage of her vulnerability. Even with the information I learned about Travis being the one to cause the upheaval in our lives, I'm not sure I'm in the right headspace. If it were any other woman—the women I normally hookup with—I wouldn't think twice. I'd fuck all thoughts from my mind. But this is Penelope. I believed for years that I hated her.

Do I hate her now?

The fury that rages through my body when I used to look at her has disappeared. How can I hate her for something out of her control? Yes, she planted the drugs in my locker that changed the course of my life, yet I think I hate myself more for losing control and calling Garrett. This is Travis' doing, and he will pay for his part.

I pull up in front of the This 'n That store. There's no way I can spend another day with Penelope dressed in skimpy clothing.

Her gorgeous curves—the roundness of her breasts, the curve of her ass—need to be covered for my sanity. Because now that I've touched her, my body is craving more. If she's covered, then hopefully this hard-on I've been walking around with can deflate.

Penelope opens the passenger door. When I don't follow, she turns to me. "Are you not coming inside?"

"I'll wait for you at the bar. I need to make a call."

"Okay. I won't be long."

As she walks into the store, I get out of the car and head over to the bar. I take a seat next to the window, pull my phone from my pocket, and dial Finn's number.

When he picks up, I can hear Avery crying in the background. "This better be quick. I have a fussy kid who needs a diaper change."

Finn has become such the doting father and husband. His daughter and wife Harper have him wrapped around their fingers. Once a man who had no interest in falling in love and finding a partner for life, now he has the perfect little family. I've never seen him so happy.

"Have you seen or heard from Travis Gilbert recently?" After I left school, I had no contact with him. Last I heard he'd moved to California. Travis had a brother in Finn's year at school who he sometimes caught up with. Maybe he'll know where I can find him.

"No. I haven't seen him in years, but I know where he is." Finn makes shushing noises I'm sure are aimed at Avery and not me.

Excellent. If I know where he is, I can pay him a visit. That fucker has payback coming. "Where is he?"

"Haven't I told you?"

"If you had, I'd know," I huff.

"Hmm. I guess being busy with Harper, Avery, and work, I'd forgotten. I don't remember who I've talked to these days." He chuckles.

I drum my fingers on the table, waiting for him to tell me. "He's in California State Prison."

I sit ramrod straight in my chair. "He's where?" I ask, because surely I heard wrong.

"California State Prison," he repeats.

"What did he do?"

"He got done for drug possession, assault, and armed robbery. Looks like he'll be locked up for many years. Why do you ask?"

I don't have to beat the shit out of him after all. Karma is going to fuck him up the ass. "There was something I remembered from school I wanted to ask him about." There's no point telling Finn about the photos of Penelope. He was in college when Travis shared them. "I'll let you go so you can settle Avery."

"Before you hang up, what's happening with you and Penny? I saw the articles online. Hayden told me you helped her at the hotel, but why was she leaving in your car with you the next morning? Stories are circulating all over the internet, and they aren't flattering for Penny."

I pinch the bridge of my nose and squeeze my eyes shut. Shit! Instead of helping her, I might have made things worse. "It's a long story. I'll fill you in when I get back to the city."

"Okay, see you later." Finn hangs up, and I toss my phone on the table and blow out a long breath.

Glancing out the window, I spot Penelope walking out of the store. Dressed in dark blue jeans that look painted onto her hips and thighs, she saunters toward the bar on tan hiking boots. A red and white plaid shirt is tied up in a knot at her waist. She's left a few buttons undone to expose a white tank top underneath. Her hair is loose over her shoulders. I swallow hard.

I knew the store only provided outdoor wear. Shapeless clothing that wouldn't have me mentally undressing her, yet the hard-on I wanted to deflate is rock solid. I shuffle in my seat to adjust myself.

Entering the bar, she scans the room. When she spots me she gives a small smile, and my heart does something it's never done before...skip a beat. What the actual fuck? At the table, she places a paper bag with what I'm assuming are more clothes onto an empty seat.

She runs a hand over her hips, looking self-conscious. "Where on earth do the women of Oaks Valley shop for clothes? All I could find were items suitable for a lumberjack." Then she takes a seat opposite me.

"It's perfect. You'll fit right in," I joke. *Although I've never seen a lumberjack look so sexy.* To get my mind off the way Penelope fills out her clothes, I point to the menu. "Are you hungry?"

She glances out the window at the cloud-filled sky as heavy raindrops splatter on the ground. "Should we head back to the cabin? It looks like the storm is about to hit."

"We'll ride it out over lunch." All I need is to be stuck in the cabin with Penelope and nowhere to go.

"Okay, I'm starving, and I need to make a few calls."

"While you decide what you want to eat, I'll go get us a couple of beers."

At the bar, Allie gives me an icy stare. It started the moment I walked in. "Are you shacking up with the city girl?"

What was once a fun hookup is now turning into something jealous and possessive. "No, I'm not shacking up with her. I'm sorry if I've led you to believe that there might be more between us. We agreed to one night, remember? No strings."

Her lips thin. "Of course. What can I get you?"

I've pissed her off. "Allie, I'm sorry—"

"I'm too busy to chat. Do you want a drink or not?"

"Two beers please." Maybe it's better this way. If she's angry with me, any romantic feelings she may have toward me will die.

"I'll bring them to your table."

I return to the table and take a seat. "Did you make your calls? Have you spoken to Darren?" Is that why she's looking so sullen?

The bastard doesn't deserve her sadness. No one deserves to be cheated on. Two years ago, I learned my father was cheating on my mother for years. She loved him and treated him like a king. He said he loved her too, yet he couldn't keep it in his pants. It was so fucked up.

Growing up, I was always told that I was just like him. Fun-loving, carefree, and easy to be around. Well, if I have his traits, what chances do I have of having a relationship? Will I screw around on the woman I say I love the way he did? That's why I'm having fun with no commitments. That way I won't risk hurting anyone.

She gives me a weak smile as she spins her phone on the table. "I haven't plucked up the courage to call anyone yet. I'm afraid of what's being said. It's easier to stay in my clueless bubble and pretend all is right in my world. Darren has stopped calling. I guess he doesn't care what he's done anymore. He's probably shacked up with Karen Featherstone."

"You look pissed." Or is it a ruse to hide her heartbreak?

Resting her elbow on the table, she drops her chin in her hand. "I am pissed. All those years together and this is what he does to me? I helped him build his brand. I got him exposure when people were looking at other athletes. And this is how he repays me?"

I sit back in my seat. "Stop me if I'm wrong, but you have said nothing about love and commitment and the life you had together. Your relationship sounds more like a business deal."

Looking taken aback by my comment, she sits up straight. "Of course I loved him. It's just...well, we had a more sophisticated kind of relationship that wasn't all PDA."

"Sounds cold and passionless." Is that what she meant when she said Darren had never looked at her or touched her the way I did? How could he not? She is gorgeous. "Tell me something. Would he have fucked you up against a boulder in the middle of a forest?"

Her gaze flicks from left to right, like she's checking to see if anyone can hear our conversation. "We didn't do that."

I roll my eyes. "Putting my cock in your pussy is the only thing we didn't do. Shall I remind you where I did put it?"

A red stain creeps up Penelope's neck and fans across her cheeks.

"Here are your beers." Allie plonks our glasses on the table, interrupting our conversation. "Are you wanting anything to eat?" She pulls a notepad and pencil from her back pocket.

"I'll have a cheeseburger with fries please," Penelope orders.

"Same for me," I say.

She scribbles our order down then taps the pencil on the notepad. "I know you," she says to Penelope. "It was bugging me all night. Then this morning it hit me. You're Penelope Aldin. That famous closet organizer or whatever you are." The redness in Penelope's face drains, leaving it white. "Never knew why people made such a fuss over you. You organize stuff. Big deal. A trained monkey could do that kind of shit." She screws her nose up. "It's not every day we have a *celebrity* in our little town." She says 'celebrity' like it's a dirty word.

"Allie, we're hungry. We need to get back to the cabin soon," I say to draw Allie's attention and harsh words away from Penelope.

She pulls a face then spins on her heels and heads toward the kitchen.

"Sorry about Allie. She's not usually so nasty."

"That's because she has a thing for you. She's jealous you're here with me."

"She knows I couldn't give her more than one night and she willingly agreed."

"Just because she agreed verbally doesn't mean her heart did."

Why can't things be simple?

"Will she tell anyone I'm here?" Penelope scans the bar like she feels people watching her.

"I doubt it. She'd probably hate you getting so much attention." I stop myself from saying out loud *because you already have mine.*

Penelope drums her fingers on the table, looking uncertain. Then she picks up her phone and takes a deep breath. "I can't put off my calls forever. If anyone knows if my location has been leaked, it will be Claudia." She taps the screen and a few seconds later says, "Hi Claudia, it's me."

"Where the hell are you? Elizabeth and I have been calling you. Your mother was ready to go to the police to file a missing person's report." Penelope doesn't have the phone on speaker, yet I can hear Claudia's shrill voice from across the table. "We didn't know if you were alive or dead."

"I'm so sorry. Cell reception isn't the best where I am."

"Are you okay? Are you still with Lucas? Is he an absolute ass?" I can still hear Claudia's words loud and clear.

Penelope's gaze flicks to me. I grin at her, waiting to hear what she has to say. "I'm good. And yes, I'm still with Lucas. He's...okay," she says, grinning back.

"You poor thing. It must be horrible having to spend time with him. After everything he did—"

"I don't have time to explain it now, but things back in school weren't what they seemed," she interrupts.

"Okay, then tell me where the hell are you?" Claudia asks again. "I'll come get you."

"Lucas took me to a small town called Oaks Valley. At the moment I'm in the town's bar, but I'm staying at his cabin for a few days to...you know...clear my head."

"A few days. There is a shitshow happening here. The things that are being said about you are repulsive. We need you here so we can try to fix things."

Penelope grows still. "What things?"

"Go online and see for yourself. Actually, no, don't do that. It will only upset you. Now that I know you're safe and in relatively good hands, I've changed my mind about you coming home. Take your time. Hopefully, in a few days, it will have blown over."

"Claudia, I have to go. Tell my mother I'm okay and I'll call her when I can."

"Elizabeth would love to hear from you now."

"I have something I have to do."

"Pen, please don't go online if that's what you're planning," Claudia pleads.

"Bye, Claudia."

Penelope ends the call and types something on her phone. As she flicks her finger over the screen and reads what's on it, the phone trembles in her hand. Her breathing is fast and shallow. Her face drains of all color.

"I need to go." She jumps to her feet and rushes toward the door. Whatever she's seen online isn't good. Not that I expected it to be.

Pulling money from my wallet, I place it on the table to cover our drinks and lunch. Chasing after her, I reach the car. Rain hits me hard in the face. Penelope is already inside. Strands of hair are plastered to her cheeks. Her legs are jutting up and down.

Sliding into the driver's seat, I turn to her. "What did you see?"

"I don't want to talk about it." Lightning cracks through the sky, flashing a golden streak across her face. She looks on the verge of tears. A crying woman is something I've never dealt with before. Better to get her to the cabin before the dam opens.

Turning on the ignition, I head home. Trees are thrashing about. Leaves tumble through the air. Even though the wipers are turned onto the fastest speed, my view of the road is blurred from the torrential rain. The thunder is loud enough to shake the car, yet Penelope is staring out the windshield, seemingly unaware of any of it.

When I pull up in front of the cabin, and before I come to a complete stop, Penelope flings the passenger door open, jumps out, and runs into the forest. I scan the sky. It's dark and dangerous-looking. She shouldn't be out in this weather. Whatever she saw online has triggered something. I need to get her and bring her back to the cabin before she gets hurt.

Getting out of the car, I rush after her. I push my way through the brush, avoiding branches swinging toward my face. A couple of minutes later, I find her in a small clearing. Tall trees with skinny, white trunks circle around the perimeter, give the area an eerie ghostly feel. Her face is tilted toward the sky, her eyes squeezed shut. Rain mixed with her tears are rolling down her cheeks.

"Penelope!" I yell over the thunderous storm. "You need to go to the cabin. It's not safe out here."

She doesn't move. Did she hear me?

I stand in front of her and take her ice-cold hands in mine. "Penny, come home with me."

Opening her red-rimmed eyes, she yanks her hands free. "Do you know what they're saying about me?" She doesn't give me time to answer. "They're saying *I'm* the one who's been having an affair. Darren's doing interviews about how heartbroken he was when he learned of my infidelity. Claiming that he only turned to Karen Featherstone one time for comfort and felt devastated by his weakness."

"We'll go back to the city and set things right. Tell them Darren is lying. I'm sure they'll believe you. Your fans love you." I try to reassure her. "Now come with me."

She clutches at her saturated hair. "No, I can't go back. I'm a laughingstock. They've chosen the most humiliating pictures. They've published photos of me in a robe at the hotel, looking hideous. Even photos of me curled up on the floor, like my devastation was entertainment for them. They've circled areas to highlight where I have cellulite on my thighs. My body is a joke. It's getting scrutinized, laughed at."

She flings her arms out to the side just as lightning cracks, making me jump. Penelope doesn't even flinch.

"They're saying I'm fat, ugly, and unhealthy, and it's only my money that is bagging hot boyfriends." The wind tosses her hair about her head. She tugs the wet shirt plastered to her skin and yells, "This is me!" Pulling the shirt open, buttons fling all around. She yanks it off her body and tosses it on the ground. "When those photos of me skinny-dipping circulated in high school I was laughed at. Ridiculed because I wasn't supermodel thin. It made me feel worthless. Even my mother makes me aware of my weight. Always recommending a more flattering outfit to wear. Darren never said it in so many words, but he'd buy me gym subscriptions for my birthday and question whether or not I should eat the cupcake."

My body tenses with rage. What the fuck! What is wrong with these people? Penelope is beautiful. One of the most gorgeous women I've ever seen. What are they not seeing?

Kicking off her hiking boots, she strips out of her jeans and tank top and throws them next to the shirt. Standing in her lacy, pink bra and panties with the shadows of the forest surrounding her, the storm raging above, and leaves tumbling around her, she reminds me of a sexy mythical nymph.

She opens her arms wide, spins in a circle, and yells, "This is me!" She slams a hand to her chest. "Me. The hair, makeup, and designer clothes are all to hide what's really underneath." Tilting her face up to the sky, sobs rack her body.

Thunder rolls. Lightning cracks. The rain is pounding. We really need to get to the cabin.

I take her hands in mine again. This time she doesn't pull away. When she stares at me, sadness is etched deep on her face. Tears are welling in her eyes and spill down her cheeks.

"Is this what I have to put up with for the rest of my life? Constant criticism on how I look?" Her voice has lowered to a whisper, and I barely hear her over the storm.

"There is nothing wrong with the way you look. Your face and body are perfect. You are beautiful. You have always been the most beautiful and desirable woman I've ever seen." The first time I saw her in high school, I couldn't take my eyes off her. Age has only made her more stunning. "Whatever those fuckers are saying online, they need to get their heads examined, because they have no idea what they're talking about."

Penelope's bottom lip trembles. "The photos show something different."

I swipe rain from my eyes and push my wet hair off my face. "Fuck the photos. If they could see you right now, they'd see what I'm seeing. A woman who is sexy and stunning. A fucking badass for stripping in the middle of a storm that can kill her." I cup her face. "You are beautiful. Don't let anyone tell you different."

Putting a palm on my chest, she steps closer. "Show me how beautiful I am."

The muscles where she touches tighten. "Penny, now isn't the best time. You're upset. You're not thinking straight. Let's go back to the cabin and dry off."

"That's the second time you've done that."

"Done what?"

"Called me Penny. Only my friends call me Penny."

"I think after everything we've been through we can call each other friends now." Would I have chased her into a dangerous storm if I truly hated her? And with things out in the open and desire flattening any animosity, I can honestly say that we are no longer enemies.

A ghost of a smile plays on her lips.

"Let's go," I say. "I can even take you back to town if you need to call someone to sort this out."

"No, I don't want to go back. I want this. You. Right now. You look at me, touch me, like no one has ever done before. When you call me beautiful...I believe you."

Rain is plastering her hair to her face and tracking rivulets down her cheeks. I brush soaked strands away. Damn, I want her. "If that's true, then you've been with losers who don't deserve you. Your body is a temple I want to worship at."

With all seriousness, she says, "Then kneel down and worship it."

Holy fuck. How can I refuse such a demand? "Are you sure? You're upset. You might regret it later."

"I have never been more sure of anything. The only regret I'll have is not being with you."

"Let's go back to the cabin where it's dry."

She shakes her head just as lightning streaks through the dark clouds. "Here. Now."

Stepping back, she pulls her bra straps down her arms, unhooks the clasp, and lets it fall to the ground. Next, she shimmies out of her panties. Standing under a stormy sky with trees thrashing about, a goddess stands before me. With her creamy skin, sensual curves, and her auburn hair whipping around her, it makes this all feel so surreal. When she reaches out and places her hands on my waist, I know this is no dream.

She wants me on my knees? Not a problem. There's nothing more I want to do right now than to taste her sweet spot. Dropping to the soaked ground, I stare up at her. "Spread your legs," I demand.

Shifting her feet out to the side, she does as she is told. Anchoring my hands on her hips, I grip tight and bring my mouth to her, licking a flat tongue along her slit.

"Oh God." Gasping, she tunnels her fingers through my hair.

It gives my ego a nice boost when I feel her legs dip with weakness. I continue to lave her, twirling my tongue around her clit and sucking her in. Rain slashes at my back, but I'm so caught up with the taste of Penny I can barely feel it.

Soft, quick gasps expel from Penny's mouth. Her body trembles, and she leans back against the tree behind her for what I'm assuming is support. My dick is so eager to be inside her, growing harder with every passing second. Yet, even with the storm raging around us, I want to take my time.

My hands move to her ass, and I squeeze her cheeks, pulling her firmer against my face so I can fuck her with my tongue.

"Lucas," she pants. "If...you...keep...doing that...I'm going to...come."

"I have more I want to do to you first."

As much as I'd love for her to come in my mouth, I want to be inside her more. Breaking away, I nibble at her pubic bone, take bites from her hips, and place open-mouth kisses over her stomach, then trail up her torso. Still on my knees, I cup her breasts and massage them, tweaking and twisting her nipples. Her body quivers.

"Your tits are perfect." If she needs to be told over and over again how perfect her body is, I'm happy to do so. Even happier to show her.

Tossing her head back, she bites her bottom lip as she arches into my hands. I love how sensitive she is. I replace my hands with my mouth, sucking a nipple.

"Oh yes," she moans. The wind whips her cry into the air.

Taking her hands, I tug so she's kneeling in front of me. I cup her face in my hands and kiss her, my tongue sweeping into her mouth. Our hands explore each other like we both need to touch every inch of one another.

Penny breaks away to pull my t-shirt over my head. Next, she reaches for the button of my jeans and then unzips the fly. Her hand slides behind the waistband of my underwear, and she grasp my cock.

Squeezing my eyes shut, I drop my forehead onto hers. When her hand pumps, my body jerks and I let out a raspy moan.

The strokes increase in pace. My hips thrust into her hand. If she keeps at it, this is how I'll come. It can't end here. "Penny, you have no idea how much I want to fuck you. I'm even risking getting struck by lightning to do it." The sky cracks golden light just when I finish speaking. "Death by pussy and lightning strike."

Penny giggles. "What a way to go."

That's for fucking sure. "Please tell me right now this is what you really want. Promise me this is something you're not going to regret." I need her to tell me again.

She cups my chin, her thumb ghosting over my bottom lip. "I want this. I want *you*."

The best words I could possibly hear. I pull her down and lay her out on the moss and leaf riddled ground. Being outside among the trees, with the rain and wind, feels carnal. Sprawled among the forest debris, she is a man's wet dream. Sexy. Beautiful. So many times I have imagined her laid out naked before me. My imagination doesn't do the real thing justice.

Quickly stripping out of my sodden jeans, I then dig my wallet from the pocket and remove a condom from it. Rolling it on, I then drop to my elbows and hover above her. My hair falls over my forehead, and she rakes her hands through it, bringing our mouths together. Leaning to the side, my hand caresses every curve I can get a hold of and I work my way to her sex. I slide my finger through her folds and press my thumb on her clit, causing her to grind against my hand. I dip two fingers inside her wet warmth, and she grinds into my palm. She grips my hip and sucks at my neck.

"Lucas...so good."

Her body is trembling, getting ready. And I'm so damn hard I can't hold back much longer. "I feel responsible for giving you the best sex you've ever had, yet with this raging hard-on and the need to be inside you, I don't know if I can."

"You have already exceeded anything I've had before." Her hand clasps around my cock, and she swipes the tip of the head with her thumb. "I need you *now*."

My chest expands with male pride. Lifting up to my knees, I nestle between her thighs, spreading them wide and then hooking them over my hips as I plunge into her.

We both gasp as I bury deep. Our mouths fuse together as I drive harder and faster. She hooks her legs around my waist like she doesn't want to let me go. There's no chance in hell I'd stop what I'm doing. Our bodies slap together. The clash of lightning and roaring thunder compete with our frenzied connection.

"Lucas...I'm...I'm..."

I'm right there with her. "Let it go, baby. Let it go."

Her pussy clenches around my cock, and I toss my head back and moan into the sky. My hips pummel into her. She bucks against me. Trembles rack her body, and she cries out her release just as another flash of gold lights up the sky.

"Oh fuck...fuck." My orgasm rips through me as my body jerks and spasms. Is the ground shaking, or is it just me? Thunder rolls in the distance. The rain is easing. I've never experienced anything so amazing in my life.

Dropping to my elbows, careful to keep my weight off Penny, I kiss her softly. I pull back to find her staring at me with a satisfied smile on her face. Yeah, I put that there. And damn, I want to do it again and again. And that's not like me at all. Fuck a woman once and I've had my fill. But I have a feeling that once with Penny will never be enough.

With her lying on the green, mossy ground, leaves and twigs in her hair, mud smudged on her creamy skin, she looks ethereal. Gorgeous. I've photographed hundreds of models and none of them, even with their perfect beauty, compares to Penny.

She starts to lift onto her elbows, but I put a hand on her chest and hold her down. "Don't move," I say. "I'll be right back."

Her eyes widen. "Where are you going? I can't stay here on my own. I'm naked. What if something happens?"

"Oh, now you're worried about being in the forest. A few minutes ago you didn't seem to care if you got struck by lightning."

She gives a sheepish grin. Thankfully, there is only the distant sound of rolling thunder. The storm has moved on.

"I have to get something from the cabin. Stay right there and *don't* move," I order.

"Fine. I'll stay put. But if a hungry bear comes sniffing around, I'm running for my life."

"Understandable." I grin. "I'll be right back."

In a flash I'm on my feet, naked and running through the woods. Arriving at the cabin, I leap up the steps and fling the door open. I grab my bag off a chair, dig into it and find what I'm looking for. Bolting back to Penny, she's exactly where I left her—looking totally fucked, messy, and gorgeous.

"What's going on?" she asks as her gaze falls to the camera I'm holding.

"You can't let the photos of you online bring you down. The bastards who took them meant to make you look like shit—got you at your most vulnerable state. That's how they sell stories. I see you for who you are. I see beauty. If you let me, I'd like to take photographs of you that will show you just how beautiful you are."

"You want to take photos of me like this? Naked?" she says with a worried frown. Her hands cover her breasts like she wants to hide. I'll never make her do anything she's not comfortable doing.

"Yes."

"I'm a mess. They'll be unflattering." She bites her bottom lip. Is she thinking about what she saw online?

"They won't be unflattering because *I'll* be taking them. And you look perfect."

"What will you do with them?"

"Nothing. You and I will be the only two people who will see them. Then if you want me to delete them, I will." This will be the test of whether or not she trusts me. She knows I wasn't the one who took the photos of her in high school, but she believed it for years. It's hard to let that trauma go. "It's okay if you don't want to do it."

"I want to."

My chest expands with pride. I've never felt so excited to take photos before. I pop the cap, adjust the lens, and stand over her. The sun peeks through the clouds and rays of light filter through the leaves, dappling Penny in golden light.

As I take a couple of shots, Penny's body stiffens. "Relax, Penny. Try not to think about what I'm doing."

"Easy for you to say. You're not lying on the ground buck naked."

I pull the camera away from my face. "No, but I'm taking your picture *buck naked*."

Her eyes scan down my body and lands at my crotch. A sensual smile pulls at her lips. Yeah, that's it. I know how to get her to relax.

"Look at me like you did when I was fucking you with my mouth," I say.

Her face softens. Her eyes grow heavy. Perfect. *Click—click*.

With her staring at me like that, my cock grows hard. Her gaze drops to it, and her tongue darts out to lick her bottom lip. If she keeps looking at me like that, I won't be able to finish taking these photos. *Focus, Lucas. You've had naked women in front of you before. Nothing you haven't seen.* Yet nothing compares to this.

"Perfect. Place your left hand over your navel. That's it." *Click. Click. Click.* "Now bring it lower, just above your pussy." I swallow hard at the thought of her working herself with her fingers. Maybe we can get to that later. "Look at me like you want me to fuck you again. Like you loved having my cock pounding inside you."

Her chest heaves. Her nipples peak into hard balls. God, I want them in my mouth again. A few more photos and I'll do just that.

"Place your right hand near your face. Good. Slightly turn your head to the side and arch your back."

My cock is growing harder. She's sexy as hell. I can't hold on much longer. I take a few more photos and put the camera on the ground.

"You're a natural." I spread her legs and kneel between them.

"Can I see them?"

"Not yet. I have something more urgent to attend to."

She smiles with innocence, yet her eyes spark with lust. "Oh really? What might that be?"

"I want to fuck you. Now." I'm painfully hard. "If you want me to." *Please say yes.*

A light sun shower sprinkles her body with glistening drops of rain.

She lifts into a sitting position and hooks her arm around my neck. "I want you to."

Chapter Ten

———◆○◆———

PENNY

We walk back to the cabin naked. Our clothes are too saturated to put on. This behavior is so new to me. I never walk around nude. Not even in my home. Never in front of Darren. I always felt the need to cover up. Hide my body away. With Lucas, I'm free. Empowered. Maybe it's the magical surroundings or the way he looks at me. Whatever it is, I'm loving the way it makes me feel.

Lucas leads me by the hand to the outdoor shower and turns the water on. I gasp as the icy water splashes over me. "Oh my God. It's freezing!"

"Now you're complaining about the cold. You didn't seem to care when you were in the middle of a raging storm."

I giggle. "I can't believe we did that!"

He taps my nose with his finger. "*You* did that. I was happy to come back to the cabin where it's warm, dry, and *safe*."

"I'm sorry. It was stupid of me. I should never have put you in danger." Yet, at that moment when he took me into his arms, it felt like nothing could harm me. Strange how after all these years of despising him, he has made me feel the safest.

Grabbing my hips, he pulls me close. His erection presses against my belly. Heat spears down to my sex. Who am I? I don't strip naked in the woods and have sex. Especially in a dangerous storm. Yet I have no remorse. It was exactly what I needed. A cathartic moment. A kind of healing.

"It was the best experience of my life. I wouldn't change a thing," he says.

Our eyes lock, and for a moment, something passes between us. I know we have moved to the friend's stage. Him calling me Penny solidified that. This right now...I can't name.

Lucas breaks the connection and brings his hand to my hair. "There's a bunch of leaves and twigs in your hair."

Mortified, I start to leave the shower. I need a hairbrush and a mirror. I must look a mess.

Lucas clasps my arm, stopping me. "Where do you think you're going?"

"I need to fix my hair."

He shakes his head, then makes a twirling motion with his finger for me to turn around. "I'll do it."

"It's fine. You don't have to."

He gives another twirl of his finger. "You can't possibly get it all out yourself."

Doing what I'm told, I turn.

He combs his fingers gently through my hair, plucking out whatever crap is tangled in the strands. After a few minutes, he brushes my hair off my neck and over one shoulder. "Shit. You're hurt."

Twisting my neck, I try to look over my shoulder. "What is it? I don't feel hurt." Maybe I'm still running on adrenaline after the best sexual experience I've ever had in my life.

"You have a few scrapes from lying on the ground," He sounds annoyed, like it's somehow his fault.

"I can't feel a thing." Then water sprays on my back and I suck in a hiss. Now that I know something is wrong my brain is signaling my body that I'm hurt.

"I thought you said you can't feel a thing?"

"It stings a little."

"I'm sorry." He clutches my shoulders and places a kiss on the side of my neck. "I should have been gentler with you."

I turn to face him. "Don't be sorry. I'm not. It was perfect."

He grins. "Perfect, huh?"

With the water from the shower running down his body and his hair plastered to his face, he's the sexiest man I've ever seen. Or had sex with. He is the ultimate fantasy come to life.

I slide my finger over his chest. "Well, maybe not *perfect*. I'd hate to give you a big head," I tease. "There's still room for improvement."

Lucas narrows his eyes, giving me a mock disgruntled expression. "You did not just say that."

I tilt my head to the side and smile sweetly. "Oh yes, I did. There is that one thing you did with your tongue that didn't quite hit the spot."

Growling, he turns the water off, picks me up, and tosses me over his shoulder like I weigh no more than a toddler.

I squeal with delight. "What are you doing?"

"I don't have a big head, but I do have a big cock." He lightly slaps my butt. "And don't worry, when I'm finished with you, you'll have *every* spot hit."

We lay intertwined in the tangled sheets. My body is too exhausted to move. Lucas hit the spot alright. Multiple times! And it was oh so good. Who knew there were so many creative things he could do with his tongue and, in his words, big cock—which he's not lying about.

I haven't felt this relaxed in years. With my work, I feel like I'm being pulled in every direction. Saying yes to everything. These past few days have forced me to stop. If having sex with someone who is only a friend is this amazing, imagine what it will be like when it's with someone I truly love. That's how I know what I had with Darren wasn't true love. How could it be when sex was more a chore than a pleasure? What I've done with Lucas I could do every day of my life.

Any affection I had for Darren has vanished. Thoughts of him and his betrayal make me sick to my stomach. There's no love lost. And it only took four days to realize it.

As appealing as it is to stay in the cabin, with Lucas as my personal sex slave, I can't hide here forever. My reputation—which Darren is destroying with his lies—needs fixing.

I will energy into my body and untangle my legs and arms from Lucas. Sitting up, I lean back against the headboard, tuck my knees to my chest, and hug my legs. Thinking about the mess I have to face back home causes an icy chill to run through my veins.

Can I even fix my reputation? With the way people turned against me, I'm not sure it's possible. Thanks to Darren spewing lies about me, and the horrid paparazzi photos with Lucas, I look like the bad guy. All the hard work I've put into my career is slipping through my fingers.

They've broken me. How do I move forward?

Lucas sits up next to me. "Hey, what's wrong?"

"Nothing."

"After the amazing orgasms I've given you, you should be grinning from ear to ear, not looking like someone's just died."

I give him an exaggerated, stiff smile. "Better?"

With a mock scared expression, he shudders. "That's horrifying!" he jokes. Then with all seriousness, he says, "Are you regretting what we've done? I know we haven't been the best of friends—"

"More like mortal enemies," I amend. Just because we've had sex doesn't mean Lucas has forgiven me for what I did to him in high school. Yes, I was set up—Lucas is off the hook for that—but me putting drugs in Lucas' locker got the ball rolling for the traumatic event to come. Will that always be something between us? "But no, I don't regret what we did. It's exactly what I needed."

"Sex with a godly stud will fix a lot of your problems." He grins.

I roll my eyes and nudge his shoulder. "You think highly of your-self."

He waves a hand down the length of his body and cups his penis. "When I have this to work with, how can I not?"

I giggle.

With a serious expression, he says, "Why were you so deep in thought?"

"I'm just thinking about all the crap waiting for me when I go home."

"Don't you have a team who can fix things for you?"

"Yes, Claudia—you remember her from school, don't you?"

He nods.

"She, along with my mother, handles that side of the business. After the last phone call and hearing what was being said about me, I didn't give her a chance to tell me what she's planning on doing. If I call her back, it will only upset me again." And I'm in such a happy bubble, I'd hate for it to burst.

"Out in the storm you were more than upset. It looked as if the world was crashing around you. Why did the photos and the stories affect you so much? Surely being so well-known you'd see a lot of crap written about you. As much as it sucks, it comes with being famous."

I rub my hands up and down my legs. "I've always been insecure about my body. When I was a kid, my mother put me in a bunch of beauty pageants. Forced me to join ballet and gymnastic classes. Anything physical. She told me it was so I would have a talent for the pageants. I knew she wanted me to lose weight to give me a better chance of winning." I pull the sheet from the bed and cover myself. "When I got on stage, the judges looked at me with sympathetic eyes. The other girls didn't bother hiding their giggles when I squeezed myself into a sparkly gown. It was humiliating."

"Why didn't you quit?"

"I tried. My mother kept entering me in them."

"She made you do that when you hated it?" Lucas says incredulously. "Why?"

"She had competed, and so did her mother. They were both winners. She wanted me to follow the family tradition." Photos of their time on stage were displayed in our house. Put there to motivate and inspire me to be just like them.

"How long did this go on?"

"I started at five. My last competition was when I was fourteen."

"What made it finally come to an end?"

"I did something to make my mother understand that I never wanted to be in another pageant again."

Lucas raises an eyebrow. "What did you do?"

"I dyed my pink gown black, wore a black wig, and sang *Zombie* by The Cranberries."

Lucas laughs.

"It was the happiest I'd been on stage." I giggle at the memory of my mother's mortified face. "I told her if she wanted me to continue doing pageants, that was my new look. She never asked me again. The embarrassment at seeing her only daughter looking like a goth chick was too much. How could she show her face to the other mothers on the circuit again?"

"So being forced to do pageants made you insecure about your body?"

"Not just the pageants. I was always the chubby kid at school. Never the pretty, popular girl. The boys never looked twice at me." I drop my head and smooth out the bedsheet. "Then the photos Travis took and sent through school were so humiliating, I guess I never got over it. Seeing the pictures of me online at the hotel brought me back to that memory and dragged up the old feelings." It took me a long time to get over that period of my life. I'm not that young eighteen-year-old anymore, but that doesn't mean the pain doesn't hit hard.

Lucas puts a finger under my chin and tilts my face up to look at him. "Just so you know, I found out that Travis is in prison for a lot of serious shit. He was a fucking asshole, and if I'd known he was the one to hurt you back then, I would have done something about it. I'm sorry he did that to you."

Travis is in jail? A sense of relief washes over me. Karma caught up to him.

"As for boys not looking twice at you, I looked *multiple* times. I couldn't stop, and I liked what I saw. Still do," he says.

Heat fans over my cheeks at his words. I wish I'd known that back then.

Lucas slides off the mattress. Naked, he saunters to the table. My eyes drink him in. His broad shoulders, narrow waist, and corrugated abs make my mouth water. I can't believe I had my hands all over him.

What a perfect rebound guy. Except, I don't see him as someone to help me get over Darren. Being with Lucas is healing. Fixing something that was broken inside me. I'll always be thankful to him. If I never see him again after we leave the cabin—a thought that squeezes at my heart—I'll always have these memories. Something to pull out when I'm not feeling great about myself.

Coming back to bed with the camera, he presses a few buttons and the screen lights up. My photos are in there! How could I have forgotten about them? Maybe because Lucas has my mind on other, more exciting, things.

He holds the camera out to me. "Take a look at these. You can't tell me there's a man alive who wouldn't look at you twice."

My hands shaking with nerves, I take it from him. I pull in a deep breath and look at the screen. Gasping, I stare at the first photo. "Oh my God! This is not me."

"It sure is."

Still staring at it, I say with disbelief, "You must have edited it or used some kind of filter." I flick through more. My eyes grow wider with every photo I see.

"No filter. It's only natural light. This is you. This is what *I* see. What the *world* should see. Not the fucking photos those bastards posted."

"I look...beautiful," I say with awe. In every photograph I'm lying on the forest floor of leafy vegetation. A ray of sunlight filters through the canopy to sprinkle what looks like golden dust over my naked body. Surely, I don't really look like this?

"That's because you *are beautiful*. Don't let anyone tell you differently."

When I'm done looking at the pictures, I put the camera on the bed. My chest fills with emotion. No one has done anything like this for me before. "Thank you for taking them. You did such an amazing job. I never knew you were so talented."

"It's easy when you have a great subject. If anyone gives you shit again, show them these. That will shut them up. Or I'll shut them up for you." His expression shows me he's telling the truth. He'd stick up for me. Look what he did for me at the hotel when he hated me; what would he do now that he likes me?

"Darren would never stick up for me like that." The comparison between the two are so different.

"Surely he's fought away paparazzi who's held a camera to your face without consent."

I shake my head. "He loved the attention. Whenever I complained about the intrusion, he'd laugh it off, saying we should be grateful for the publicity."

"Why the hell were you with such an asshole?" Lucas rakes his fingers through his hair.

Getting up, I take the shirt Lucas gave me to use as a pajama off the chair and put it on. I stand by the bed. "A few years ago, a mutual friend introduced us at a party. I was getting my career off the ground. I had a regular gig booked on a morning show. My first book was releasing. Darren got noticed on the football field and had signed a contract with the New York Dragons. We were both in a position where all the glitz and glamour was new, scary, and exciting. We bonded over being the new kids in our industries. Our careers grew, and we stayed friends. He was charming and we got along well. Then one thing led to another, and it moved past friendship. When he asked me to marry him, I believed it was the next step for us. We were comfortable. Our relationship didn't take too much time away from work. When I think back, he wasn't always a jerk."

Taking my hand, Lucas leads me back to bed. I sit next to him. "When did it change?"

"Nothing big happened. That's probably why I didn't see it coming. I never noticed the lack of affection and intimacy. We weren't kids, so I didn't expect we'd be groping every chance we got."

"He should have been all over you twenty-four seven."

I smile. "Well, it wasn't until I spent time with Harper and Alyssa that I noticed the way Finn and Hayden looked at their wives. Like they are goddesses. In public they can barely keep their hands off each other, so I can only imagine what they get up to in the privacy of their own homes."

Lucas shudders. "Don't remind me. I've accidentally walked in on them a time or two, and they were *not* in their bedrooms."

Giggling, I say, "It's so obvious they're in love. Now that I've stepped away from my relationship with Darren, I know what we had wasn't love. It was easy. Convenient. Our jobs constantly pulled us away from each other for days, sometimes weeks, at a time, yet we never planned a schedule to make sure we weren't apart too long. The only time Darren insisted we be together was when I had an important event to attend. He enjoyed rubbing shoulders with celebrities and getting his photo taken." I frown at the thought. "He showed more interest in that part of the relationship than he did in me."

Was that the only reason he proposed? To reap the benefits of my career? He'd asked me to marry him after he'd gotten injured in the Super Bowl and thought he might never play again. Did he do it because it was a way to stay in the limelight? Nausea coils in my stomach. He used me.

"Is that why you don't seem heartbroken over the affair, because the relationship wasn't about love, or are you still in shock?" His brow creases like my answer is important. I know he's worried he's taken advantage of me during a vulnerable state. He couldn't be more wrong. Being with Lucas is exactly what I needed.

I'm not sure when it happened, but my body is pressed against Lucas' side, my head rests on his chest, and his arm is wrapped around my shoulder. I could get used to this. The affection Lucas has shown me within a few hours blows away any attempt Darren ever made. What the heck was I thinking staying with him for so long? Comfortable and easy isn't what a relationship should be based on. Learning about Darren's affair has done me a favor. What if I'd married him? I'd be in a loveless marriage and would never have experienced this moment. If this is the only time I feel secure and desired, at least I have something to hold on to.

"I'm not heartbroken. Deep down, I think I knew something was off. After what he did, my heart should have shattered. It didn't. I'm more annoyed at the mess he has made of my reputation." And I'm disappointed that I wasted my time with him when I could have experienced so much more.

"It sounds like you're better off without him." His fingertips softly brush up and down my arm. "And it's time you stop thinking about him."

"How do I do that?"

"I know a thing or two we can do to get him off your mind."

I tilt my face up to look at him. I grin because I know he has something sexual in mind and I'm ready for it. "Are you going to make me forget?"

"Absolutely," he says with playful arrogance.

"How are you going to do that?"

He rolls me onto my back, leaning on his elbows on either side of me. Hovering above, his eyes burn into me. "I'm going to kiss every part of your body and then fuck you so hard you'll forget your own name. Is that what you want?"

Heat pools between my legs. "Yes please!"

Chapter Eleven

LUCAS

The next morning, I wake up in an empty bed. My head swivels from side to side in search of Penny. I sigh with relief when I see her in the corner of the room, buttoning up the blue plaid shirt she bought from the store. For a second, I thought she'd left, and for that brief moment, I hated the thought of her leaving.

How quickly I've stopped despising everything about her. What happened in the past—the photos, the accident—was all out of our control. I can't keep blaming her for something she had no fault in. It was my decision to run wild. It was Garrett's decision to defer college. Our choices. Not Penny's.

Like she feels my gaze on her, she turns her head toward me and smiles. Damn if that smile doesn't do funny things to my insides. "Good morning. Did you sleep well?" she asks.

We only managed a few hours, yet it was the best sleep I've had in this cabin in years. Usually I'm plagued by nightmares about the car accident that caused Garrett's death. "I'm sorry," I say instead of answering her question.

Penny raises a querying eyebrow. "What are you sorry for?"

Sitting up, I swing my legs off the mattress. "For blaming Garrett's death on you."

Her shoulders sag and she comes and sits next to me on the bed. "If I hadn't gotten you expelled—"

"Still not your fault," I interrupt. "How I dealt with it were my choices. Garrett wanting to stick around was his choice. It was a freak accident."

"Do you really mean it?" Her bottom lip trembles.

Cupping her cheek with my hand, I gently kiss her mouth. "Yes."

With that one word, years of hate lifts off my chest, finally letting me breathe with ease again. The one person who I blamed for everything is the person who has helped me let it all go. I'll never forget Garrett. But instead of rehashing the bad memories, I have so many good ones to remember.

"Thank you." A glistering of tears shine from Penny's eyes. I can tell it means a lot to her. "Yesterday, what I saw out on the ridge, that was about Garrett wasn't it?"

"Yes. It's the anniversary of his death. I come to the cabin every year and trek to that spot as a tribute to him."

"He was lucky to have a friend like you."

"I was pretty lucy too." I shake of the melancholy. "Now, let's go into town for breakfast," I suggest. "I'm starving."

"Bless your heart. I thought you weren't going to feed me. I'm hankerin' for a cream cheese bagel."

I chuckle at the hint of an accent that peeked through. "I'd forgotten you're from the south."

"My accent slips out sometimes." She giggles. "My mother and I practiced for years to tone it down. She thought it would help us fit in when we moved to New York City."

I rise from the bed, hold onto Penny's hand, and pull her to her feet and wrap my arms around her waist. "Well, if you want to bring out the southern belle within you, I'm sure it's sexy as hell."

Tapping me on the chest, she pulls a faux offended expression. "Why Mr. Alessi, I do believe you're positively sinful." Her voice rises slightly and has that southern twang.

Oh yeah. Sexy as fuck. "I have a lot of sinful things I want to do to you." I tug her close.

She wiggles free from my grasp and takes two steps back. "Hold that thought. I plan for you to do every devilish thing you can think of to me. But it has to wait until we get back. I'm hungry."

I pull clothes from the wardrobe and get dressed and swipe the car keys off the table. "The quicker I get you fed, the quicker I get you in bed."

With a grin, she opens the door and races from the cabin.

⸻◆⸻

On our drive into town, Penny stares out the passenger side window. She's quiet, and I'm wondering what's on her mind. "Are you ready to go home, or do you need a few more days at the cabin?" Normally, I'd be heading back by now, but staying with her is more appealing.

I navigate the car around a small tree that has fallen partially on the side of the road. Probably a casualty from last night's storm. I inwardly shudder. How we didn't get struck by lightning or crushed by a tree I'll never know.

"Do you mind if we spend another day or two here?" she asks.

That shouldn't make me as happy as it does. "Sure thing, Pixie."

She turns to look at me. "Pixie?"

"That's exactly what you looked like in the forest and in the photos. Like a pixie controlling the storm. A *sexy* pixie."

Covering her face with her hands, she laughs. "What was I thinking? That was so not me, yet it was the most amazing experience of my life. Claudia tried dragging me to an artist workshop once to get a nude painting done. Told me it would break me out of my comfort zone. I locked myself in my apartment and wouldn't come out until she left me alone. Yet I succumbed to you so easily."

"Did you not trust her or the art studio?"

She shakes her head. "I trust Claudia with my life. But after what happened in high school, doing something like that freaked me out."

"You hardly know me. Why didn't you freak out when I aimed the camera at you?"

She shrugs. "I just knew I was in safe hands. No one else would stay with me in a raging storm and risk their life to bring me down from the ledge I was stepping off."

My chest expands. Something warm fills my heart. Holy hell, what is that? That's never happened before.

Poking a finger in my arm, she says with a playful tone, "Those photos can *never* be shown to *anyone*. Delete them, or I'll torment you and make your life miserable."

"They are fucking amazing. The world should see how beautiful you are, but I'll delete them if that's what you want."

"That's what I want," she insist.

"It will be a shame to destroy them."

"Promise me you'll delete them."

I rub the back of my neck. "I hate the thought of deleting my art."

"Promise me," she demands.

"Okay, I promise."

"Cross your heart." She smiles.

I take one hand off the steering wheel and make a cross sign on my chest.

When the town comes into view, I make my way to the diner and park out front. We step out of the car and head inside the Hop and Bop. It's like we've literally stepped into the 1950s with its black and white checkered floors and faded, vintage movie posters on the walls. Pastel blue and pink booths fill the room, and white stools line the silver counter. This wasn't done deliberately to give a nostalgic nod to the past. This place hasn't been touched since it first opened seventy years ago. We slide into a cracked vinyl booth and pick up the plastic menus.

Penny takes in the restaurant. "I feel like I should be wearing a poodle skirt and bobby socks." She laughs.

"I have no clue what those things are." I chuckle.

"And you should be wearing a black leather jacket with your hair slicked back into a ducktail."

"Never going to happen."

"It all looks original," she says, gazing at the restaurant's décor.

"That's because it is."

She taps her fingers on the menu with a contemplative expression. "With a bit of a spruce up, reorganizing, and repairs, this diner would look amazing. People try to replicate things like this all the time. This is the real deal. Something that can't be copied."

"I'm sorry to say, I haven't followed your career and don't have a clue how you got started." I know little about her life after I left school.

Penny props her elbow on the table and rests her chin on her fist. "It happened by accident. It's never what I thought I'd be doing. I wanted to be a nurse."

"What changed?"

"I went to college to study nursing. I didn't party, so when I wasn't buried in my books, I got creative in my spare time and started refurbishing old furniture and reorganizing my cupboards. I baked a lot too. One night, out of boredom, I decided to record myself organizing my closet, and I posted it online after a couple of red wines when the liquid courage kicked in. It did okay, so I posted a few more videos and gained a following. For years I felt invisible—in high school and college—then suddenly people knew who I was. I felt validated, and it felt good. After a couple of years, I dipped my toes into other social media platforms and things exploded. I got flooded with opportunities I could only ever dream about. Eventually I quit college and followed this path instead. I still pinch myself." She drops her hand in her lap. "It's probably all gone now."

"You don't know that for sure. After the shit blows over, no one will remember what happened."

"I hope so." She doesn't sound confident.

"Good morning, Lucas. I heard you were back in town." Louise, our waitress, strolls to our table with a notepad and pencil ready in hand. "What can I get you two?"

"I'll have a pancake stack, two fried eggs, banana muffin, and coffee please." Last night's activities has built up an appetite.

"And for you, sweetheart?" Louise asks Penny.

"I'll have a bagel with cream cheese please, and arrhh...can you add chocolate sauce on it?"

Louise's pencil pauses on the pad as she gives Penny a strange look. Hell, it's probably the same baffled look I'm giving her.

"Sure, no problem. I'll be right back with your orders."

When she walks away, I say, "Who puts chocolate sauce on a cream cheese bagel? It sounds disgusting."

Penny shifts on her seat. "Don't knock it until you try it."

"There's no way I ever will. That's something kids would eat." I screw my nose up with disgust.

She shrugs her shoulder. "Speaking of kids, why isn't a guy like you married with children yet?"

"A guy like me?"

"You know, successful, rich, talented, sweet, sexy."

"Wow, anything else?"

She rolls her eyes. "Conceited, bossy—"

I hold my hand out like a stop sign. "Okay, I think I like the first list better."

We both laugh.

I fiddle with the cutlery on the table. "I don't want marriage and kids."

She raises an eyebrow. "Never, or not in the near future?"

"Never."

"I know marriage and kids isn't for everyone, but is there a reason you don't want to go down that path?" she asks.

As I think of the reason, my skin tightens and my jaw clenches.

"You don't have to answer that if you don't want to," she adds as if she senses my tension.

"It's okay. I don't mind talking about it. I don't want marriage and kids because I'm exactly like my father and he's an asshole."

Her eyes widen. "What do you mean?"

Blowing out a long breath, I scrub the back of my neck. I hate what he did to our family—what he did to my mother. "A few years ago, I learned that my father constantly cheated on my mother. The worst part was when he was with one of his mistresses while my mother lay dying in a hospital room asking for him. When we contacted him, he told us he was out of the country for work and wouldn't make it back in time."

Penny covers her mouth. "Oh my God. That's…that's…"

"Fucked up," I supply as she struggles with the words.

"Did they have a troubled relationship?"

"That's what's really messed up. Looking at them, you'd think they were madly in love. Always laughing and affectionate with one another. He'd often tell me and my brothers stories, when Mom wasn't around, about how he played the field. How he never wanted to settle down until he met our mother. Dad said he'd found the love of his life and had to marry her. I think in some sick way, he believed he loved her."

"Why would he cheat if she was the love of his life?"

I shrug. "Because there's something seriously wrong with him."

She frowns. "So, because your father was unfaithful you don't want to get married? You're not him."

Letting out a mirthless laugh, I say, "Yes, I am."

Her frown deepens. "Why do you say that?"

I trace a crack on the table with my finger. "All my life I've been told I'm exactly like him. My looks. My personality. My behavior. *Everything*. His friends always told me I'm a chip off the old block. So, if I'm just like him, I don't want to hurt anyone the way he did. I'd rather stay single all my life."

Penny reaches across the table and places her hand over mine. "You are two different people who share similarities. That doesn't mean you'll do the same things. If anything, you know what *not* to do."

The comfort of her hand burns away the icy chill that smothers me. "I'm not taking the risk."

Before she can say anything more, Louise arrives with our breakfast. As she puts the plates on the table, Penny's attention drifts over to something out on the street. "What's going on out there?"

I look out the window. Cars and vans are lined up in front of Allie's bar.

"Is the bar usually so busy this time of day?" Penny asks.

"No. It doesn't open until eleven." I glance at my watch. "It's only nine. Who are they?"

Penny gasps and holds her hand over her mouth. "We have to leave. Now!"

"What? Why?"

"They're paparazzi," she says, her voice rising with agitation.

"Oh fuck." Without hesitation, I jump out of my seat, pull my wallet out of my pocket, and toss money to cover breakfast on the table. I grab onto Penny's hand, lifting her to her feet. If we stay by the window, it won't take them long to spot us. I pull her toward the back of the diner, out of view. "Hey Louise, is there a back way out of here?"

She points toward a door. "Through the kitchen. What's wrong?"

"Sorry, I don't have time to explain. Tell no one you saw us," I call over my shoulder as I pull Penny behind me.

We race into the kitchen, ignoring the cook's surprised expression. I open the door just a crack to check and see if anyone is waiting for us out back. It looks clear. If they're waiting for us at the bar, hopefully no one will think to look for us here.

Stepping outside, we creep around the building until we have a view of the road. The photographers are still hovering around the bar, which is dangerously close to my car. If we make a run for it, they'll see us.

"What do we do now?" Penny asks, nibbling at her bottom lip.

Shoving my fingers through my hair, I say, "I don't know."

"I was really looking forward to my bagel." She sighs.

Chuckling, I say, "It's gross. You're better off without it."

She pulls a face, which makes me laugh out loud.

"Sshh." Her eyes widen as she takes a peek at the bar. "They might hear you."

We need a distraction. Something to get them away from the bar.

"Wait here. I'll be right back." I turn toward the door that leads into the kitchen.

Penny puts a hand on my arm, stopping me. "What are you going to do?" she whispers.

"Get rid of the vultures."

I race inside and find Louise serving an older couple. When she's done taking their order, I pull her aside.

"Louise, I need your help. I have to get out of town without being seen."

She crosses her arms over her chest. "What trouble have you gotten yourself into, Lucas? Seeing you with that nice lady, I thought you were settling down. But you're still as wild as ever."

"I'm not in trouble. I'm helping Penny—the woman I'm with—get away from a bad situation. Will you help us?"

Her face softens. "Of course I will."

I breathe a sigh of relief and tell her what I need her to do. Then I rush outside, thankful to see no one has spotted Penny.

"Everything okay?" she asks with an anxious expression.

"It will be." If Louise does as I asked, I hope to get to the car unseen and get Penny out of town.

"What did you do? How are we getting out of here?"

Glancing toward the bar, I wait for Louise to do her thing. "You'll see."

Right on time, Louise ambles from the diner with the cook and heads toward the bar. With a voice loud enough for the paparazzi to hear and to carry toward us, she says, "I can't believe Penelope Aldin is in the diner! She's the first celebrity I've ever met."

Penny gasps. Swinging her head toward me, she narrows her eyes. "What did you do? We're supposed to get away from them, not lead them straight to us."

"If my plan works, it will lure them away from you. Do you trust me?"

Without hesitation, she says, "Yes."

I watch the paparazzi take the bait and scurry to the restaurant. Penny is bouncing on her toes, ready to bolt. I grip onto her hand. "Not yet."

As they get closer, we watch as they pile inside. After the last person disappears, I pull her by the hand. "Run!"

We race to the car. When we reach it, we open the doors and dive inside. I glance back at the Hop and Bop. Through the window, I see the paparazzi are wandering around the diner searching for us. One looks back out onto the road and sees us. He points and says something, and a second later all eyes are on us.

"Shit!" I turn the ignition, reverse from the parking lot, and gun it up the road.

Looking in the rearview mirror, I see the men and woman scurrying out of the diner and piling into their vehicles.

"Fuck, they're following us," I say. Of course they would. More photos for them to sell.

Penny turns in her seat and looks behind us. "How did they find me?"

"Someone must have tipped them off."

She flops around with exasperation and sits forward. "It was Alison. She must have told them."

I keep an eye on the rearview mirror. We have a good head start. If I keep this speed up, they won't catch us. "She wouldn't do that."

"How can you be so sure? She recognized me. Hates me because I'm staying with you. It's the only explanation."

Allie has a jealous streak, one I'd never witnessed before. Would she do something so catty?

"Have you called anyone other than Claudia? You told her where you're staying, maybe she tipped them off," I say.

"No. Claudia would never betray me. Someone else in the bar must have recognized me." We drive past the road that leads to the cabin. "Are we not going to get our things?" she asks.

"No, they'll trap us there. I hope you had nothing important in your luggage you might need." Thankfully I never go anywhere without my camera. It's sitting safely in it's bag on the backseat.

"Nothing I can't live without. Where to now? Do you have any other secret hideouts?"

The last car disappears from my rearview vision, and my grip on the steering wheel relaxes. "We're going to hide in plain sight."

"What do you mean?"

"We're going back to New York City."

"Do you think that's a good idea?"

I take a right turn, keeping a watchful eye behind me. "It's time to face the music."

She rubs her palms up and down her thighs. "I'm not ready."

I glance at her for a beat. "You can't hide forever."

She blows out a long breath. "I'd like to try, but you're right."

"What's the security like at home?"

She scrubs her hands over her face. "Do I even have a home? For all I know, Darren has moved Karen in there. I can't go there. Looks like I'll have to book a room at a hotel until I can kick Darren out."

"Not a great idea after what happened to you at the last hotel you stayed at."

"I could probably stay at Claudia or my mother's apartment." She sounds unsure. "Although anyone can get into their buildings."

"Not an option. You're staying with me. Security in my building is tight. No one can get in, much less to the penthouse suite, without me knowing. There's also a sneaky back entrance to slip in and out of." I've never had a woman stay in my apartment before. Not even for a night. Yet with Penny, I didn't even hesitate to offer.

"I couldn't put you out. You've done so much for me already and gotten caught up in my mess. I bet you regret helping me at the hotel."

Taking my attention off the road for a moment, I gently squeeze her thigh. "I don't regret it. If I hadn't taken you with me, I'd still be holding onto so much anger over Garrett's death. Putting blame where it shouldn't be." Up ahead I see a gas station and I pull in. "Will you stay with me?" My heartrate picks up speed as I wait for her answer.

I'm not ready to let her go.

Because when she walks away, I may never see her again.

Chapter Twelve

PENNY

"Penny, wake up." I feel a nudge on my shoulder, and I jolt up in the seat. Blinking heavily, I stretch my arms in front of me. The long drive and stress of the morning had lulled me to sleep.

Glancing around, I see we're in a dim parking garage. "We're at your apartment already?" I ask.

Lucas chuckles. "The travel time goes fast when you sleep through most of it."

I give him a sheepish grin.

"Come on. Let's get you settled. I have a private elevator that takes us straight to my apartment. No one will know you're here."

Lucas was right when he said I can't hide forever. And I will show my face again. I guess I have to arrange a meeting with Claudia and my mother to work out how I get back out there after the lies that have been said about me. Until then, I want to enjoy whatever time I have left with Lucas before we go back to our normal lives.

There's so much I need to think about, but for now, all I want to do is take a long, hot shower with Lucas and curl into bed with him. It's amazing after only spending a few days together he seems to be all

I want to think about and spend my time with. It's funny how quickly I've become comfortable with him.

Getting out of the car, we make our way to the elevator. He punches a code into the keypad next to the door. A moment later the doors slide open, and we step inside. As soon as they close, Lucas presses me against the cool mirrored wall, his body melding into mine.

His lips hover above my mouth. "I've been wanting to kiss you for hours."

"Then do it." I'm not one to argue.

Lucas tunnels his fingers through my hair, pulling me forward. Our lips meet on an urgent kiss, like we haven't touched each other in days not hours. I wrap my arms around his waist, holding him tight.

How does this feel so right? I've never felt so alive in a man's arms. If I'm not careful, I'll want this forever. But Lucas isn't offering forever. He isn't even offering a relationship, because he doesn't believe in them.

I can't imagine Lucas treating a woman he loves the way his father treated his mother. Not when he's shown me—a woman he originally hated—compassion and care. I think he'd be great relationship material. Not with me though; I'm not ready to jump into another one. I'll enjoy this moment and every other moment before it comes to an end.

His hand floats down to my chest, and he massages my breast in a slow, circular motion and brushes a thumb over my nipple, pulling out a long sigh from me. Oh, he's so good with his hands. I'm going to miss this.

All too soon, the elevator dings, announcing our arrival. We pull apart and I adjust my top before the doors slide open.

"We'll continue this inside," he says like he can sense my disappointment at having to stop.

Taking my hand, he leads me along a small corridor until we reach two enormous timber double doors. Once again, he enters a code into a nearby keypad and pushes the doors open. We step into a luxurious foyer with white, marbled flooring and a huge chandelier. Photographs of beautiful mountains, forests, and beaches—I'm assuming photographed by Lucas—line the walls. I want to stop and admire his work, but he keeps pulling me along with urgency.

As we enter the living room, we pull up short. Lucas' family is in the room. Finn and Harper are sitting on a caramel leather couch. Finn is bouncing their daughter Avery on his knee. Hayden and Alyssa are sitting on the floor with their daughters Lily and Sadie. Sadie is lying on a plush blanket while Lily is dangling a soft toy above her head. They all stop what they're doing when they see us. Huge grins spread across their faces.

"What the hell are you all doing here?" Lucas asks.

"We thought you'd never get here. We've been waiting for ages," Hayden says, not answering the question. He pushes himself off the floor and saunters to us. First he shakes Lucas' hand, and then he gives me a quick hug. The rest of his family follows.

"What are you doing here?" Lucas asks again. "My code is supposed to be used for emergencies only. You can't walk in here whenever the hell you want. I need to change the code to my apartment and tell security to ban you all," he threatens, though his words hold no heat.

"We wanted to see you. Make sure you didn't need anything," Hayden says.

"I told you on the phone on the way home that we're okay. We didn't need a greeting party."

"Admit it, you're happy to see us," Alyssa says. Sadie has fallen asleep on her shoulder.

Lucas playfully rolls his eyes. "Don't you have better things to do with your time?" He aims the words at all of them. "Because I know I have," he mumbles for only me to hear. I bite back a giggle.

"Nope. Being here and finding out what the two of you have been up to these past few days is more interesting." Alyssa wiggles her eyebrows like she knows there's saucy information to be shared. Did Lucas tell them anything about us?

Harper takes a seat back on the couch, cradling Avery, who has also nodded off to sleep. Lily, Hayden and Alyssa's eight-year-old daughter, sidles up to her stepmother. Alyssa is the only mother Lily has ever known. Her own left her with Hayden as a newborn. "Mom, can I go in the theatre room and watch a movie?"

Alyssa brushes her hand over Lily's hair. "Only if Uncle Lucas says it's okay."

"No problem, Lily. The Disney channel is set up."

Hayden laughs. "You watch the Disney channel?"

Lucas shuffles his feet. "I got it for Lily."

With a dubious expression, Hayden says, "Right...it's for Lily."

Lucas shrugs with a huff. "Fine, I got it for myself. There are some great movies. Have you watched *The Lion King*? It's a tearjerker."

Everyone bursts out laughing.

Lily bounces on her toes. "Thanks, Uncle Lucas." Then she runs off.

"That girl has so much energy I can barely keep up," Alyssa says.

But since Alyssa is a professional dancer and dance teacher, I doubt the truthfulness of that statement. Alyssa is probably fitter than all of us put together and she had a baby five months ago.

"How about you boys organize some food and drinks so we girls can chat," Harper suggests.

"Food sounds amazing right now. Nursing makes me so hungry," Alyssa says.

"Sure thing." Lucas chuckles. "Any suggestions?"

"Anything cheesy and greasy," Alyssa offers.

"Coming up. What about you, Pixie? Want a cream cheese bagel? I still owe you one." He winks and walks away. Finn and Hayden follow him.

I can feel Harper and Alyssa's stare on me. My face heats. Although Lucas' suggestion of food sounded innocent enough, there was an innuendo that couldn't be masked.

Turning to face them, I'm met with huge grins. Oh yeah, they've picked up on something.

"As much as I want to hear what that's all about—" Alyssa says then taps her hand on the seat next to her. I sit. "I want to know how you're doing after, you know...the publicized...*incident*. We haven't had a chance to catch up. After the show we couldn't reach you."

"Thank you for your messages. Things were so chaotic. I wasn't in the right headspace to talk and needed time to myself. Then at Oaks Valley cell reception was bad, and I only called Claudia to check on things. I'm sorry I never responded."

Harper waves a dismissive hand. "Don't apologize. We understand it was a difficult time. If you don't want to talk about what happened, you don't have to."

"No, I don't mind."

From the moment I met Harper and Alyssa while organizing a party for Harper's family, we immediately clicked. I've only known them for a few months, yet it feels like years. Apart from Claudia, I've never had other girlfriends to talk to. Trust. Open up with. It's a great feeling to have so much support and friendship.

I fill them in on how Lucas found me at my lowest, surrounded by paparazzi at the hotel. How instead of going on what would have been my honeymoon with Claudia I couldn't because more photographers were waiting at the airport. So Lucas took me to his cabin. I tell them about going online and reading what was being said about me. Seeing humiliating photos, and how I let go of pent-up emotions I'd been holding onto. I don't go into detail about how Lucas brought me from a dark place. Or how he kissed me. Touched me. Those moments are private and will live in my heart forever.

"Thank God Lucas was there to help you," Harper says.

I'll always be grateful for everything he's done—and is still doing—for me.

"Have you spoken to Darren? I can't believe the rubbish he's spreading about you having an affair." Alyssa rolls her eyes, clearly not believing his lies. "He and Karen Featherstone should be ashamed of their disgusting behavior."

"No. Not since I left the apartment. I never want to speak to him again. How did I not see what a douchebag he was?"

"Love is blind," Harper offers.

I shake my head. "That would be true if I loved him. If anything, his affair made me open my eyes and face how I really feel about him. I'm ashamed to admit it, but being with Darren was convenient. Comfortable. The video made me mad because he humiliated me. I confused it for being heartbroken. I wasn't—I'm not. I don't miss him. I don't love him." It only took a couple of days and being with Lucas to realize it.

"I hate the humiliation you went through to get to the place you're at. No one should be treated that way. I'm glad you didn't go through with the wedding. It would have been a disaster," Harper says as she pats Avery's diaper when she stirs.

Sighing, I slump back into the couch pillows. "Me too." I hate to think what my life with him would have turned into. I inwardly shudder. "Can we talk about something else? I don't want to think about Darren anymore."

"Then how about we talk about the cute nickname and wink Lucas gave you before going into the kitchen," Alyssa suggests. "Alone in the woods and secluded from everyone, did you and Lucas get up to anything fun and exciting? Tell me you had amazing revenge sex." Alyssa gives me a playful grin as she rocks Sadie in her arms.

Heat flames my cheeks, and I avert my eyes for a beat.

Alyssa's grin grows wider. "You did! I knew it. As soon as I saw the two of you together I could see sparks flying. Something about the way you looked at each other. This makes me so happy."

"Now Lucas is my brother-in-law, so I don't want to know all the juicy details—"

"I want to hear them and he's my brother-in-law too," Alyssa interrupts Harper.

"That's because you're sick." Harper laughs.

Alyssa shrugs, not looking offended at Harper's comment. "Was it fantastic? Who initiated it? How many times did you do it? Wait..." Alyssa pauses and frowns like a thought just hit her. "Don't you and Lucas hate each other? I should be asking if you nearly killed each other."

I could play dumb and avoid the questions. But I don't want to. If I don't share something with someone, I'm going to explode, and who better than my friends? "Yes, it was fantastic. I initiated it. Lost count of how many times. We nearly did kill each other. Now there's no more hate."

We all burst into giggles.

It feels wonderful to be so free with close friends. Claudia and I have been friends for years, and there's not much we don't know about each other, yet when was the last time we had girl talk and giggled like we were teenagers? Lately all we seem to talk about is work.

"I love this so much," Harper says gleefully. "Lucas needs a woman like you in his life."

I jerk back. "Arrhh. Don't get too excited. This isn't turning into anything."

"Why not?" Harper raises an eyebrow. "There's obviously chemistry zapping between the two of you."

"I can't deny the chemistry, but that's all it is."

Alyssa scratches the side of her face. "Why are you staying in his penthouse if nothing is happening?"

"I needed a place to stay, and he offered his apartment. When I get things sorted, we'll go our separate ways."

Harper and Alyssa stare at me with confusion.

"What about the sparks and the zapping?" Alyssa waves her hand around.

"That's all. It's just sex."

Harper looks unconvinced. "If it's just sex, why has he brought you home with him? He could have dropped you off at your mother's or Claudia's if you didn't want to stay at another hotel after what happened."

"There's no security at their homes. Lucas suggested I stay here until I can get Darren out of my apartment and ramp up security in my building," I explain.

Alyssa narrows her eyes as she stares at me intently. "I sense something else simmering under the surface. Like this is all a plan for Lucas to keep you here because he has feelings developing."

"I agree," Harper says. "Lucas never has women stay over. He wouldn't invite you here unless he cared."

No, Harper and Alyssa are wrong about him having feelings. "Sure, he cares as a friend. That's all."

"What about you? How are you feeling about Lucas?" Alyssa asks.

There's nothing more than friendship. Right? "Thinking about the past few days, with everything that's happened and everything he's done for me, he's become an important person in my life."

Then I remember the way he smiles at me. Touches me. My heart pounds against my ribs.

Or am I falling for him?

Chapter Thirteen

LUCAS

In the kitchen, Finn and Hayden take a seat at the breakfast counter. I open the fridge and pull out three Budweisers and pass them on. Twisting off the cap, I toss it into the sink and take a long pull of my drink.

"Okay, hit me with it." I know for a fact my brothers have a lot to say. Better to get it over with.

Hayden twists the bottle in his hands. "The media has gone nuts over you and Penny. Some are calling you the greatest couple of all time. Others think you're a home-wrecker and Penny is a cheater who doesn't deserve a man like Darren, and that's putting things lightly."

I rub my fingers up and down my forehead. It's been days. Why hasn't there been another celebrity scandal for the media to move on to? "You said you were getting the PR team on it? Can they make it go away?"

With a shake of his head, Hayden says, "We put out a statement on your behalf stating that Darren's accusations were false, but with all the photos and video evidence of you and Penny together, plus his statement about the two of you having an affair which drove him into Karen's arms, there wasn't much they could do. It was dying down until they spotted you in Oaks Valley." Hayden blows out a breath. "We've lost two major clients because of this. Hopefully no one else leaves us or we could lose a ton of money."

I slap my hands on the counter. "Is that all you're worried about—the money?" As head of finances, sometimes all Hayden sees is dollar signs.

"Of course not," Hayden retorts. "What I'm trying to say is that if we're losing clients because you've been seen with Penny, I can only imagine what damage is happening to her company. The media are ripping her apart."

"This isn't her fault. That asshole is to blame."

"We know that. The media doesn't. The juicier the story, the better. They will milk it for every drop they can whether it's true or not. Destroying people's reputation isn't a concern for them," Hayden says.

Leaning against the counter, I cross my arms over my chest. "How do we fix this? Penny has worked too hard for her career to be tarnished."

"Why do you care so much?" Finn asks. "I thought you hated her."

"Things have changed."

"What things?" Finn gives me a curious look.

I never told my brothers why I hated Penny so much. After what happened I didn't want to think about her or speak her name. It was better to forget she ever existed. So without going into detail, I say, "We had the time to talk and work through some misunderstandings."

Thankfully they don't pry and ask questions about what those misunderstandings were.

Finn takes a sip of his beer and sets it on the counter. "How the hell did you end up in this mess?"

"Photographers surrounded her. The assholes wouldn't let up. I couldn't leave her in such a vulnerable state." I don't tell them that I nearly did a couple of times. Something inside me kept pulling me back to her.

"I'm surprised you took her to the cabin during Garrett's anniversary. You never let anyone join you. Not even us," Hayden says.

"I didn't have much choice. It's not like I could have dumped her at some random hotel. The paparazzi were hounding her everywhere she went."

Hayden rubs a hand over his chin. "She could have called someone she knew to pick her up and take her somewhere secluded. Then you could have wiped your hands of the situation. Is there something you're not telling us about Penny?"

"Like what?"

"Well, it didn't take long to see there's some kind of connection between the two of you. Are you finally realizing that all the bullshit people say to you about being like Dad is exactly that—bullshit—and you're in a relationship with her?" Hayden questions.

I slide my hands into the pockets of my jeans. "We're just friends."

Although, something tugs at my heart, telling me this could be more. I mentally shake myself. No, it can't go any further than what it is. Because if I try having a relationship with Penny, I'll only break her heart. She's too important to me to hurt. It's better not to risk it.

Hayden and Finn give me a dubious look.

"It's true. She's just come out of a serious relationship, and I'm not looking for one." I try to sound convincing, but even to my own ears I'm not sure I'm buying it.

"Well, maybe a relationship with Penny will turn things around." Hayden drums his fingers on the counter in thought.

I push away from the counter. "What do you mean? I just said we're not together."

"If the public thinks you are, then do it."

Frowning, I glance at Finn to see if he's following. He shrugs his shoulders and looks as confused as I feel. "You still don't make any sense," I say.

"We get PR to make up a story about how Penny's relationship with Darren was over a few weeks ago, and she didn't have an affair with you. They'd broken up before you got together," Hayden suggests. "It will be your word against Darren's."

"Then, what if instead of Penny hiding, you're seen together as an enamored couple. Confess your love for each other. You already have half of her fans on your side, you only need to convince the other half. People go nuts over a great love story. They'll soon forget about the scandal because they'll be invested in what the two of you are doing. You'll be the next golden couple in no time." Finn points his bottle in my direction and smiles like he's solved the problem.

Could it be as easy as that? I take a moment to think. The attraction is undeniable—no pretending there. Hell, I can't keep my hands off her. But fake love? That's a problem. I haven't a clue what love is. Sure, I've seen it between my brothers and their wives. All loved-up expressions and loving touches. If I pretend, can I make it look real? Or will the media see right through me?

"What if Penny doesn't agree to it? Hell, I'm not sure if I want to do it." That means spending more time together. Not seeing other women. It sounds too complicated, yet being with Penny longer sounds better than spending time with dozens of different women.

Finn shrugs. "If you think of a better way to get out of this mess, let us know. We'll do whatever it takes to help."

My brothers are my best friends. We've bonded even more over the loss of our mother and the betrayal of our father. We are by each other's sides in a flash. Or sticking our noses in each other's business. With their wives added in the mix, we're stronger than ever. What would it be like to have that connection with a woman? Loving only one person for the rest of your life. Pure love radiates from Finn and Hayden when they look at Harper and Alyssa. Never could I imagine them cheating on their wives like our father did. But they were never told they were like him. Not like I was.

All my life I heard:

"You're the spitting image of your father."

"When you grow up, the girls are going to fall at your feet like they did for your father when he was younger."

"Your father was wild in his youth, just like you."

"You're a lucky man to have the charm of your father. Women love it."

"Don't get a girlfriend, they don't like it when you have a wandering eye."

That last comment hits hard now that I understand it. Not only did my father have a wandering eye, but he also couldn't keep his dick in his pants even when he was married and proclaiming his love for his wife.

If that's love, I don't want it.

The kitchen door opens and Alyssa walks in. She glances around at the empty beer bottles on the counter. "I thought you were organizing something for dinner?"

Shit! We've been discussing what to do about Penny and we'd forgotten about food. "I'll call the restaurant downstairs and have them send up pizzas." I pull my phone out of my pocket.

She gives me a hard stare. "Fine. I want one with extra anchovies and mozzarella cheese. Pay them extra if necessary to speed it up." Like the dancer she is, she gracefully spins on her heels and sashays from the room.

Hayden watches her leave. A huge grin spreads across his face. "Man, I love that woman."

"I can tell by the goofy expression on your face," I remark.

"One day you'll be wearing one too and you won't even be sorry." Hayden grins.

One day you'll be wearing one too.

Not if I can help it.

Chapter Fourteen

⧫

PENNY

After Lucas' family leaves, I help him gather the empty pizza boxes and glasses and take them into the kitchen. The room is huge with a large, white marble bench, charcoal cabinetries lining the wall, and top-of-the-line, modern, stainless-steel appliances. Soft ambient lighting from strategically placed sconces gives the room a cozy feel in such a large space.

"Do you do a lot of cooking and entertaining?" From what I've seen of his penthouse so far, the apartment is way too big for one man. You could easily fit a dozen more people.

"I don't cook a thing." He chuckles. "Not when I can have the restaurant downstairs deliver almost anything."

"The penthouse seems so big for one person."

He places the pizza boxes on the counter. I take the glasses to the sink then stack the dishwasher.

"I travel a lot for work. When I'm home, my brothers and their families are here a lot. I need all the space I can get when they're around," he jokes.

At dinner the brothers messed around with each other, calling one another names and poking fun. All done with love and affection behind their disparaging shit talk. There's no doubt they are tight. Seeing them all together had me wishing for that kind of connection. What would it be like to be part of a big, loving family?

"Speaking of family, I need to call my mother and Claudia. They must be wondering where I am after the run-in with the paparazzi at Oaks Valley. Is there a room where I can make some calls?"

"Sure. You can use my office."

Lucas leads me through the apartment decorated with stunning paintings and artwork. When he opens a door and I step into his office, I gasp. And it's not because of the magnificent floor-to-ceiling view of New York's city lights, it's because of the blown-up photographs arranged haphazardly on the walls, propped up against furniture, and sitting on easels. It's like I've stepped into a gallery.

On the walls I take in the photos of beautiful women dressed in Alessi designs. They're not your normal catalogue photos. They're artistic. Different from anything I've seen before. The locations look like they've been pulled from fairy tales. Mystical and magical. Photos propped against the furniture are of nature; mountains, valleys, and I recognize the area around the cabin.

"These are stunning." I walk to one of a woman wearing a white, flowing, silk dress, lying on a bed of pink roses. Diamonds and pearls are draped around her neck and wrists. She's looking into the distance with a whimsical expression. "You are so talented."

"Thank you." He dips his head like the comment embarrasses him. Surely he knows he's great. He must get told so all the time. "I'm including them in an exhibition in a couple of weeks."

"You're displaying your work? That's amazing. People are going to love them."

If I hadn't asked him to delete the photos he'd taken of me in the woods, would they be added to his collection? Displayed so people can look at them? A shiver travels over my body at the thought. After my experience in the past, I could never show mine. Even though I know they were beautiful and tasteful, I'd never be brave enough.

He wraps his arms around my waist and pulls me so my back is pressed against his chest, resting his chin on top of my head. Like he knows what I'm thinking, he says, "I would have put your photos somewhere more private."

Turning in his embrace, I tilt my face up to look at him. "And where would that have been?"

He grins. It's so sexy I feel it down to my toes. "Blown up and put on my bedroom ceiling so I could look at it every night and—"

"Have sweet dreams?" I interrupt, knowing where this is heading.

Heat flashes in his eyes. "More like kinky ones."

Playfully, I lightly pinch his chest. "I thought they were meant to be artistic photography?"

"All depends on the audience." He wiggles his eyebrows.

I shake my head with mock disappointment. "You're too much."

He tugs me close, and I can't miss the bulge pressing against my stomach. "That's not what you said last night. If I recall, you screamed you wanted a lot more."

He nuzzles his face in my neck, and goosebumps explode over my body. I'm not sure I'll ever get enough of him. It's a shame our time together will end soon. I can't stay here forever. My life has been put on hold long enough. As much as I'd love to stay in this bliss bubble, it's time to put a pin in it. And that means making some calls.

I pull away, and Lucas narrows his eyes. "Come back here. I have a fantasy of fucking you on this desk. First, I have to carefully remove the photographs, then you're getting sprawled out on it."

Laughing, I shake my head. "So you're not sweeping everything off like they do in the movies?"

"They're important photos." His tone is serious, yet his eyes sparkle with mirth.

"As hot and tempting as that sounds, I have calls to make. If I don't, my mother will send a search-and-rescue party out for me." I float my finger over the fly of his jeans, pulling a hiss from his lips. "When I'm done, I'll wait for you right here." I point at the desk.

"With the photographs carefully removed." His lips twitch.

"Of course."

"I'm holding you to that." He pierces me with a long, lustful stare.

Oh, I won't change my mind. Not when he looks at me like that. "I'm leaving tomorrow, so I'm going to make the most of tonight."

He cocks an eyebrow. "You're leaving tomorrow? I thought you needed somewhere private to stay?"

"I can't rely on your generosity indefinitely. If I don't show my face, things might get worse."

"Be my girlfriend," Lucas fires. His eyes widen, and he looks as shocked as I feel at his outburst. He clears his throat. "I mean, be my *fake* girlfriend."

Confused, I ask, "What are you talking about?"

Lucas shuffles his feet. "Finn seems to think if we pretend we're in a relationship, people will forget about Darren and what he's saying. He thinks if we're seen together, everyone will fall in love with us as a couple, and our reputations will be restored."

Needing to take this information in, I walk to a plush, caramel settee free of photographs in the corner of the room and drop down. "Do you think it will work?"

He shrugs. "I don't know. It might."

"Are you seriously considering doing it?" Hasn't he done enough for me already? Surely he wants to get back to his life.

"It's worth trying."

"And then what? We *pretend* to break up?"

"After things settle down, we wait until the media has moved on to something bigger and better and we amicably part ways."

"You've already done so much for me. I can't ask you to put your life on hold," I say.

He has a reputation of regularly being with different women. Doesn't he want to get back to that? Jealousy wells up inside me at the thought. Oh, that's not good. This is going to end. He will move on.

Lucas sits next to me. "You're not asking. I'm offering. I'm involved in this too. My photos are plastered online along with yours. Being in a relationship might fix my reputation of being an Alessi playboy." He gives me a cheeky grin.

I nudge his shoulder. "Oh, I'm sure that's a reputation you pride yourself on. Our *fake* relationship might ruin that for you."

"I'll risk it." He chuckles.

With seriousness, I say, "Thank you for trying to fix my life. I should deal with this myself. Hopefully things aren't as bad as I think. After I speak with Claudia and my mother, I'm sure they'll have a plan on how I move forward from here."

Lines crease between his brows. "Are you sure?"

I nod. "Yes. Who knew you had such a sweet, caring side to you?" I tease.

Leaning toward me, his eyes zero in on my lips. "There's nothing sweet about what I'm thinking. Forget making calls, come to my bedroom and I'll show you what's on my mind." His mouth lands on the racing pulse on my neck. His tongue flicks out and glides to my ear.

Breathless, it takes effort to form words. "What about the desk?"

One of his hands skims the side of my torso until it reaches just under my breast. His thumb ghosts over my peaked nipple. My eyes roll back into my head before they flutter shut.

"Changed my mind. I want you in my bed, because I'm keeping you there all night," he murmurs against my neck.

"As much as I love the sound of that, I can't keep ignoring my responsibilities." Using all the effort I can muster, I place my palms on Lucas' chest and push. "Save it for later. I really do need to make some calls. When I'm done, I promise we can get back to this."

With a heavy sigh, he rises from the settee. "Fine. Make it quick."

"I will."

When he leaves the room, I reluctantly pull my phone from my pocket. I stare at the screen—so many missed calls and texts. Should I call Claudia or my mother first? My mother will probably only make things more dramatic than what they are. Better to call Claudia; she'll keep her cool while telling it to me straight. Selecting her name, I put the call through.

She answers on the first ring. "My God, Pen, why haven't you returned my calls? Your mother is going crazy because you haven't contacted her. Are you still at the cabin, or did the paparazzi find you there? Everything is falling apart. You don't know what we've been dealing with here. We've been trying to put out all the fires you've made, but it's out of control. You're losing everything!" Claudia's frantic voice shrills through the phone.

The breath gets knocked out of me. So much for Claudia keeping her cool. For her to be in such a panic mode, things must be bad. "Claudia, calm down. What fires have I made?"

"Calm down! Calm down! How can you tell me to calm down? We've barely spoken, and then we see photos of you gunning it down main street in a freaking middle-of-nowhere town. I thought you were hiding out so no one could find you? Being seen again has only stirred things up more." I hear her sniff. Oh no! For her to get emotional, I've really hurt her feelings by not contacting her sooner.

"I'm sorry. I told you when we last spoke I had no reception at the cabin. Things got so crazy this is the first chance I've had to call you." I tell her a little white lie. I could have excused myself from Lucas' family when we arrived. They would have understood. I just wasn't ready for reality, and I was enjoying my time with them. "So tell me what's going on. What do you mean I'm losing everything?" My stomach clenches as I wait on her response.

"First, tell me where you are so I can get you. We can talk better face to face."

I tuck my legs up onto the settee. "I'm staying at Lucas' apartment."

Claudia is silent for a beat. "You're in the city? Why haven't you gone home or at least come to mine or Elizabeth's place?" I hear the hurt tone in her voice.

"I was worried there'd be too many paparazzi there. Lucas' apartment has super-tight security. Anyway, it's only for the night. I'll work out my living arrangements tomorrow. Darren probably hasn't left—even moved Karen in." I own my home. Darren moved in with me. But now, after he had sex with another woman in there, I don't want to step foot in it again. Although, that doesn't mean I'm going to let him get comfortable. I'd rather burn it down than let him live in it.

"You're right about Darren living in your apartment, but not with Karen. They've gone their separate ways. Although he's still sobbing about your affair to whoever will listen."

Great. If he keeps talking, it will take even longer for the media to move on. Once I kick him out of my apartment, I never want to have anything to do with him again or give him another thought.

"Tell me why I'm losing everything," I say. Surely she's being overly dramatic.

"Oh, Pen. Your TV series deal has fallen through. Why air a show about a wedding that's not taking place? And they no longer believe in your squeaky-clean image. Also, the book contract your publisher was sending out for you to sign has been withdrawn."

I spring from my seat. "What? They can't do that! I did nothing wrong. Darren is the one who got caught bare-assed having sex with another woman, yet I'm the one being punished? How is that fair?" I can understand about the show, but the book? That hits hard.

"The photos of you with Lucas, and Darren's statement saying you had the affair first, is making you look guilty. Your image is damaged. No one is prepared to commit to you anymore."

I drop my head in my hand and rub my fingers across my forehead. This is worse than I expected. Anger burns in my gut. All my hard work is ruined. What the hell am I supposed to do now?

Be my fake girlfriend.

Lucas' suggestion rings through my head.

Would pretending to be a couple help with my reputation? Will people love our relationship enough to forget about the mess with Darren? I don't have to fake being attracted to Lucas. The chemistry between us is electric. With people watching our every move, could we pull it off?

What other option do I have? I need to do something to save my business and reputation.

"Claudia, I have to go."

"Wait...what do you want us to do? We need to put some kind of plan together."

"I have something in mind. I'll fill you in when I know more." Before she can ask questions, I quickly say goodbye and end the call.

Leaving the office, I go in search of Lucas. The apartment is massive, and it takes opening a few doors and peeking inside rooms until I find the one he's in. The bedroom boasts magnificent views of the city, like every room I've seen. Lucas is sitting on a lush, king-sized bed propped with pillows, looking at his phone. When he sees me, he smiles. That smile makes everything inside me weak and tingly.

"Let's do it," I say.

Lucas' smile spreads across his face. He tosses the phone on the mattress and then flicks the top button of his jeans open. "You don't have to tell me twice."

I shake my head. "No, not that. Well, yes, that will happen. What I mean is, I want to be your fake girlfriend."

"Are you sure?"

"Yes. Everything is falling apart. I have to try something."

"Want to talk about it?"

That's the last thing I want to do right now. "No."

Swinging his legs off the bed, he saunters toward me and backs me up against the wall. He links our fingers together and raises my arms above my head, pressing his body against mine. His tongue darts out to swipe his bottom lip, like he wants to devour me, and I absolutely want him to. Then, with quick movements, he drops my hands. He picks me up by the waist, and in two long strides, he's at the bed. He tosses me on the mattress, and I squeal with delight.

Next, he slides down the zipper of his jeans. "It all doesn't have to be fake."

Propping myself onto my elbows, with one hand I reach out and hook my fingers in the waistband of his underwear. "If I'm agreeing to this, I expect some benefits."

"I'll give you anything sexual you want. Multiple times. In every position you can imagine."

My body thrums with wanting.

Tugging at his underwear, I yank hard, and he drops on top of me, carefully keeping his body weight on his elbows. His pelvis presses against mine, securing me to the mattress. There's no mistaking the hard length of him.

With the tussle of getting tossed on the bed, my shirt has gone askew, exposing a shoulder and the top of my breast. His gaze zeros in on my heaving chest. His tongue darts out to swipe his bottom lip like he's waiting for my hard nipple to pop out so he can lick it. I shimmy my shoulders so the fabric moves lower, exposing my breast even more.

Instead of putting his mouth on me, to my annoyance, he pushes himself onto his knees. What is he doing? My face must show a frustrated expression because he chuckles.

"Patience, Pixie. I want you naked before I fuck you." He unbuttons his shirt so slow I want to groan with impatience. While I'm waiting for him to finish, I tug his jeans and underwear off his hips until his erection, large and heavy, spills free and into my hand.

I stroke him from root to tip, pulling a long moan from his lips. Pumping his hips into my hand, our eyes lock. His body tenses, and I can tell that he's trying to hold it together. When has sex ever been this exciting before? When have I literally held a man in the palm of my hand and felt like I could make all his sexual fantasies come true?

Never. Nothing has ever compared to this. To the way Lucas makes me feel. To the way my body sings whenever he's near. This fake dating with benefits could be dangerous. If I'm not careful, I could fall off the edge of friendship and land somewhere I have no business being.

Lucas pulls away, steps from the bed, and shuffles out of his jeans, tossing them on the floor. Next, he takes condoms out of the nightstand and throws them onto the bed. I shrug out of my shirt and jeans and toss them aside. He wants me naked. I'm giving him naked. Never have I been so confident in my body before. In his brightly lit room, I'm not trying to cover myself under the sheets or keep an item of clothing on to shield myself. Lucas looks at me like I'm the most beautiful woman he's ever seen, and I believe him.

Before he joins me again, he holds onto my ankles and drags me to the edge of the bed. Hooking my legs over his shoulders, he dives between my thighs. The flat of his tongue glides along my slit right before it flicks and sucks at my sensitive nub. My hips buck. I clutch his hair and squeeze my eyes shut and take in the sweet torture of his mouth.

"Lucas," I say on a strangled breath. His mouth works me over. His tongue delving deep between my folds. "Oh...Lucas...Lucas."

He pulls away long enough to say, "Yes, Pixie? Do you like that?"

"Don't...stop...ever." I take deep breaths between each word.

He chuckles and I feel the vibration against my sex.

My hips thrust with the rhythm of his mouth. If he keeps doing magical things with his tongue, I'm not going to last much longer. When his hands travel up my thighs and he adds his fingers, I nearly levitate off the bed.

Like he senses how close I am to finishing, he says, "Easy, Pixie, I'm not ready for this to end."

Unhooking my legs from his shoulders, he joins me on the bed, and we shuffle to the top of the mattress. He rolls on top of me, my legs automatically spread, and he nestles between my thighs. He captures my lips with his mouth, and for a moment I relish in his kiss and the weight of him on my body.

His kiss alone can make me orgasm. Who am I when I'm with him? Someone whose sexual prowess has laid dormant for years and it's getting released in such an oh-so-exciting way.

Lucas glides his tongue along my neck, sucking over my collarbone before he closes his lips around my hardened nipple. I gasp as his tongue flicks and his mouth sucks. He floats his hand over my stomach and to my other breast and massages in slow circles. My body is trembling. Every part of me is on fire. I grasp at his hair as he laves me up. My legs fall open, ready and waiting for his next move.

Lucas lifts his head to look at me. "You're gorgeous, Penny. Every inch of you is fucking perfect."

My heart flutters at his words.

"I want to take my time with you and lap you up from head to toe. But every time I touch you, I'm a fucking ball of lust and need to be inside you," he says through gritted teeth, like it's an effort to hold back long enough to speak. He slides his hand between our bodies and dips a finger inside my sex. My body jerks with sensitivity. "You're so wet." He pulls his hand away, his finger glistening with proof. "Tell me you're ready."

"Not yet."

He groans with frustration.

I push at his shoulders so he lies on his back. I pick up the foil packet from the bed and tear open the condom. With it in my hand, his eyes darken as he can tell what I'm about to do. He folds his arms and places his hands behind his head like he's relaxing, yet he's taking deep breaths through his nose. As I roll it on him, his eyes flutter shut and he bites his bottom lip. I love how I have this effect on him.

Straddling him, I stay on my knees. I clasp my hand around his penis and guide him to my sex. Inch by excruciating slow inch, I lower myself until he's buried deep. For a moment we don't move, only stare at each other, our breathing coming out in labored breaths.

Slowly, I circle my hips one way and back the other. Lucas grips onto my hips, encouraging my movement. Arching my back, I pick up the speed as he grinds into me.

"You feel so good," he groans. "I want to see you touch yourself."

I'm a little surprised at his suggestion, but it also excites me. "Where?"

"Wherever you want."

Timidly, I caress my hands over my stomach and up to my breasts. With an unexpected thrum of satisfaction, I massage them. My thumb and fingers tweaking and swirling around my nipples.

Lucas' pelvis thrusts up and down as he grips my hips hard. "Do you like touching yourself?"

"Y-yes. Yes," my breath escapes on a gust of air.

He growls, "Fuck, that's hot, but I can't take this much longer."

Lifting himself up, he flips me onto my back. I bounce once before he hovers above me, the muscles in his arms bulging as he holds his weight. In a swift motion, he's back inside me, and I bite down on the curve of his neck.

With each thrust, my body is coiling into a tight ball of lust. "I-I don't know how much longer I can last."

He bends his head and closes his mouth around my nipple.

I dig my nails into his back. "More," I say. He moves on to the other breast and gives it equal attention as his hips don't break from their pace, but I need even more. "Faster," I demand.

He grinds hard and picks up speed. Our bodies slap together, my breasts bounce on my chest. Gripping onto his butt, I hold on tight. My body is tightening. My vision blurs.

Squeezing around him, I scream, "Yes, Lucas, yes!" At least, that's what I think I'm saying. My mind is going blank. I can only feel. And I feel Lucas beginning to lose control. With his head tilted back slightly, his mouth falls open. His pounding into me grows harder with each thrust.

Our eyes lock as an orgasm rips through me, tearing a moan from my mouth. Right with me, Lucas is jerking as we both fall over the edge together. He slumps on top of me, keeping his weight on his arms, his warm breath fanning my face.

"Fuck, you're amazing," he declares, and I can't help the grin spreading across my face.

"You're not so bad yourself." He's magnificent. I think—no, I *know*—he's ruined me for future men. My grin drops. How can I think about what's to come when I have something this great? Yet this isn't real. It's fake.

I'm his pretend girlfriend.

But why does this feel like the real deal?

Chapter Fifteen

PENNY

When I wake the next morning, I turn to reach out for Lucas but find the spot next to me empty. Raising onto my elbows, I search the room. Lucas isn't here. The clock on the nightstand reads ten AM. Oh wow, how did I sleep in so long?

Then the answer immediately hits me. Because Lucas kept me up until early morning. That man has a truckload of stamina. My body is still tingling in all the good places. I could easily get used to this.

I flop on my back and stare at the ceiling. I have to keep reminding myself I'm his fake girlfriend. Except the mind-blowing, toe-curling sex is far from fake. If I'm not careful, I could do something stupid like fall for him. That would be a mistake, wouldn't it?

Yes! A huge mistake. Too much is happening in my life. I need to sort it out before I can think about another relationship. Also, Lucas has made it clear he's not looking for love. I'm just letting all the amazing orgasms cloud my mind.

Rising from the bed, I pull on Lucas' t-shirt that's laying crumpled on the floor where he tossed it last night. In the en suite bathroom, I brush my teeth and freshen up then go in search of him.

I find him in the living room surrounded by clothing laid out on the furniture and hanging on portable clothing racks. He's dressed in jeans and a navy t-shirt, his hair damp from a recent shower. I wish I'd woken up to join him. Maybe that's tonight's activity.

Goodness, will I ever get enough of him? I don't want to think too deeply on the answer. I'll take what I can get for as long as I can.

"Good morning," I say.

He turns toward me. "Hey, Pixie. I thought you were never getting out of bed. I was giving you another ten minutes, then I was coming to wake you up." He waggles his eyebrows, and I know exactly how he'd wake me up. Why did I have to get up?

"What's all this?" I wave my arm at the clothes.

"You had to leave your stuff at the cabin. I didn't think you wanted to go back to your apartment to pick up some things and face Darren yet, so I had a few things brought to you."

I float my fingers over the stunning Alessi garments arranged carefully on the couch. "A few things? It looks more like a clothing store on steroids. This is too much."

There are multicolored cocktail dresses, workout gear, and a mixture of casual yet elegant outfits. On the floor next to the clothes racks are heels, sandals, and sneakers. Bags with lingerie brands are placed on the floor.

"What use is owning a fashion house if I can't reap the benefits? In the bags on the table are hair products, makeup, and toiletry items. If there is anything I've missed, let me know and I'll have it brought to you."

Lucas has thought of everything. There's enough stuff to last months. We never discussed if I would stay for more than a day now that I'm his pretend girlfriend. I assumed I could still move into a hotel somewhere and still put up the façade of being a couple. By the looks of everything Lucas has bought is he thinking of a longer stay?

"I can't believe you did all this."

"I want you to be comfortable."

"There are a lot of clothes and products. Am I right to assume I'm staying a little longer than a day?"

"I thought it would be easier to carry out our plan if we were living together. You know, so we're seen coming and going from the building. But if you don't want to, we can arrange another place for you."

Was that a flicker of vulnerability across his face? Does he really want me to stay? "Thank you for all of this. I'd love to stay longer. You're sweet."

He reaches for my hand and tugs me to him so that our chests bump together. "There's nothing *sweet* about what's on my mind while looking at you wearing my t-shirt." He slides his hands along the backs of my legs until he reaches under the shirt to clasp my butt. Nuzzling at my neck, he murmurs, "I wish I had time to fuck you, but Hayden is already busting my ass to get to work. I should have been there two hours ago."

Gliding my hand between our bodies, I rub over his erection. "What's a few more minutes?" He might be gone for hours. I've told myself I'm getting what I can get while I can.

His eyes darken, and I'm pierced with hot lust. "You're right. Hayden can fucking wait." Spinning me around, he bends me over the couch. "This is going to be hard and fast. Are you up for it?"

I'm already dripping wet thinking about it. I hear the zipper of his jeans and the crinkle of the foil packet. The anticipation is building. He pushes my shirt up—I'm not wearing any underwear—and he palms my butt. Spreading my cheeks, he dives into me until he's buried deep.

With hard, fast thrusts he pounds into me. My face his pressed against the cool leather of the couch, and with one hand he twists my hair and pulls until my head is tilting backward. With his other hand, he's clutching at my hip. Nuzzling his face in my neck, he bites and licks over my racing pulse.

I'm moaning...screaming with each thrust. How can I be turned on so quickly? Because it's Lucas. He's a magician with his hands and body.

"Fuck, I love being inside you," he pants.

I love it too. Way too much. Once this is over, will I be coming off a high like a drug addict? Desperate for more? Will I do anything to get it?

My brain turns to mush when he reaches around me and presses on my clit. "Oh...Lucas!" I cry. The pressure builds and I'm there trembling and jerking through another orgasm. Lucas pounds a few more times and groans his release.

Pulling me up to face him, he adjusts my shirt then cups my face in his hands. "I hope I wasn't too rough."

"No, it was wonderful."

He gives me a cocky grin, like he wants to say *yeah, it was.*

Placing a kiss on my nose—which feels so cutesy after what we just did—he excuses himself to use the bathroom to clean up. My legs feel a little weak, so I lean my hip on the couch. Not for the first time, I wonder how this is going to end. When will it end? The sooner I can get my life on track, the sooner I can go back to normal before I get too attached.

A few minutes later, Lucas saunters back into the room. Jeans buttoned, t-shirt back in place. He looks like a dream with or without clothes.

"I really have to get to work before Hayden drags me there himself."

"Is there a problem?"

"We need to do some damage control. A couple of clients have cancelled."

"Oh no! This is all my fault for dragging you into my mess." Things are getting worse and worse. It's one thing for me to lose business, it's another for Alessi Fashion, especially when all Lucas has done is help me.

Taking me by the shoulders, he says, "None of this is your fault. Stop blaming yourself."

"If you hadn't gotten involved—"

He gently squeezes my shoulders. "My decision. I'd do it again if I had to."

The fierce look on his face tells me he means it. Warmth spreads across my chest. "But your brothers are paying for it now."

"Don't worry. It will be fine. The clients were assholes to deal with. I'm happy to see the back of them."

I gnaw on my bottom lip. Lucas places a finger on my mouth, stopping me.

"You worry too much," he says. "Everything will work out in the end. We'll win everyone over with our fairy tale romance. You'll see. Now, I won't be long. I can work mostly from home, so I'll be back in a couple of hours. Is there anything you need before I go?"

"Do you mind if Claudia and my mother come over?" We need to talk about mine and Lucas' plan.

"You don't need to ask to have guests." He points to a phone attached to the wall. "Press zero and it will connect you to Samuel.

He's security. Give him the names of your visitors, and he'll let them up. He'll also arrange a car for you to leave the building undetected if you need to go anywhere. When you're hungry, press one on the phone and it will take you to the restaurant. I've already had them send up cream cheese bagels with chocolate sauce." He screws his nose mockingly with distaste. "It's in the kitchen."

"Thank you." There he goes being sweet again. I will never be able to repay him for everything he's done for me.

He swipes his phone and keys from the coffee table and slides them into his pockets. "Call me if you need anything." Walking to me, he cups my face in his hands and kisses me softly on the lips. "See you later, Pixie."

He saunters away and out of the apartment. I'm left frozen on the spot. Up until now our new friendship was based on sex, and soon to be, a fake relationship. My heart is knocking against my chest, because that gentle goodbye kiss didn't feel so fake.

<hr>

"My God! I thought I was going to have to donate a kidney to the Dwayne Johnson look-alike security guard to let us in. He asked us a hundred and one questions and wanted two forms of identification before he let us into the elevator. You'd think the president lived here," Claudia huffs as she gives me a quick hug. Then her gaze takes in the luxurious room. "Holy shit! I think the president does live here." And it's only the entrance. Wait until she sees the rest of the place.

My mother follows close behind Claudia, looking like a picture of elegance, dressed in a white, fitted bodice with a flared skirt emphasizing her slim frame. Chunky gold and pearl jewelry drape around her neck. Her platinum blonde hair falls in perfect waves past her shoulders. Anyone would think she's dressed for an important event, not a visit with her daughter. This is what she calls 'casual'.

"Hello, sweetheart." My mother gives me air-kisses on each cheek. "Nice of you to call me while you were away." Her words have an undertone of pissed although the botox doesn't show how upset she really is with me.

I lead them into the living room, which I've tidied up. I hung all the clothes in a closet in a bedroom I found. Just because I stayed the night in Lucas' bed doesn't mean that while I'm living here, that's where he wants me every night.

"I'm sorry, Mom. Things got hectic, and the cell reception was bad."

She tilts her chin. "Well, it would have been nice to know if you were alive or dead."

I mentally roll my eyes at her dramatics. I know Claudia would have let her know we'd spoken. "I'm sorry," I repeat. No point arguing over it. "Can I get either of you a coffee?"

"No thank you," Claudia says.

"I'm fine for now," my mother says as her gaze trails me from head to toe. "Is that a new outfit?"

"Yes, it is." My body tenses as I wait for her criticism.

Because I'm not planning on leaving the apartment, I chose something more casual from the Alessi collection. I look down and self-consciously smooth out the fabric of the navy, wide-legged, high-waisted trousers. Then I fiddle with the blue and white striped silk shirt, which is rolled up at the elbows and tucked into the waist-band of the pants. Cinching my waist is a tanned belt. When I'd looked in the mirror I thought I looked stylish and cute. Now with my mother's scrutinizing stare, I'm not so sure.

"It's lovely. The shape is flattering," she says.

I wait for the 'but' that always follows. My mother rarely gives a compliment without it being followed by a criticism. *That shape is flattering on you* but *it's clinging too tightly to your hips. Are you sure the size is right?* When she doesn't follow it up with anything else, I turn to Claudia and raise an eyebrow—she knows exactly what my mother is like. She shrugs and gives me a surprised look.

Gesturing for them to take a seat on the couch, I sit on a wingback chair opposite them. They probably have a million questions they want to ask. How do I answer them without giving away too much? Do they need to know how close Lucas and I have gotten? No doubt Claudia will know that we've had sex. I can't hide much from her.

First, I need to ask about the company and how bad a shape it's in. "Hit me with it. How much is lost?" I ask.

My mother adjusts her skirt to cover her knees. "I'm not going to lie. Your bookings for live shows have dried up. The book deal is still being negotiated."

"Claudia told me it fell through."

My mother nods. "Yes, the publishers wanted to let it go. I'm trying to convince them they shouldn't. If it goes ahead, they'll offer half of what the original sale was. I'll see if I can negotiate more. If they don't budge, I guess it's better to lose some money than all of it. And with the way things are going, you need all the money you can get."

Okay, that's not so bad. There's still a chance my book will get published.

"The TV series isn't happening. No matter how much I tried to win it back with other ideas to film since the wedding fell through, the production company wants nothing to do with you. I'm plumb tired of trying to get them to change their mind."

I clutch the armrests. "They have to fulfill the terms of the contract."

"You represent home and family. You promised a squeaky-clean image. That image broke when you had an affair."

Springing from the chair, I throw my hands in the air. "You know I didn't have an affair."

"The photos of you with Lucas Alessi, and Darren's statement, paints a different picture. Your reputation is tarnished. It's going to take time, or even a miracle, to fix this. What in the world were you thinking traipsing around with Lucas Alessi? If you wanted to take out your revenge on Darren, you could have done it discreetly." My mother narrows her eyes at me.

Looking at it from the outside in, it looks suspicious. Yet I would have hoped my mother didn't believe what was posted. In all fairness, I didn't fill her in on what really happened.

"I wasn't trying to get back at Darren. I'd accidentally locked myself out of my hotel room and got surrounded by paparazzi." The thought of that night still makes me shudder. "Lucas was staying in a room opposite mine. When he saw the predicament I was in, he stepped in and helped. Those photos aren't what they seem. We weren't in some lovers' tryst. As usual, the media likes to tell stories without facts." I go on to tell them that Lucas wanted to drop me off at the airport to meet Claudia only for the paparazzi to be there too. "That's how I ended up at his cabin. He thought we'd be safe from the media because it's so secluded." But they somehow found us again. Did Alison call them? Of course she did. Who else? She was the only one who knew who I was.

"Whether or not the photographs of the two of you are innocent, they've done a lot of damage. With your disappearing act, not even Claudia can put you in a better light."

I rub the back of my neck and sit down. When I talked to Lucas last night about the 'fake dating' plan, it sounded like a good idea. But now that I have to relay it to my mother and Claudia, I'm nervous as to what they might say. Will they think it's a stupid idea? Well, they haven't come up with anything better.

"I may be able to do something that will change everyone's opinions of me," I say.

My mother places her forearms on her thighs and leans forward with a dubious expression on her face. "What is it?"

I glance between her and Claudia and take a deep breath. "Lucas suggested that since everyone believes we're dating we should go out and be seen together. He thinks if people see us as a couple they'll get invested in our relationship and forget about the scandal." My mother and Claudia sit in silence, staring at me like I've lost my mind. "What do you think?"

"*Are* you and Lucas Alessi dating?" my mother asks.

"No. It will be fake."

"I thought you and Lucas hated each other. Surely that hasn't changed within a few days. You do remember *why* you hate him?" Claudia gives me a knowing look.

"You hate him? Why?" My mother looks confused.

"It's a long story, Mom. A silly high school misunderstanding that got blown out of proportion." I never told her about the naked photos or how I got Lucas expelled from school. I was so ashamed about everything I wanted to pretend it never happened.

"What changed?" Claudia asks.

"We talked and the truth came out." Even though I hate what's happening with the media, if it weren't for them, I would have never had this time with Lucas and our pasts wouldn't be healed.

Claudia gives me a look I don't understand. Is she not convinced that Lucas didn't take the photos? She's probably worried about me and still a little suspicious of Lucas.

"How are you going to convince people you're in love? It has to be believable or it won't work," Claudia says.

We have off-the-charts sexual chemistry. Can that pass as love? "That's something we can work on before we venture out in public."

Will I be able to look into his eyes and not fall a little bit in love with him? What if pretending turns into the real thing? My heart already goes crazy every time he looks at me.

"Do you think it will work?" I ask.

"It might. Before you make your couple debut we need to post a statement," Claudia suggests.

"Another one? Didn't you post one when this all started?"

"That was more of an 'I'm shocked and saddened by the recent events and would like privacy at this time' kind of statement. This time you need to tell everyone how sorry you are for your indiscretion and apologize."

My spine prickles and my jaw clenches. "I'm not admitting to and apologizing for an affair I didn't have."

"Sweetheart," my mother says. "We know you're innocent in this. The statement will appease people and stop them from trying to keep proving it's true. Then once it's published, if you want to go with the plan Lucas suggested, we'll work something out. We'll fix this the best way we can."

I thought my mother would be more upset about the breakup and maybe even suggest I work things out with Darren. Yet she seems understanding and on my side. Sometimes I put walls up around her. I have to remember she's not out to bring me down.

"So, Darren gets away with what he's done?" I say. "He should be the one apologizing."

"Darren has always been the golden boy. He knows how to charm people and have them eating from his hand. Of course he comes out of this looking like the good guy," Claudia says with resentment. She sounds more hurt about the situation than me.

"If I go ahead with the statement, what do I say?" I hate the idea of it. But if both my mother and Claudia think it's the right way to go, I have to trust their judgment.

Claudia pulls her phone from her purse, swipes at the screen, and types something. When she's done she hands the phone to me. "What do you think of this? If you approve it, I'll post it right away."

I read what she's written.

I deeply regret my hurtful and embarrassing behavior which has affected those I care about. It was never my intention to cause any pain. For that, I'm truly sorry.

Nausea coils in my gut. I hand the phone back. I never thought I'd be dealing with something like this. It makes me want to go back to that invisible girl who no one paid any attention to. My life would be private and no one's business.

"You haven't admitted to the affair outright, yet it is implied. I'd wait a couple of days after I release it before you go out with Lucas." Claudia screws her nose up slightly. She clearly has a problem with something.

"Do you not like the plan? Or doing it with Lucas? If I'm making a mistake, you'd tell me, right?"

Claudia smiles, yet something is stiff about it. What's wrong with her? It's risky; maybe she's just worried.

"We have to try something," she says. "The only way we can hopefully pull it off is with Lucas since he is part of this mess. So, do I post the statement?"

Feeling defeated, I shrug my shoulders. "Do it."

Claudia types on her phone. "Done."

"It will all work out. You'll see," my mother says with optimism that I'm not yet feeling.

"If we're going to convince the public you and Lucas are a couple, you need to explain what's been happening the past few days. How has the relationship developed? Are you still frosty with one another or more friendly now that you've talked? If you're staying in his apartment, are you on good terms?"

My face heats, and I hope they don't see what our relationship has really developed into. How do I tell them I went from being engaged to one man and four days later in the bed of another?

Claudia stares at me suspiciously. If there is anyone who can read me, it's her.

I rise from the chair. "Would anyone like a drink?" Without waiting for an answer, I turn my back to hide any telltale signs and walk to the bar in the corner of the room.

"No thank you," both Claudia and my mother say.

Pulling out a bottle of water from the mini fridge, I turn back and take a seat, hoping that my expression has settled. "We're on good terms and have become friends."

"I still don't understand if he hated you so much the night you got locked out of your hotel room, why did he help you?" my mother asks.

Twisting off the lid of the bottle, I take a sip of water then say, "Just the kind of man he is. He saw I was distressed and couldn't leave me there. Then after learning what was happening in the media, I had a little meltdown. Lucas pulled me through." I take another sip of water. That day in the woods will always be the most memorable and important of my life. If anything good comes from what's happening, it's that moment feeling powerful in my own skin. "We're on such good terms now, he even took photographs of me." Crap! I didn't mean to say that. I was trying to express that we're friends, and I just blurted it out.

My mother's eyes widen. "What kind of photographs? I thought he only worked with models."

Of course she'd be surprised he'd want to take photos of me when he had such beautiful women to shoot instead. "Nothing interesting. Just some shots in the woods. It was raining, the lighting was good—or so Lucas said—and I posed for him." That's the PG version of what really happened that day.

"Ooh, sounds sexy. Are they good? Did he print them? Can we see?" Claudia's eyes light with excitement as she fires off her questions.

"They were beautiful. I asked him to delete them because I was showing a little skin and didn't want anyone finding them." More like a whole lot of skin.

"That's a pity," my mother says. "It would have been a nice change to see something artistic printed of you in the media instead of the ghastly ones the paparazzi posted. Anyway, I need the bathroom. Can you tell me where it is please?"

"Follow the hallway to the end, take a right and it's the second door on your left." I know because I went in search of Lucas last night.

When my mother leaves and is out of earshot, Claudia's smile drops, and she leans forward. "I can't believe you're shacking up with Lucas Alessi." Her tone is filled with disgust. "Especially after what he did to you in high school. He took naked photos of you for the whole school to see," she says as if I need reminding.

"I told you, we talked." I go on to explain how Travis was the one who took the photos and set Lucas up.

She frowns. "Why would he do that? What would he get out of it?"

That's something I don't understand either. "He probably didn't like Lucas and assumed I'd retaliate somehow." Which I did in a big way.

Claudia gives a dubious look. "Seems far-fetched. Okay, so you don't hate him anymore now that you know the *truth*." She says the word 'truth' like she's skeptical that it really is. "But why doesn't he hate you anymore? You got him expelled. Although, I still don't know why he took it so hard and hated you so much for it."

"I still feel guilty about what I did, especially now that I know he was innocent. Even if he wasn't, it was still a horrible thing to do. He lost so much and blamed me for Garrett's death. That's why he was so angry."

Claudia jerks back like I'd slapped her. "What the hell? How dare he blame you for something you had no control over. Garrett's death was an accident."

"He realized it wasn't fair to blame me. And he's forgiven me for getting him expelled."

Claudia crosses her arms over her chest and leans back into the cushions of the couch. Giving me a knowing look, she says, "You've slept with him." It's not a question. "Elizabeth might believe this is all sweet and innocent and he's only helping you out of a bad situation, but I can see the truth on your face. What I want to know—is it more than just fucking or are you really a couple?"

We've been best friends too long to not tell her the truth. I'm not surprised she figured it out. "Yes, we have slept together, but we're just friends. We're not a couple. I'm staying in his apartment because it will be easier for what we need to do."

Claudia's eyes narrow as she scrutinizes me. "While you're playing the happy couple, don't go and fall in love with him. That man is a notorious player and has a new woman every week. He'll toss you aside as soon as this is over."

That's the problem. I'm not sure if I haven't fallen a little already.

My mother walks back into the living room, thankfully interrupting our conversation before it gets too deep. I don't need Claudia questioning me about how I'm going to get through these next few days or weeks when I'm not sure myself.

"I walked into Lucas' office by mistake. My goodness, that room is amazing. There are so many gorgeous photographs I could spend hours in there looking at them. It's a shame yours aren't among the collection."

It wouldn't surprise me if she'd snooped in his office on purpose hoping to find them. "Yes, he's talented," I say. I'll never forget how beautiful the photos he took of me were.

Taking a seat, my mother places her palms on her thighs and sighs. "Back to business. Things have changed. Getting your career back on track is like starting from scratch. Even worse, because you have a history now. After you're seen out with Lucas, and hopefully the majority of the response is good, I'll talk to people about booking you jobs. It won't be easy, nor can you ask for the same amount of money."

Back when I was making videos for YouTube it was my way of not being invisible. Most of my life I was looked over. Never beautiful enough for pageants. Never pretty enough or skinny enough for my mother. Not popular enough to be included with the cool kids at school. It took videos of me making things and organizing closets to finally be seen. People sat up and noticed. I had a talent—one people were excited about and wanted me to teach them. Now it's getting torn away from me.

If this plan with Lucas doesn't work, will I go back to being invisible? The thought doesn't scare me. Probably because when things in the entertainment industry go wrong, the repercussions are like a landslide, taking everything in its path with it. This is a part of fame I've never experienced before. If being seen comes with so much destruction, is it really what I want anymore?

"I appreciate everything you both have done and are doing for me. I couldn't get through this without you."

"You're welcome, sweetheart," my mother says.

"Anything for you, Pen." Claudia smiles.

My mother taps her thighs. "I'd love a cup of coffee now please, Penny."

I rise from the chair, grateful to be doing something else other than wallowing in the living room about my failing career. "Sure, I'll be right back. Anything for you, Claudia?"

"I'll have a coffee too please."

"I'll come with you. I'm dying to see if the kitchen is as fabulous as the rest of the penthouse." My mother follows me.

Did she really need to use the bathroom, or did she snoop around the whole apartment? I wouldn't be surprised if she gave herself a tour.

When Claudia stays seated, I ask, "Are you coming?"

She picks up her phone and waves it. "I have a call to make. I'll be there soon."

We leave her in the living room and enter the kitchen.

"Oh wow, this is gorgeous. Look at those fancy appliances. This kitchen doesn't look cooked in," she says as she slides onto a chair at the breakfast counter.

I pull three cups from a top cabinet and place them on the counter. "That's because it hasn't been. Lucas gets his meals from the restaurant downstairs." I turn on the coffee machine and wait for it to brew.

"You know how to whip up a good meal. Lucas might appreciate it. It would be easy to get comfortable living here with him. He's a handsome young man." She gives me a teasing look.

"Mom, this is temporary. How could you even suggest such a thing when I only broke up with Darren a week ago?" Is she so concerned I'm going to be put on the shelf collecting dust and no man will ever want me?

She waves a hand. "I was kidding. Just trying to lighten the mood."

Now I feel like a jerk for snapping at her. The coffee is ready, and I pour it in the cups, passing one to my mother. I take the other and sit next to her.

"All jokes aside, how are you, sweetheart? We haven't had a chance to talk about what Darren did and how you're feeling. I'm sorry he cheated on you and so publicly. You must be heartbroken." Even though my mother focuses on my appearance, I know she loves me.

"I'm fine. Taking time away from everything made me realize that marrying Darren would have been a huge mistake. Not just because he was cheating on me, but because I was never truly in love with him. It was all too easy and comfortable, so I believed the next step was marriage. Finding out about the affair before the wedding was a blessing. I just wish it wasn't so public."

How did that video at my event get played? Why would Darren do such a thing and risk the backlash he might receive from it?

My mother gives my hand a pat. "He ain't got the sense God gave a goose, and he won't be able to make it without you. His injury ended his football career. Unless he finds another woman to carry him, his world will fall apart soon enough."

"I'm sorry my career is ruined over this." This affects her too as my 'momager'.

She makes a tsking sound. "Don't be sorry. It's not your fault. You'll get through this and come out better than ever."

I smile even though I know she doesn't truly believe that.

"Claudia must still be on the phone. Let's join her in the living room. We'll be more comfortable."

Picking up our coffee cups, we take them with us. When I enter the room, I stop short. Lucas is walking into the living room. "Oh, hi. I wasn't expecting you back so soon. Is everything okay?" I place my cup on the coffee table and hand Claudia hers, resisting the urge to run to him for a kiss. *Stop thinking stuff like that!* I mentally give myself a forehead slap. We are not a real couple.

Lucas smiles, and my heart squeezes. He's so gorgeous and kind and funny. It would be so easy to— *Again! Stop letting your thoughts trail into dangerous territory.*

"Everything is fine. A statement is out. It's in the hands of our PR team." He turns to my mother and smiles. "You must be Ms. Aldin. I'm Lucas Alessi."

My mother slips her fingers through the ends of her hair. "Please call me Elizabeth. It's lovely to finally meet you. I'm in love with your fashion label."

"Good to meet you too, and thank you. I see you're wearing one of our creations. You wear it well."

My mother blushes like a schoolgirl and giggles. *Giggles!* "You're too kind."

Next he turns to Claudia. "Nice to see you again, Claudia. It's been a while."

Claudia smiles back, but it looks a little stiff. Even after I've explained everything to her, why is she still mad at Lucas? Does she not believe him?

"Hi, Lucas. Yes, it has." Claudia's words are just as stiff as her expression. Maybe she needs time for all the information to sink in. It takes time to let go of the past even when you know it was lies. "Well, we're done for the day, so I'll head home." She hooks the strap of her purse over her shoulder and stands. "Let me know if you need anything, Pen."

"What about the coffee?"

"Sorry, don't have time. There's something I need to do."

Okay, that's weird. Was it something to do with the call she needed to make? If it was something about the business, she'd tell me, right? I hope nothing is wrong with her. In case it's something private, I don't ask any questions. I'll call her later and check in on her.

"Claudia is my ride, so I better go too." My mother kisses me on the cheek. "I'll talk to you tomorrow." Then she beams a smile at Lucas. "I hope to see you again. Keep my Penny with you for as long as possible. She needs the support of a good man like you."

"Mom!" I groan.

Lucas chuckles, and I want to hide from embarrassment. "She can stay here as long as she wants," he says.

He turns to me with a piercing gaze. When he looks at me like that, I never want to leave. Lucas feels like home. A feeling that is new to me. With Darren, we shared an apartment. A life. Yet, when I looked at him, I never felt a sense of belonging—a desire to put down roots.

"Who would have ever thought that the two of you—who despised each other—would now be playing house?" Claudia's trill laugh—sounding anything but joyful—breaks through my musing. What is her problem? "How times have changed. It's amazing what time alone in a secluded cabin can do."

I don't miss the innuendo in her words. Luckily, my mother is too starstruck by Lucas to notice. Then Claudia disappears into the foyer.

My mother hurries after her. "Goodbye, sweetheart," she says as she sails from the room.

"Coffee?" I pick up Claudia's untouched cup and offer it to Lucas.

"Thanks," he says and takes it from me. I pick up mine from the coffee table and we sit on the couch.

"I'm sorry about Claudia. She's not normally so frosty. Even after I told her you weren't responsible for the photos, I don't know why she's still angry with you."

Lucas takes a sip of coffee. "That's the most she's said to me since I turned her down at a party in high school, which was weeks before she thought I spread your photos around."

My cup pauses at my lips, then I lower it. "What are you talking about?"

"Before the photos, and before I got expelled, we were at a party. She followed me into the bathroom and wanted—well, she gave me a lot of options to choose from."

I lean forward and set my cup on the coffee table, no longer having the strength to hold it. Shifting in my seat, I hook my leg on the couch and face him. "She wanted to have sex with you?"

Lucas places his cup next to mine. "Yes."

"I don't believe you." He must be mistaken. Claudia would never do that. Especially when she knew how much I liked him.

Shrugging, he says, "Well, she did."

"She must have been drunk." That's the only explanation. She didn't know who she was hitting on.

"From what I remember, she was steady on her feet and appeared sober. She told me what she wanted to do to me in detail without a slur or stutter in her voice."

Shocked at what I'm hearing, I cup my hands over my cheeks. "What did she say?"

With a raised eyebrow, he says, "Something about starting on her knees and ending bent over the vanity."

I gasp. My gut churns at the betrayal. "And you refused?" I can't hide the cynical tone in my voice. How many eighteen-year-old boys would turn down sex?

"Yeah, I refused." He looks affronted at my cynicism.

"Why?"

"Because I liked *you*. If I fucked your best friend, what chances would I have of getting you?" he says like the answer is obvious.

My heart does a little jig behind my ribs. *He liked me.* "Why didn't she tell me about this? We tell each other everything."

"Maybe she was embarrassed she'd gotten rejected."

"Or she was ashamed she hit on you behind my back when she knew I liked you."

I thought I knew everything about Claudia. Every crush. Every hookup. Every heartbreak. Every dream. But all these years she's kept this secret from me. Now I'm keeping one from her too. A big, fat one. I haven't told her, and I'm not sure I will, that I'm liking Lucas more and more each day.

"Or because you'd be pissed she tried swooping in," Lucas says.

Is that why she was so insistent about putting drugs into Lucas' locker—because he rejected her? Would I even have thought about that kind of revenge if it weren't for her? She was the one to supply the goods. My mind is exploding with this new information.

"Anyway, enough about Claudia. Tell me how much you liked me in high school."

I roll my eyes and giggle. "No. I'd hate to give you a big head."

He shifts closer to me, and our thighs brush. "Did you want to kiss me?"

My gaze lands on his lips. *Yes! Still do.* "No," I lie with a grin.

"Did you want to put your hands down my pants to feel how *big* I was?"

That pulls out a laugh. "No," I lie again. I'd thought about it too many times.

He shuffles even closer, and I sink back into the couch cushions. "Did you want to fuck me?"

Brushing a lock of hair from my face, he skims his fingers down the curve of my neck, across my shoulder, and over my breast. I swallow hard, unable to speak.

"Because I wanted to kiss you, touch you, and fuck you. I thought about it every single day," he says. Pushing me onto my back, he lays on top of me. "I plan to do just that. Every day until you tell me to stop."

Chapter Sixteen

LUCAS

Today's the day we venture out in public. Time for the world to see us as a happy couple. Hopefully they'll fall in love with our relationship.

If it were up to me, I wouldn't give a fuck what the media said. It's not the first time they've written shit about me. I'm doing this for Penny. She deserves better. Her business and reputation shouldn't suffer because of what her ex did.

Why I feel so strongly about helping her, I'm not sure. Or I just don't want to delve into it. If I did, what would I discover? Something I'm not ready for. Something I'm not made for—monogamous love.

"I still can't believe you agreed to that bullshit statement you let Claudia post." I tug on my boots.

Penny stops shimmying into a pale blue skirt. "We had to do something."

Watching her stand in my bedroom in only a bra and skirt, I want to say *to hell with everyone*, rip off the little clothing she's wearing, and throw her in bed and fuck her for hours. It's exactly what we've done the past three days. Eat, sleep, fuck. And I've loved every minute.

Judging by the smile Penny wakes up with every morning, I'd say she's having a great time too.

Never in my life have I wanted to spend more than a few hours in bed with a woman. Yet with Penny, I never want her to leave it. I spend every minute wanting to be with her. Not only in bed, but talking with her. The conversations we've had about our childhoods, careers, and everything in between is more than I've learned about anyone besides my family.

Unfortunately, if we cross the line from friendship to a relationship, I'll only hurt her. So, when this is over, I will say goodbye. That way we can stay friends. I'd rather cut off my right arm than cause her pain.

I rise from the chair and slide my hands into my pockets. "You apologized for something you didn't do."

A white blouse is on the edge of the bed, she picks it up, puts it on, and ties it in a knot at the waist. "Should my statement have been more like yours?" I had her clothes moved into my bedroom. She belongs in my room. In my bed.

"Nothing wrong with telling people to worry about their own lives and fuck off out of mine."

Shaking her head, she rolls her eyes. "Thank goodness your PR manager said it more eloquently than that." She turns to the mirror and adjusts her clothing, finger-combs her hair, and applies lip gloss. With a heavy sigh, she says, "Do you think this is going to work?"

I walk to her and slide my arms around her waist. Resting her back against my chest, I prop my chin on the top of her head. We look at each other through the mirror's reflection.

"There's a good chance it will," I say. "It might take time though."

Her chest heaves up and down. "It's been nearly two weeks and Darren is still riding the media wave. People are on his side."

"This is why we can't hide away anymore. Let's show our faces. Act like we're in love." My heart pounds in my chest. Somehow I feel like I won't have to do much acting. "They'll get over what happened, and everything will go back to normal." And she'll be out of my life. It's selfish of me to want this to drag on. But I do.

"What if it doesn't work and it only makes things worse? My business is suffering because of this. It can't take much more. *I* can't. This has broken me." Tears shine in her eyes, and she bites her trembling bottom lip.

Her tears are like a spear through my heart. Never do I want to see her upset again over this. Her ex needs to pay for what he's done and for what he's putting her through.

Spinning her around so I can face her, I hold on tight when I say, "If there's one thing I've learned about you, it's that you are *unbreakable.* You have survived nasty beauty pageants, naked photos, a humiliating breakup, and a media circus hounding you. Not many people could get through all that without major damage. You're the strongest person I know. You've got this."

She gives me a small smile. "After all the years of hating each other, never in a million years would I have thought we would be here like this."

"We're meant to be—" I bite my tongue before I say *we're meant to be together.* She looks at me intently, like she's wondering what I was about to say. "We're meant to be friends," I correct myself.

She nods, her eyes downcast. Is she disappointed? God, I hope she's not feeling things other than friendship and lust for me. Feelings I can't return.

Having her living in my apartment is blurring the lines between friendship and love. We're saying this relationship is fake, yet we're sleeping in the same bed every night. Having breakfast together. Talking about our lives, our goals, our dreams. I spend more time working from home than in the office. When I'm in the office I'm excited to get home because I know Penny is waiting for me.

Just like a real couple.

Dropping my hands from around her waist, I step away. I need to pull back and put some distance between us—keep emotions out of it. Shit! This is the worst time. We are about to walk into a pack of wolves. All eyes on us. Every move will be monitored. This is not the time to fuck this up.

I clear my throat. "Are you ready?" Am I? I have to be. This was my idea.

"Yes." She picks up her purse from the dresser, and I follow her out of the room. Her hips sway with each step and my gaze follows. I breathe a sigh of relief. I don't think I'll have a problem proving I'm into her.

<hr>

Stopping in front of the restaurant, I grip the steering wheel and stare out the windshield. This is it. When we get out of the car it's game on. No backing out.

"Hey, you've been quiet all the way here. Is something wrong?" Penny asks as if she senses my unease.

"No," I say.

"Are you sure? Because you've been frowning since we left the apartment. If you don't want to do this, it's okay. You have done so much already. This is my mess to fix. I'll think of another way to win back the public's affection."

I give her a quick glance. "I'm a little nervous," I admit.

Putting her hand on my thigh, she says, "Me too. Let's turn around and go home."

I shake my head. "No, we're here now. Let's see it through." I reach for her hand and give it a gentle squeeze. I don't need to hold her hand; no one can see us. Yet my instincts have me touching her every chance I get. "Are you ready to go inside?"

Biting her bottom lip, her gaze locks on mine, her eyes a little wide with fear. I bring her hand to my lips and kiss her knuckles to try and steady her nerves. Hell, it's to steady mine too. So much for keeping my distance. This is not pulling away.

"Ready as I'll ever be," she says with a too-bright smile.

"That's my girl," I say, and her eyes snap to mine. I keep doing and saying things I shouldn't, yet every fiber of my being is screaming she *is* my girl! I drop her hand and open the door. "Let's do this."

We get out of the vehicle, and I move around the hood of the car to Penny. Once again, I take her hand. It's small and soft in mine. This time I'm holding it for no other reason than for show.

Yeah, right. Keep telling yourself that, buddy.

A valet hurries to the car, and I hand him the keys, and we make our way inside.

We chose the Italian restaurant for its location. It's not a hotspot in the center of the city where celebrities go to be seen and photographers line the streets to get a photo. If we turned up at a place like that, it might look too obvious that what we're doing is all an act. This restaurant is still busy enough to get noticed in a more subtle way. If all goes well, the paparazzi will get wind we are here.

The hostess greets us with a smile before she does a double-take. Okay, here we go. She's recognized us. That's a good sign. She picks up leather-bound menus and guides us to a booth in the corner of the restaurant and in front of a window. We are exposed to the diners and to whoever walks past outside. Claudia picked the restaurant and arranged for this table, said it was the perfect position to be seen.

As we take our seats, I glance around the room. People are looking our way and whispering to each other behind their hands. We've attracted their attention. It won't be long before they take what they think are sneaky photos of us and upload them online.

With jerky movements, Penny opens her menu. Her face is pale and stiff. This is hard on her. I hate that she has to go through all of this because she picked an asshole for a fiancé.

"Hey, Pixie," I say, my voice lowered. "You won't convince anyone we're in love if you're firing daggers at the menu."

Her head snaps up. "They're talking about us and staring."

I nod and smile like she's said something sweet. "Yeah, that's the plan."

"Like *really* staring. They're not even trying to hide it," she says with disgust.

Brushing a lock of hair from her face, I tuck it behind her ear. At my touch, her face softens. "Pretend they're not here and focus on me. You *are* with the hottest guy in the room."

Laughter springs from her lips. That's better. This is real.

With an amused expression, she says, "Is that so? I think the guy in the gray suit at the next table is super-sexy."

I quietly growl and nip at her jaw. Her body quivers. Yeah, she's relaxing. "You only have eyes for me, Pixie." I know she's only joking, but the thought of her looking at another man makes my gut churn. I selfishly want all of her attention.

Before she can respond, a waitress comes over to our table. "Hello, Ms. Aldin, Mr. Alessi. Are you ready to order?" Her attention flicks from me to Penny, and I can tell she's taking us in. Probably fishing for juicy details to pass onto the other staff.

We pull apart to look at the menus, my thoughts far from food. I give it a quick glance. Penny orders penne alla vodka, and I order the same. We both could do with a drink, and I ask for a bottle of merlot.

Like we hoped, it doesn't take long for word to get out. Through the window and past the garden edge, paparazzi are arriving and setting up their cameras. After getting Penny to relax, her body stiffens again and fear is etched on her face.

I lean toward her, making out as if I'm nibbling her ear, and I whisper, "Relax. This won't work unless it looks real."

Turning her head to face me, she says, "I'm used to people looking at me. It's part of my job. These people are scrutinizing us. I feel like an ape in a zoo."

"Want me to throw shit at them?"

Her head tosses back, and she laughs out loud. The sound warms my chest. Penny is getting under my skin, and I'm not sure how to stop it.

"Look at me. Not them," I say.

She does what I say, and I get caught in her gaze. This is dangerous territory for me. Because while I'm looking in her bright blue eyes I'm scared I'll fall in.

"As long as they keep their distance and don't abuse me for being a whore, I'll be okay." She adjusts the collar of my shirt and places a light kiss on my cheek. Now she's getting into the spirit of things.

"When you're with the hottest guy in the room—no, in all of New York City—they're thinking what a fucking lucky bitch."

She tosses her head back and laughs. "Conceited much?"

I shrug. "Just stating the obvious."

If this banter keeps a smile on her face and convinces everyone this is the real deal, I'll keep it up. For Penny. For show. This is not for me, I remind myself.

"Do you think it's working?" She gnaws at her bottom lip.

I take her chin in my fingers and place a light kiss on her lips. Before I can deepen it like I've wanted to do since we've sat down, the waitress arrives with our meals. The interruption keeps the kiss at a PG rating.

The waitress gives us a big, approving smile and places our plates on the table. "I love the two of you together. I'm so happy for you both," she says before she walks away.

"It looks like it's working," I say. "We could win an Oscar for our performance. Our acting is brilliant."

A shadow crosses Penny's eyes. "Yes, we're good," she says with a smile that looks stiff on her face. I hate how this is taking a toll on her. She picks up her fork and starts eating her pasta.

A few moments later, Penny's attention is drawn to the front of the restaurant. Her mouth drops open on a gasp.

Following her gaze, my jaw clenches tight. "What the fuck is Darren doing here?" Word must be spreading. He's not the attention we want to attract.

"I don't know." Her voice shakes like she's dreading what's to come.

He walks toward us, but before he reaches our table, I stand up and shield Penny from him. There's no way I'm going to let this piece of shit near her. When he reaches us, he tries to step around me, but I block his path.

"Get out of my way," he demands.

If we weren't sure whether we grabbed the attention of the diners before, we have it now. All eyes are focused on us.

"Not going to happen. You lost your right to Penny when you fucked another woman," I say loud enough for everyone to hear. I want them to know what a scumbag he is and stop pointing the blame at Penny.

"Get the fuck out of my way. Penny is *my* fiancée." His mouth twists with anger.

Everyone has stopped eating. Cameras are pointing in our direction. Shit! This is not good.

"Penny isn't your fiancée anymore. She's *my* girlfriend. If you don't turn around and leave, I'll personally toss you out on your ass."

"Penny!" he calls out, trying again to step around me.

I stand my ground and don't let him pass. "One last warning...fuck off." Rage is bubbling inside me, wanting him to give me an excuse to put my fist in his face.

Penny puts her hand on my back. "Lucas, it's okay. Let him tell me what he wants so he can leave."

Every muscle is vibrating in my body, telling me not to move, but I step aside for Penny to stand next to me.

"What do you want, Darren?" she asks.

Like nothing has happened, like he hasn't slandered her name, ruined her reputation, and betrayed her, he steps forward with his arms out wide, going in for a hug.

I reach out and put my hand on his chest, stopping him from coming any closer. "Do. Not. Fucking. Touch. Her." I grind out each word. The threatening tone in my voice makes him retreat.

He shuffles his feet. "I've seen things online. I wanted to check out if it was true. You really *are* involved with him." His unimpressed gaze travels up and down the length of me.

Asshole, she's upgraded to first class. You're not good enough to be put in baggage.

"Looks like it didn't take you long to shack up with him after you tore my heart out," he sneers.

Penny, along with the diners, gasp with shock. The onlookers aim their sympathetic gazes at Darren. I need to get him out of the restaurant before he ruins everything we're trying to fix.

"Darren, leave. Now." I control the anger in my tone and try to stay as calm as possible.

"This is a public place. I have a right to be here. Maybe I'll join you for lunch," he says with a mocking tone and a smug smile. He crosses his arms over his chest like he's challenging me to do something. It's taking all my self-control to not kick him out.

I lean toward him, and he flinches like he's scared I'm going to hit him. *Not so tough under all that bravado.* Keeping my voice down, I say, "You're only here to cause trouble for Penny. Don't you think you've done enough to her? Get lost before things get ugly." I nod my head in the direction of the entrance.

He ignores my warning and looks at Penny. "How could you do this to me? After all the years we were together, don't you think flaunting your affair in public two weeks after what should have been our wedding day is a little insensitive?" He said the words loud enough for everyone to hear. I wouldn't be surprised if the chefs in the kitchen heard.

Penny's gaze darts around the room, her face turning bright red. "Can we go somewhere private to discuss this?"

"There's no way I'm letting you go anywhere with this asshole. He needs to fuck off and keep his distance. He's here to humiliate you, and it's working." I step between them. "Get the hell away from *my* girlfriend. If you so much as come near her again, you'll be eating through a straw."

Darren pokes a finger into my chest. "Make me."

Rage is running through my veins. I shove at his chest. "Don't tempt me."

Darren's fist flies toward my face. Lifting my left arm, I block it then slam my right fist into his gut. He buckles at the waist with a groan, clutching his stomach and wheezing for air.

Gasps and chatter spreads through the room.

Penny's eyes are wide with fright, and her hand is covering her mouth.

The hostess comes scurrying over with a worried expression on her face. "I'm going to have to ask you all to leave. We can't have this kind of behavior in our restaurant."

I pull my wallet from my pocket and toss money on the table. "I'm sorry for the trouble." But not sorry for punching the asshole.

I clasp onto Penny's hand, nudge Darren out of the way, and lead her out of the restaurant.

Outside, we're greeted with the frenzied sound of clicking cameras pointed in our direction as the photographers yell our names out at us like we're going to stop and pose for photos. Fuck! With all the commotion, I'd forgotten about them.

I signal for the valet to bring the car around and hope we don't have to wait long. Glancing at Penny, I see that all color has drained from her face. Her body is trembling, and I'm betting she's trying her damned hardest to keep it together. I wrap my arms around her and use my body to shield her from the cameras. Pressing her face into my chest, I hear her sniffle. All I want to do is protect her. Fuck everyone for doing this to her.

As soon as the car arrives, I usher her inside. Jogging to the driver's side, I slide in next to her and try to pull out onto the road. The paparazzi surround the car, pointing their cameras at us. I slowly drive forward, tempted to run them down, and finally get onto the road. We drive in silence until we arrive at the apartment building. Pulling into the entrance of the garage, I park and turn off the ignition. No one moves. We just sit in the dim silence.

Finally, she turns to me and says, "We can't do this anymore."

"What?" The soft light in the garage shows me she's getting some color back in her face.

She waves a hand between us. "Pretend to be a couple. I don't want you thrown into my mess of a life. It's not fair for you. You should have walked away from me that night you found me in the hotel hallway."

Incredulous at what I'm hearing, I twist in my seat. "You never asked me to do this. It was my choice," I remind her.

"You have gone above and beyond. It's time we end this. I'll kick Darren out of my apartment and get on with my life, no matter the outcome." Her phone rings, and she pulls it out of her purse and looks at the screen. "It's Claudia. She's probably seen what happened at the restaurant." Penny declines the call. A second later, it rings again. She glances at the screen again, then blows out a frustrated breath. "My mom."

"Don't answer. You can call them back later. We need to talk."

"If I don't answer, she'll only keep calling." She accepts the call and presses the phone to her ear. "Hi, Mom. Before you ask me a thousand questions, I'm fine. I'm back at Lucas' place. Love you. I'll call you later." She hangs up and gives me a ghost of a smile.

"Wish I could deal with my family like that. You need to teach me," I joke, pulling a bigger smile from her. There's my girl. And there's that thought again...*my girl*. She's not my girl, except the more time I spend with her, the more I see her that way. Maybe it is time for her to go. Not when I can't offer her anything more than a fake relationship.

Am I ready for her to walk out of my life?

No.

And that's fucking selfish.

Chapter Seventeen

PENNY

In Lucas' apartment, I toss my purse on the coffee table and flop onto the couch. Lucas stays standing, his hands on his hips. He wasn't pleased with my suggestion of ending things and moving out. Why? Our living arrangement is only about the crises I'm in. He's made no mention of turning what we have into something real. If I stay any longer, I'll get too attached. Who am I trying to kid? I am attached. This is something more to me than friendship.

When Lucas told Darren I was his girlfriend, my heart leaped with joy. We've talked about doing the fake relationship thing, but hearing the world 'girlfriend' said out loud was bittersweet. How wonderful if those words were true? It's not hard to imagine what kind of life that would be. Especially with how he looked and touched me at lunch.

It's easy to get lost in the fantasy of it being real. And the way he protected me from Darren, shielded me from the paparazzi while waiting for the car, is something I'll never forget. Being in his arms makes me melt. The world around me disappears. Never have I felt so safe. In that moment I was his and he was mine.

"Are you really considering leaving?" he asks.

"Yes."

"Why?"

Was he not listening to me in the car? "I can't keep pulling you into my drama."

"Like I told you, it is my choice."

"Don't you want to go back to your daily routine? Have your apartment to yourself…date?" The word 'date' clogs my throat. I don't want to picture him with another woman. Another sign I'm getting too close and now is the right time to back away before I fall too hard.

"I don't date," he says flatly.

"I know you said you don't want marriage and kids but surely you date. I've seen you with women."

Sitting on the arm of the couch, he crosses his legs at the ankles. "I haven't dated in years. Ever since I learned about my father's affairs. I fu—have one-night stands," he corrects himself.

I don't miss that he almost said 'fuck'. Just because we haven't been in each other's lives for years doesn't mean I haven't read about him being a playboy in the tabloids. "You don't see a woman more than once?"

He shakes his head. "Rarely."

It gives me a thrill that he's changed all that for me, but I say, "Living with me must be a huge inconvenience to your life. Don't you want things to go back to normal?"

Before he can answer, his cell phone rings and he glances at the screen. "Yes, Samuel." He listens to what the security guard is saying. "That's fine. Thank you." Ending the call, he tells me, "Claudia is on her way up."

What bad timing. I want to finish this conversation. Now it will have to wait. "We'll talk about this later?"

He gets to his feet. "Sure. I'll give you and Claudia some privacy." His face is expressionless, his voice monotone. I can't make out what he's thinking.

"You don't have to leave. Whatever she has to say will probably involve you."

"Fill me in later. I have work to do. If you need me, I'll be in my office."

I watch him walk out of the living room. Something has shifted with him. Does he not want me to leave? Why wouldn't he? If he's used to a revolving door of women, I'm in the way.

A couple of minutes later, there's a knock on the door. I get up to answer it and Claudia barrels inside, storms into the living room, and paces. "Why are you making my life so difficult? Are you doing it on purpose?"

I raise an eyebrow. This is a tone I've never heard from her before. "Excuse me?" I'm the one who had to go into hiding. Whose career is slipping through my fingers. And she's telling me *I'm* making *her* life difficult.

She makes an annoyed huffing sound. "Have you seen what's online now? How am I supposed to fix your career if you keep doing stupid things? God, Pen, can't you do anything right?"

Jerking back, I stare at her incredulously. The situation I'm in has been stressful for everyone, but there's no excuse for Claudia to speak to me like this. "You need to calm down or leave. Come back when you have something useful to say." Never have I had to put Claudia in her place. Yes, she is my friend, but she's also my employee. This is a time where we need to put our friendship aside.

She blows out a breath and sinks onto the couch. "I'm sorry, Pen. I shouldn't have said that."

I take a seat next to her. "I haven't looked online. Are things that bad?" Of course they are; she wouldn't have barged in here with so much attitude if they weren't.

"The good news is, you've convinced people you and Lucas are a couple and not just a casual fling."

"Great." That was the point of being seen together. I know there is a *but* coming.

"But..." There it is. "There's bad news. That scene in the restaurant is everywhere. Darren is made to look like a heartbroken man trying to reunite with his ex-fiancée. While Lucas is portrayed as a home-wrecker. I can't believe he punched him. He's only helped Darren by acting like a neanderthal. Everyone is sympathizing with him. More so than before."

I sink my head in my hands. All this work, and our lives put on hold, for nothing. Things have only gotten worse. I can't keep doing this. It's not fair to Lucas. It could even affect his business even more.

"Darren provoked Lucas and threw the first punch. Did no one see that and post about it?" I ask.

"Not that I've seen. Apparently, the punch to Darren's stomach is more entertaining."

"Darren started it," I try to plead Lucas' case.

"Doesn't matter. Darren is buckled over in pain and gasping for breath. You and Lucas are seen leaving the restaurant like lovers on the run."

I scratch my fingers through my hair. "What do we do now?"

"You should talk to Darren *without* Lucas. Try and work things out," she suggests.

My head snaps up. "You want me to get back with Darren?" My skin crawls at the thought.

She waves her hand. "No. Definitely not. He's a pig. You should talk to him about what he's doing. Ask him to stop. Offer him money. Let him keep the apartment. Do anything to get him to shut his mouth. Otherwise, he's going to keep milking this. We know that after his injury his sponsorships dried up. The sport has lost interest in him. This is giving him the attention he craves."

Lifting my legs on the couch, I wrap my arms around my knees. "Do you think offering money will work?"

Claudia shrugs. "Worth a try. You can't keep living like this. Especially with Lucas. He's such a man whore he'll probably ruin this 'fake relationship' by screwing some other woman and getting caught."

Didn't he just tell me he only does one-night stands and never dates? How long will it take for him to miss that life? He might say he is in this with me, but he'll soon tire.

"You can't trust him to see this through," Claudia says bitterly.

My spine stiffens as I remember a conversation I had with Lucas. How Claudia hit on him at a party behind my back. "Speaking of Lucas..." I don't agree with what she's saying because I *can* trust Lucas. He might eventually want to go back to his normal life, but he won't destroy what we've worked on to get there. "Why didn't you tell me you tried having sex with him while we were in high school?"

She gives a nervous, surprised laugh and doesn't look me directly in the eye. "What are you talking about?"

Oh, she knows exactly what I'm talking about. I see the guilt on her face. "Lucas told me you wanted to hookup at a party. Described in detail what you wanted to do to him. And he refused."

Claudia rolls her eyes and flippantly says, "That was years ago. Who cares now?"

"I do." High school feels like a lifetime ago, but this information is fresh to me, so I care. A lot.

She gives me a look as if to say *seriously?* "I can't remember what happened."

"You knew how much I liked him. There wasn't a day that went past that I didn't talk to you about him. Why would you do that behind my back?"

"You always had a sick obsession with him. It's no surprise you finally got your wish," she says, avoiding the question.

Tiny pricks trickle up and down my spine. I hate that she's brushing this off as nothing. If I had found out about this back then, it would have been a big deal. Maybe big enough to end our friendship. I would never have forgiven her.

"Why did you hit on him?" I want an answer.

Tossing her hands up, she says, "He kept flirting with me. Asking me to dance. Getting me drinks. I was drunk. Who wouldn't want to fuck the hottest guy in school? When I saw him head to the bathroom, I followed him. I wouldn't have tried anything if I was thinking clearly. It would have ruined our friendship, and I'd never jeopardize it for a boy. You're not upset with me, are you?" She gives me a pleading look as if asking for forgiveness.

Deep down in my gut I know she's lying. In one breath she tells me she doesn't remember anything, and in the next she's telling me how she followed him into the bathroom. And seems to remember the night vividly. Except Lucas mentioned nothing about getting her drinks and asking her to dance. Yet I believe his story over Claudia's. Something in my gut doesn't sit right.

For now, I let it go. Is there any point dredging up the past? What's done is done. She was a teenager who made a mistake.

"No, I'm not upset with you. Just curious," I say.

"Why is Lucas bringing that night up? Does he want to cause trouble between us?"

"Why would he do that?"

She shrugs. "Who knows? Maybe he gets a kick out of other's misery. This is why you need to leave. We don't really know him."

"I think you're wrong about him wanting to cause trouble. It just came up in conversation, that's all."

Claudia gives me a skeptical look.

"Anyway, I've already decided it's time to move out," I say.

The thought sits heavy on my chest, crushing the air from my lungs. Why does walking away from Lucas feel wrong? Why does everything inside me want to spend every minute I can with him? The answer is within reach. But I'm not ready to grab on to it. Not when nothing has changed between us.

We're friends who are fake dating. Nothing more.

"Excellent. I'll help you pack. The sooner you're out of here, the better." She stands. "Where's your room?"

I'm sharing Lucas' room. Even though Claudia knows we've slept together, my gut is telling me not to tell her our sleeping arrangements. Will she read too much into it? Ask questions I'm not ready to answer?

Like she can read my mind—or my facial expression gives it away—she narrows her gaze. "You're sleeping in his room, aren't you?" She blows out an exasperated breath. "What are you doing? Sex with him is one thing, but to share his bed every night is something deeper. Are you falling for him?"

Flicking my gaze in the direction of Lucas' office, I focus on keeping my voice down. I don't want him overhearing this conversation. "I'm not sure how I'm feeling. All these years I hated him and now... Well, now that I know the truth, and we've spent so much time together, things are shifting into—"

Claudia tosses her head back and scoffs. "Oh God. Please don't say love." She screws her nose up in disgust.

What is her problem with Lucas? For the first time ever it makes me not want to talk to her about this kind of stuff. We have always been open about the crushes we've had, the men we've dated, relationships we're in. But with the hostility vibrating off her, I want to keep things to myself, yet I feel because of our close friendship I have to give her something.

"I was going to say, shifted into more than friends. I just don't know what. He hasn't mentioned if he's feeling the same way."

"Lucas Alessi is a player. Because he's committed to this 'fake relationship' bullshit, he can't play his usual game. So guess what you are?" She doesn't give me time to answer. "You're his live-in sex toy. Why would he give you more when you're giving him everything he wants without leaving the apartment?"

If she'd stuck a dagger in my chest, I'd be less surprised. Where is this cruelty coming from? I've never seen this side of her before. So harsh and unforgiving. Once I could confide in Claudia with everything; now I feel I'm being judged.

"I shouldn't have mentioned anything," I say. "You obviously have issues with Lucas, and you'll never see what I do." A man who has stopped his life for me. One who has cared and protected me and opened up his home.

Sighing, she takes my hand. "I'm sorry. I never meant to make you feel bad about what's happening, or not happening, between you and Lucas. I'm just worried about you. It's no secret what he's like. I'd hate for you to get hurt because you've fallen for him and he's broken your heart."

I squeeze her hand and smile. "Thank you for caring. I know what I'm getting into. "He's *not* going to break my heart," I emphasize. Do I say that to convince her or myself?

"So, he's going to stop this 'fake relationship' and make it a real one? If I can see you're falling for him, surely he can too. Will he let you keep this up knowing this?"

Oh no...no...no. He can't know. Not when this is temporary. Not when he's not offering anything more.

"He probably knows you have feelings for him, yet he's keeping you here. Exploiting them for his own selfish reasons. Unless he's ready to stop pretending and make things official, he needs to let you go." She gives me a quick hug, like that's supposed to soothe her words. "You are my best friend. If I can't tell you the truth, who can?"

I give her a ghost of a smile. Her comments masked under the guise of being my best friend don't make the hurt any less. "I need to talk to Lucas."

Claudia rises from the couch. "Good idea. I'll go so you can get it over with."

I follow her to the foyer, and we say our goodbyes. When the door closes behind her, I lean against it, my heart beating rapidly. I'm falling in love with Lucas. I can't keep ignoring my feelings. This wasn't supposed to happen, and yet I couldn't stop myself. Now I really can't stay. If I do, it will only be harder to leave.

Walking to Lucas' office, I knock before I enter. He's sitting on the edge of his desk, fiddling with a camera. When he sees me, his face lights up with a smile. Oh God. His smile shoots an arrow through my heart. I want him to look at me like that forever.

He points the lens at me and says, "Strike a pose."

I cross my eyes and stick out my tongue.

The camera clicks a few times, and Lucas laughs. "That photo will be the showpiece for the next Alessi Fashion catalogue."

"Whenever you need a model, you know where to find me. Although, with my talent, I don't come cheap," I joke, but my heart is heavy in my chest.

"I'll pay whatever you're asking." He grins. It's so sexy I feel the buzz from it travel all the way to my toes. "I'm assuming Claudia's gone."

I nod and take a seat by the window. Far enough away so I'm not tempted to place myself between his legs and kiss him until we both can't breathe and forget about telling him I'm moving out.

"Lucas, we need to talk."

"Uh-oh. Sounds serious. Did Claudia give you more bad news?" He places his camera on the table and gives me his full attention.

"Darren's appearance at lunch and the fight is all over the internet. He's getting more sympathetic votes."

Lucas runs his fingers through his hair and sighs. "Why on earth did that fucker show up at the restaurant? Hasn't he caused enough damage? How much longer is he going to make your life miserable?"

"Claudia says I need to talk to him. Offer him money to stop him from doing anything else."

Lucas propels from the desk. "The fuck you will. You're not getting near that asshole or giving him money."

I throw my hands up. "I have to do something. Going out to lunch as a couple only caused more drama. I'm running out of options."

Pacing in front of me, he says, "We'll think of something."

I get to my feet and go to him. Holding his hands in mine, I stop him from wearing out the floorboards. "I have to talk to him. I need to get my apartment back."

"You're moving back into the apartment?"

I couldn't think of anything worse. "No. Not after what he's done in there. But it's mine and he has no right to live in it."

"So you've changed your mind, you're not leaving?"

I shake my head. "It's time I go."

He swings his head to the side to stare out the window. When he turns back there's a hint of sadness in his eyes. "You really want to leave?"

No! I want to scream. *I see my life here with you.* "I can't stay forever."

My heart stops for a beat, waiting for him to say forever is what he wants with me. I wish he didn't believe he was like his father. Maybe things could have been different.

"Penny, you're welcome to stay as long as you want. I'm not kicking you out if that's what you're worried about."

No, I'm worried that I've fallen head over heels in love with you and you'll never reciprocate my feelings.

"Thank you, but it's time," I say.

Rubbing the back of his neck, he blurts out, "I don't want you to leave."

"You don't?" I hold my breath, waiting for him to say more.

"No, not when things are still bad. I can't let you face it on your own. I'm involved too. Moving out is not the way to fix things."

I exhale a shuddery, disappointed breath. That wasn't the declaration of love I was hoping for. "Staying here won't fix things either."

Shoulders drooping, he gazes at me with something I can't decipher. Is it longing? Conflict? Whatever it is, he appears to be struggling with his thoughts. Then he says, "Where will you go?"

"I'll find a hotel secure enough to keep the paparazzi away."

"What about your apartment?"

"I'm selling it. I can't stand the thought of living in it after Darren has tainted it."

"That's if Darren leaves."

I rub my forehead with my fingertips. A headache is brewing. Darren turned my life upside down. The least he can do is give me back what's mine. "He will."

Lucas raises a dubious eyebrow. "What makes you so sure?"

"If he refuses, I'll offer him money. With the loss of sponsorships, he'll need it."

Lucas tosses his arms up. "Are you fucking kidding me? Hasn't he taken enough? He doesn't deserve a dime from you."

Feeling depleted, I drop onto the couch. "I don't know what else to do."

With a heavy sigh, Lucas sits next to me. Putting his arm over my shoulders, he pulls me to his side. Tears sting the backs of my eyes at his comforting gesture. My heart shudders. How am I supposed to walk away from this?

"I'll get him out of your apartment," Lucas says.

Tilting my face up to him, I see he's wearing a hard expression. I cup his cheek. At my touch, his face softens. "You need to keep away from him. Look what happened at lunch. He'll try to provoke you into doing something you'll regret."

"I'll never *regret* beating the shit out of him if I get the chance." His jaw tightens.

"This is why you can't be near him."

"I won't touch him."

I find that hard to believe. "Really?"

"Not much." He smirks.

I can't help laughing. I playfully poke my finger into his ribs, causing him to squirm. "You'll get yourself into trouble. Darren is my problem. Let me deal with him."

"But I'd actually enjoy paying him a visit," he says with a twinkle of mischief in his eyes.

I poke harder and he bucks. "Not funny. Stay away from him. Darren is mine."

Lucas grips my wrist, knocks me onto my back, and pins my hand above my head. His face is like iron. "Never say he's yours again."

I open my mouth to explain what I meant, but he clamps his lips on mine, sucking any words and breath from my mouth.

Like he's claiming me.

Wanting me to be his.

And only his.

If only that were true.

The kiss ends as abruptly as it started. His face hovers above me, his chest heaving, his eyes locked with mine. A connection is binding us. He looks like he wants to say something. Like he's struggling with thoughts that are on his mind. Then, as if something snaps, he lets me go, pushes off the couch, and gets to his feet.

"Are you sure you don't want me to come with you?" he asks. "You don't need to deal with him alone."

All desire and emotion is wiped clean from his expression. How can he change in a blink of an eye? Was I mistaken in thinking a bond is building? Or is this only two people stuck in a shitty situation and needing each other to pull through it? Is this all one-sided on my part, or is he fighting feelings he doesn't know how to deal with?

"I'll be fine."

"If he gives you any trouble, call me and I'll come right over."

I smile. "Thank you. I will." I get to my feet. "Well, I should get this over with."

When I walk past Lucas to leave, he holds onto my wrist and stops me. "I hope you get what you want." Why does it look like it pains him to say that?

I bite my bottom lip, stopping myself from saying *what I really want is you*.

◆

Lucas arranges for a driver to take me to my apartment building. What will I do without him when this is all over? I toss that thought away for another time, because right now I have bigger problems to face.

I step from the car and rush into the building. Keeping my hat pulled low and my sunglasses on, I find a quiet area of the lobby to wait for Darren. I can't believe I had to call him to let me into my own apartment. My keycard for the elevator and door is in my suitcase which I left at Lucas' cabin.

I send Darren a text to let him know I'm in the lobby and I take a seat behind a potted palm and wait. Watching people come and go, I'm pleased no one takes any notice of me.

After fifteen minutes and two more texts reminding Darren I'm still waiting, he finally arrives with a smug grin on his face like he takes great pleasure having me wait.

I'll wipe that smile off your face when I kick you out.

Getting to my feet, I narrow my eyes at him. "What took you so long?"

"Busy," he says unapologetically. He was so desperate to talk to me at the restaurant and now it's like he has no interest that I'm here. His behavior is strange. What is going on with him?

"I told you what time I'd be here—" I stop myself from making a scene. "You know what? It doesn't matter. Let's get this over with." With both of us standing together, I notice some people are looking our way. "Let's talk in my apartment."

He puffs out his chest. "Whatever you have to say, you can say it here."

Oh, he's trying to act like a tough guy. I may be small in height, but I will not let him intimidate me. I can't believe I thought I loved this man. Even wanted to marry him! What was I thinking? He can't compare to Lucas even if he tried.

Is always comparing men with Lucas going to be my life now?

Unfortunately, the answer is yes.

Pulling myself up as tall as I can get, I stare him dead in the eye. "We will talk in the apartment now, or I will make a scene. One that won't make you look good in the eyes of the public. And we know what a fame whore you are, don't we?" I tilt my chin up, challenging him to argue.

His eyes widen as he scans the area around us. Like the weak, little man he is, he nods and turns toward the elevator. Once inside, he swipes the keycard and presses the number to my floor. On the way up we don't say a word. Being in such a confined space with him makes me uneasy, and as soon as the doors open, I burst from the cart.

Walking into my apartment, it feels like I haven't been here in months not days. Lucas' penthouse feels more like home than this space. That's because Lucas is living in it.

There are empty pizza boxes, Chinese take-out containers, tubs of ice cream, and beer bottles on every surface. Every piece of furniture is covered with dirty clothing and trash. And there are numerous stains on the carpeting where it appears drinks have been spilled or food has been dropped.

"What have you done to the place?" I sniff with disgust.

"The cleaner hasn't been by yet."

"And you let it get to this state in only a couple of weeks?" I'm going to burn the place down with everything in it.

He shrugs. "Doesn't bother me."

It's then I take a better look at Darren. He isn't looking so great either. Once a well-built, muscular, good-looking athlete, he now looks disheveled and a little thicker around the middle. Lack of exercise and eating like a college frat boy wouldn't help with his appearance.

I don't even try to find a clean spot to sit down. The place is filthy. I'd rather stand. The quicker I get this over with, the quicker I can get out of this dump.

"Darren, you need to move out." Better to get straight to the point.

His eyes widen with surprise. Did he think I'd let him live here forever? "I'm not moving. This is my place."

Is he kidding? He has never contributed to any of the finances.

"This is *my* apartment. I want you and your stuff out because I'm moving back in." He doesn't need to know I'll never live here again.

He drops his hands on his hips. "I thought you were shacking up with that peacock fashion designer." He curls his top lip.

"It's none of your business what my living arrangements are. This is my apartment. You've outstayed your welcome. You need to leave."

He smirks. The revolting gesture makes me shudder. "Already having trouble in paradise?" His gaze scans up and down my body with an unflattering expression. "I've seen the women he fucks. You're not exactly his type."

I swallow back the nausea rising to my throat. He knows where to hit me in the place I'm most vulnerable. What I won't do is let him see how his words affect me. Never will I let him put me down again and make me feel like I'm not good enough.

"My relationship with Lucas is not your concern," I state.

He scratches his cheek, his face filled with confusion. "I know you weren't fucking him when we were together. You made it clear you hated each other. Yet suddenly, out of nowhere, you're playing the loved-up couple. Doesn't make sense." Then, after a beat, amusement glints in his eyes. "Unless... you've done something stupid like pretend you're in a relationship to gain your reputation back."

I must have pulled a face because his mouth spreads into a mocking smile.

"You have! It's all fake." He laughs out loud. "Look at you, the squeaky-clean America's sweetheart being so sneaky."

I scoff. I can't let Darren have these thoughts. If he tells anyone, the charade is over, and I'll be dealing with another fire to put out. "Believe what you want if that makes you feel better. What Lucas and I have is real. Something *we* never had. He loves me for who I am. Not for what I can give him. It wasn't hard moving on."

I hope my performance is convincing. Lucas may not love me, but he has shown me I deserve so much better.

To deflect the conversation away from my relationship with Lucas, I say, "What I don't understand is why you're being so vengeful and cruel to me. It was *you* who cheated on me and played the video in front of my audience. What did I ever do to you to deserve such treatment?"

He shrugs. "Nothing."

I wait for more. When he doesn't expand on his answer, I say, "That's it? All you have to say is *nothing*?" I shake my head. "You know what? I don't care anymore why you did it. I just want you out of my apartment and to never see you again. I'm giving you two days to pack up your things and leave. And take all this rubbish with you," I add as I wave my hand out to indicate the trash filling the area.

With that, I march into my bedroom. I open the closet, pull out a suitcase and toss a few items of clothing in it. Even though Lucas practically bought me an Alessi Fashion boutique, I still want a few items of my own. At the dresser I take jewelry from the drawers and my favorite perfume. I don't want Darren taking anything valuable that doesn't belong to him.

Once I've filled the bag with everything I need, I make my way to the living room. Darren is sitting on the couch with his feet propped on the coffee table, looking as if he hasn't a care in the world. Yet underneath the bravado is a scared man. I can tell by his slightly wide eyes and stiff facial features. Without me and my money, he has nothing.

I open the door. I turn back around and say, "Two days. If you're not gone, I'll have you removed." Forget about offering him money. He doesn't deserve it.

"I didn't plant the video at your show," he says before I close the door.

This stops me in my tracks. "You expect me to believe that?"

"Why would I ruin a good thing?" He holds his arms out wide to take in the apartment. "With you I had everything."

An icy chill prickles the back of my neck. It was never about love and commitment to him. I was his ticket to fame and fortune.

"If you didn't do it, who did?" I ask. "Karen Featherstone?"

"She was just as surprised and pissed as you."

I doubt that. "If not you or Karen, then who?"

"Someone who hates you enough to want to tear you down."

For a beat I'm frozen. Who would want to do that to me? Apart from Lucas, I've never had a problem with anyone. It had to have been Darren. He's trying to play with my head. Making me suspicious of everyone in my life.

I point a finger in his direction. "I want you gone in two days."

He salutes me with a grin.

God, I never want to see that man again.

Chapter Eighteen

—⋅◦⋅—

LUCAS

Soon after Penny left to see Darren, Hayden and Finn showed up at my door, convincing me that what I need to take my mind off what was happening in Penny's apartment was hitting golf balls. And if I refused, they'd take pleasure in dragging me from the apartment by my feet. I take their threats seriously. It's not the first time they've done something similar. Now here I am at the driving range, pulling my phone from my pocket for what feels like the tenth time, waiting for Penny to respond to my text. Smashing balls has not distracted me. I desperately want to know what's happening.

As Finn takes a swing and watches his ball sail into the netted driving range, I look around me. The place is filled with mostly middle-aged to elderly men.

"What happened to us going to bars and drinking alcohol...lots and lots of alcohol?" I ask.

Hayden plucks a ball from a bucket, tosses it in the air, and catches it. "We're married and fathers now. Those days are over."

I screw up my face with disgust. "Doesn't mean you have to turn into boring, old men."

"This boring, old man is happy." Hayden puts the ball on the tee, gives a practice swing, then hits it.

"Nice shot," Finn says.

It's my turn for a hit. I pick a ball and place it on the tee on the synthetic grass. Before I position myself to take the shot, I pull my phone from my pocket and check it just in case I didn't hear the notification sound. Still nothing. Is she okay? Does she need my help? Is he trying to convince her to go back to him? I'm so distracted with thoughts swirling in my head when I swing at the ball, I miss. Shit! That's embarrassing.

Hayden and Finn burst out laughing. "Concentrate on the ball, not your phone, then maybe you'll hit it," Finn suggests with a grin.

"In case you don't know, it's the little round thing near your feet," Hayden jokes.

I flip them the bird. "Assholes."

My response causes more laughter.

"Penny will contact you when she's ready," Finn says.

"What makes you think I'm waiting to hear from Penny?"

Hayden clasps a hand on my shoulder. "You cried like a baby because you didn't want to leave your apartment in case Penny came home. And you haven't stopped checking your phone since we arrived at the range. Who else would you be waiting on?"

Giving up on hitting the ball, I slide my club into the golf bag. "Maybe I'm meeting up with someone tonight." That sounds lame and unappealing even to my own ears.

Hayden and Finn glance at each other then burst out laughing once again. Slapping his thigh, Finn chuckles, "You're joking, right? You're a man in love, and it's with Penny. There's no way in hell you're going elsewhere."

The breath gets knocked from my lungs. "What did you say?"

"You're not going elsewhere—"

"No...not that."

Finn smiles. "You're a man in love."

I scratch my fingers through my hair. "You're mistaken. I don't... I'm not..."

"Don't look so shocked. It's better you accept it now. There's no point fighting it. I know from experience. I wasted so much time denying my feelings for Harper. Love will always get you."

I clear the lump in my throat. "What makes you think I'm in love?"

"You can't keep your eyes off her. You've changed your whole life for her. The thought of her with Darren is driving you nuts. The past three days you should be at work, yet you rush from the office to get home early." He counts the reasons on his fingers. "Oh, and you're glowing."

What the fuck? "I'm not *glowing*."

"Like a lightbulb," Finn teases.

"Fuck you. You don't know what you're talking about." *I'm not in love with Penny. Love isn't an option.*

"I know exactly what I'm talking about. So does Hayden. We've been through it. We recognize the signs."

Hayden nods in agreement.

"You know I'm helping her. That's all," I say.

Hayden and Finn both wear dubious expressions.

"You're reading too much into things." I try to convince them.

Hayden leans on his golf club. "Are you saying you don't have any feelings for Penny?"

"Nothing more than friendship." My gut twists into a tight knot like something is trying to tell me I'm lying.

"So, when she moves out and eventually finds another guy you'll be okay with that?" Hayden looks at me intently.

At the thought of another man's hands on her, heat boils my blood. The words *she's mine* ricochet through my mind.

Finn points his golf club at me. "By the thunderous look on your face, I'd say the thought makes you want to punch a hole in something."

My phone buzzes in my pocket with a text. Knocking Finn's club away from me, I step away to read it.

I'm on my way back to the apartment. I'll tell you all about what happened when I get home. Penny

That's it? That's all she has to say? I've been waiting anxiously, and she can't give me something? She said we'll talk when she gets back. There's probably too much to say over a text.

I'm out with my brothers. I'll leave now.

Before I hit *send*, Finn snatches the phone from my hand. "What the fuck? Give that back!" I demand.

"I knew it!" Finn exclaims as he looks at the screen. "You're hurrying home to be with her."

I try to grab the phone, but Finn holds it out of reach. "So? You rush home to be with Harper all the time."

"Yeah, because she's my *wife* and I *love* her." A huge, shit-eating grin spreads across Finn's face. "What's your excuse?"

I'm tempted to pluck a club from the bag and whack him over the head with it. "Give me back my phone."

His fingers fly over the screen as he types something. *What the hell?* I propel forward only to be pulled back by Hayden. When Finn is done, he tosses the phone to me. Hayden lets me go in time to catch it.

"I changed your message to tell Penny you'll see her in an hour or so," Finn says unapologetically.

"You had no right to do that," I fume.

Finn rolls his eyes. "Relax. It won't kill you to spend a little time apart."

"Why did you tell her I'm coming home later?"

"Because we need to talk," Finn says.

"*We need to talk*? Are we teenagers? Should you braid my hair while we're *talking*? Maybe Hayden can paint my nails." I hold my hand out to inspect it. "He's got experience with that." Hayden often comes to work with different-colored fingernails. Courtesy of his daughter Lily, who he can't say no to.

"I'd recommend shimmering gold. It will match perfectly with your skin tone," Hayden jokes.

I scowl at him. I'm not finding the situation amusing. All I want is to go back to the apartment. I need to know if Penny's okay. Hold her in my arms if she's not. Fuck that—hold her in my arms either way.

Taking a seat, I cross my ankle over my knee. "You wanna talk? Let's hear what you have to say." They won't drop it until they've said their piece. The sooner we have the conversation, the sooner I can see Penny.

They take a seat opposite me. "Tell us how you're really feeling about Penny." When I open my mouth to speak, Finn cuts me off. "And don't give us any bullshit about it being nothing but a fake relationship or how you're just friends. We know you. You'd never do this with any woman. Something is happening."

Dropping my foot to the ground, I rest my elbows on my thighs and let my hands fall between my legs. "We've gotten close."

When I don't elaborate, Hayden waves a hand for me to continue. "*And...*"

"*And*...she's leaving. Then things will go back to normal."

What will normal be like? Work—I'll go back to traveling for photoshoots. Play—casual hookups and drunken weekends aren't appealing anymore.

"Will you keep seeing Penny?" Hayden asks.

"As friends. If she wants to. That's it."

"That's bullshit," Finn fires at me. "You've moved beyond friendship, and I don't mean because you're sleeping together. There's a connection between the two of you. We can all see it."

They better not mention me being a man in love again. Because they're wrong. Aren't they?

"What could you have possibly seen in the few hours we were together?" I ask. The night we arrived back from the cabin we had dinner and drinks. Conversation was flowing among us all. It wasn't like I had my hands all over Penny or whisked her away for private time.

"We saw everything we needed to. It didn't take long to understand what was happening," Finn explains. "Why aren't you pursuing this?"

Staring at the ground, I toe at the synthetic grass. "Maybe she doesn't want more. She's said nothing about taking the next step."

"You didn't give her the 'I'm just like Dad' speech, did you? Because if you did, of course she wouldn't tell you if she wants more," Hayden says.

"It's true. I am like Dad."

Finn and Hayden both roll their eyes. They've heard my reasoning for not doing relationships before. They always thought it was bullshit.

With a huff, I get to my feet. "I'd only break Penny's heart."

"Just because you and Dad share similarities doesn't mean you'll do what he did. He never loved Mom, no matter how many times he said he did. You don't treat someone you love like that," Hayden states.

"I can't risk it."

"Do you love Penny?" Finn asks.

I turn my back on them and stare sightlessly at the driving range. Do I love her? Penny has made me feel things I've never felt before. But I can't fall in love. Not when the outcome could be disastrous.

Before I get to answer the question, both Finn and Hayden's phones buzz with a text. Turning around, I find them checking their messages.

"The girls want us home. They're planning dinner for us all," Hayden says, rising from his seat.

Finn follows. "That includes you too. Apparently they've already told Penny and she's on her way to Hayden's house."

"I thought we were hanging here for a couple of hours?"

Finn grins. "When my woman calls, I run to her." And he says it with such affection, like being pussy-whipped is the best part of his life.

Hayden pats me on the back. "Think hard about what you want. Don't let Dad's misdeeds cloud your mind. You're onto a good thing with Penny. You should see where it takes you." With that, we leave the driving range and head toward our women.

⋅•◦O◦•⋅

At Hayden's house, we're met with music blaring from the speakers coming from the living room. Following the sound, we find Harper, Alyssa, and Penny dancing around the room.

Alyssa is holding Lily's hand, and she spins her around like a ballerina in a music box. Harper is lifting Avery in the air as they bop to the beat. When I take in Penny, a train-sized force slams into my chest. She's swaying to the music with Sadie cradled in her arms. Our eyes meet across the room. She smiles her sweet smile my way, and I want to drop to my knees and give her anything she wants.

Don't let Dad's misdeeds cloud your mind.

Hayden's words repeat over and over in my mind. When I look at Penny, all I want is to have her in my life.

Then fear grips at my chest and strangles my throat.

Lily skips over to me. "Come and dance with us, Uncle Lucas."

Hayden and Finn are already wrapping their arms around their wives, getting into the swing of things. How can I refuse the request from my gorgeous niece?

I take Lily by the hands, and we move to the beat. I show off my best sprinkler move, causing Lily to giggle uncontrollably.

When Lily moves on to dance with her dad and Alyssa, I shimmy over to Penny. Moving behind her, I wrap my arms around her waist, rest my cheek against hers, and we sway from side to side.

"You've got some serious skills on the dance floor," she jokes.

"I'm a man of many talents."

Sadie is cradled in Penny's arms, and she stares up at us with sparkling green eyes. Holding Penny like this feels so right. My heart is full. I can't imagine her walking out of my life and never having her this way again.

This life is within reach.

If only I had the balls to take it.

During the next few hours, we overeat on pizza, drink beers, and laugh. I love watching Penny interact with my brothers and their wives. It's like she's already part of the family. She fits right in. It's the best time I've had with them in a long time. Sure, I enjoy our time together, but I often feel like the odd one out. They're on a different path than me. They talk about feeding schedules, baby stuff, school projects. Things I have no clue about. Women and partying was all I was interested in. Now things are shifting. Those days are blurring, and I'm left wondering if I really enjoyed that kind of life.

Or I made myself believe it was all I deserved.

Sitting on the couch, Penny rests her head on my shoulder and lays a hand on my thigh. I slide my arm around her, and she nestles in closer. It's all so natural. We've gone beyond pretending.

On the other side of me, Hayden nudges my arm. Turning my head toward him, he gives me a look that says *just friends*? I scowl at him. I hate when my brothers are right.

I have the sudden urge to get Penny back to the penthouse and into my bed. Strip her naked and get lost in her. I haven't had the chance to talk to her about Darren, but that can wait until later.

"Let's go home," I say. *Home*. My apartment never felt like home until she moved in.

She nods her head in agreement.

Rising, I take her hand and help her to her feet. "We're leaving."

Alyssa looks at her watch. "It's only eight o'clock."

"It's been a big day. I'm tired," I say as an excuse.

Hayden gives me a knowing grin. "You golfed for two minutes, how tired can you be?"

Ignoring his question and everyone's knowing grins, I say, "We'll see you later."

Penny gives everyone a goodbye kiss on the cheek.

As we leave the room, Finn calls out, "Sweet dreams."

A chorus of laughter follows us out.

The drive home seems like it's taking forever. Finally, my building appears in my view, and I've never been so happy to see it. We barely make it into the apartment before stripping each other out of our clothes.

Whisking her off her feet, with our lips fused together, I take her to the bedroom. I place her gently on the bed and lay next to her. Propped on an elbow, I brush her hair from her face and stare down at her. My breath escapes in a rush. She is the most beautiful woman I've ever seen. It's getting harder and harder to suppress my feelings.

She reaches up and cups my face, a small, worried crease forming between her brows. "Is something wrong?"

I shake my head. "Everything is perfect. You're perfect." And damn my heart is ready to explode in my chest. I want to tell her everything I'm feeling, yet the words still can't leave my mouth.

"Lucas...I..." Is she going to say it? Is she going to say she loves me? How will I respond? "I...I think you're perfect too."

My shoulders sag. Is it with relief or disappointment? I'd say the latter. How would it feel to hear her say those three little words?

How would it feel to say them?

I press a kiss on her lips then swipe my tongue to open her mouth. Her hands slide up my back to clutch behind my head, and the kiss deepens. Breaking away, I kiss along her jaw to her neck, feeling her pulse beating against my tongue. Her hands skim up and down my back, and when my head dips and I take a hard nipple into my mouth, she digs her nails into my skin.

"Oh God." Her body squirms beneath me.

My tongue flicks over the nipple before pulling it in deeper, causing her to quiver. Moving onto the other breast, I give it the same attention. Penny's soft moans urge me on. Making me want to hear those sounds every damn day. My mouth is lapping her up, and one hand skims down her belly and between her legs to her sweet spot. As my fingers slide between her sex, her body jerks off the mattress.

"Lucas...yes..." she pants.

I love how responsive she is.

My thumb presses on her clit, pulling another moan from her. "I need...more." A tremble is racking through her body. She's on the edge.

"Not yet, Pixie. I need to taste you first."

Kissing my way over her quivering stomach, taking nibbles from her hip bones, I settle myself between her legs. I spread them wide then dip my head and place my mouth on her sex. My tongue takes a long swipe over her folds before sucking her clit into my mouth.

Her legs open wider, her fingers tunnel into my hair, and she rocks her pelvis in time with my tongue.

"So...good," she moans. "How did you get so good at this?" She shakes her head. "No...no...no...don't answer that. I don't want to know."

A lot of meaningless sex taught me the skill. Over time, knowing how to pleasure a woman became easy. Yet nothing has ever felt this good. I've never wanted to please a woman as much as I want to please Penny. It had always been about fucking with no attachment. Sex with Penny is so much more.

I continue to lave her with long, slow strokes, bringing her close to the edge, yet not close enough to fall. While my mouth is lapping her up, my hand caresses along her body to her breasts, massaging them, and flicking and pinching her nipples.

Tugging at my hair, she pulls me up to her. Our kiss is long and deep, our tongues battling it out with each other. She breaks away, gasping for breath. "It's your turn."

Not giving me time to question her, she lifts up and pushes at my chest until I'm on my back. The heat in her eyes tells me exactly where this is going, and I'm rock-hard just thinking about it. Hovering above me, she dots kisses on my neck, across my chest, over my stomach, and hesitates at my aching cock. Her warm breath fans over my blistering skin, and my erection twitches with anticipation.

Licking her lips, she takes me into her mouth, sliding down and up. My hips jerk at the soft touch, and I clutch at the bedcovers. Her tongue twirls over the tip and then licks down the length, back up, and she takes me into her mouth again. I wrap her hair in my fingers and hold on tight.

"Fuck, Pixie...you're going to kill me," I groan. I couldn't think of a better way to die.

Gripping her hand at the base of my erection, she slowly pumps as her mouth works me over. I watch as her head bobs up and down, picking up speed as my cock fucks her mouth. My body tightens; I'm ready to come. But not like this. I gently tug at her hair, pulling her off. If I wasn't so hard and ready to fuck her, I'd laugh at her disgruntled expression.

I sit up and place her on my lap. I stop myself from sinking deep into her to pull the drawer open on the nightstand and pluck out a condom. Penny takes it out of my hand and rips it open. My head drops forward to watch her roll it on my cock.

Once in place, I swiftly flip her onto her back and settle myself between her open legs. Positioned above her, our eyes lock. I see more than lust for a good time shining from her eyes. Is she seeing the same from mine? Because every nerve in my body is screaming for me to claim her, and not just her body. Never in my life have I wanted anything as much as I want Penny. I'm so consumed by her she's on my mind from the moment I wake up until I go to sleep at night. Hell, she's even in my dreams. I can't get enough of her.

She wiggles beneath me, telling me she's ready for more. Inch by slow inch, I enter her, both of us moaning when she's taken all of me in. Our breaths hitch. Our bodies tremble.

Dropping my head, I kiss her as I begin to rock. Slowly at first. Taking my time. Feeling her tight pussy squeeze me. Her hands caress my shoulders, my back, and dig into my ass. She pushes her pelvis up, encouraging me to pick up speed. Hooking her legs around my waist like she wants to keep me there. No problem. There's no place I'd rather be. I pick up the pace even more. Our bodies slapping together. Our breathing labored.

"Oh...yes...yes!" she screams with each thrust. She's so fucking close. *I'm* so fucking close.

"Fuck me!" I groan as my body convulses and I pound harder into her.

"That's it...I'm...I'm..." Her mouth falls open as an orgasm rips through her body, whipping away whatever she was going to say.

We thrust, buck, quiver until every ounce of our bliss is wrung from us. Dropping on top of her, I'm careful to keep my weight on my elbows. I rest my head on her shoulder, breathing in the sensual scent of sex, sweat, and her sweet floral perfume.

Perfection.

Rolling off her, I pull the condom off and toss it on the floor—I'll dispose of it later. Gathering Penny into my arms, I hold her close. As I drift off to sleep thoughts of her being in my life is as important as breathing.

I can never let her go.

Chapter Nineteen

PENNY

The next morning, when I open my eyes, I'm nestled in Lucas' strong arms. Tilting my face up, I'm met with his beautiful smile. Oh, I could wake up to a sight like that every morning. I can also spend my nights having him make my body sing. The things he can do with his hands and mouth are pure magic.

"Morning, Pixie. Sleep well?" His voice is husky from sleep.

"Like a baby," I reply.

I've never slept so well as I have sharing a bed with him. It's either because he's put me in an orgasm-induced coma, or it's because of the safety, security, and love for him I feel in his arms. If I had any doubts about my feelings for him, last night's lovemaking blew them all away. There was something about the way he kissed me, touched me, that was different. Sex with Lucas is always sensational, but this time there was something more. Like he was pouring his feelings for me into every moment.

Or am I just imagining it?

How does he really feel about me? I know he cares. He wouldn't be doing all that he's done if he didn't. Is what we have more than friendship to him?

Without a doubt, I've fallen in love with Lucas Alessi. This is the man I want to spend the rest of my life with. Plan a future with. Have his babies. The works. If only Lucas didn't think he took after his father and wasn't capable of a relationship. If only he could see what I see in him. A man who is compassionate, strong, and kind-hearted. Someone who would do anything for the people he cares about...loves. Not hurt them. My heart squeezes in my chest.

Does he love me?

If I tell him how I'm feeling, would it scare him off? Break any connection we are building?

His fingertips swish up and down my arm. "We never talked about your visit with Darren. How did it go?" he asks.

The question pulls me out of my musing. "The place was a mess, and I told him he had two days to clean it up and get out."

"Will he do it?"

"Not sure. If he doesn't, I'll toss his stuff in a dumpster and change the locks. And if that fails, I'll send in the big guns."

Lucas bends his arm at the elbow and pumps up his bicep. "Me?"

"Of course." I giggle.

"Seriously, did he give you any trouble?"

"No, only a little attitude." Something Darren said niggles at the back of my mind. "He said he didn't leak the video nor did Karen."

Lucas' body stiffens against mine. "Then who did?"

"He said probably someone who wants to tear me down."

"It must have been Darren. I can't imagine you'd have other ene-mies like that. You're too sweet. Although, I have been on the end of your sharp tongue." He chuckles.

"That's because you were enemy number one until I learned what a softy you really are."

"Softy?" he chokes. "There's nothing soft about me." Which is clear by the erection laying on his stomach and the hard muscles rippling through his body. He rolls on top of me, and his penis lands hot and heavy on my thigh. "Shall I show you I'm no softy?"

Oh yes, I would like nothing more.

He trails kisses down my neck and along my collarbone.

My phone rings.

"Ignore it." He closes his mouth around my nipple.

My eyes flutter shut. "It's probably my mom or Claudia. If I don't answer, they'll just keep calling."

"Turn the phone off, then it won't interrupt us." He kisses over to my other breast.

With a shuddery breath, I push at his shoulders. "Better to deal with them now."

He flops onto his back with a heavy sigh.

I pluck the phone from the nightstand and check the caller ID on my screen. "Hi, Mom," I answer. "What's up?"

"Good morning, sweetheart. It's been a couple of days since we've spoken, and I wanted to catch up to discuss work."

I roll onto my back and scrub my hand over my face. "I thought there wasn't any work left."

Having a break is refreshing. Not having to run from one commitment to another, working seven days a week, is time off I needed. I haven't had a break since my career exploded. I'm in no rush to get back out there.

"I've booked a job for you. Claudia and I are on our way to Lucas' apartment. Please let security know to let us up."

There goes a morning of sex with Lucas.

"See you soon," she says and hangs up.

Blowing out a frustrated breath, I toss the phone on the nightstand.

"Bad news?" Lucas asks.

"Yes."

Lucas springs up, concern etched on his face. "What is it?" He looks like he'll face whatever it is with me. God, I love this man.

"Relax. Mom and Claudia are on their way. So we'll have to continue what we were about to start a little later."

He deflates and lies back down. "That is bad news."

I giggle. "She said she has something booked for me that we need to discuss."

He leans on his elbow and props his head on his fist. "Sounds promising."

"I hope so." Reluctantly, I get out of bed and pull Lucas' t-shirt on. The smell of his woodsy cologne surrounds me. I wish I could stay in bed with him all day and forget about the real world. But I can't live in this bubble forever. "I'm going to take a shower. They'll be here soon."

"I have work to do too. I'm meeting with Antonne, the gallery curator, to go over a few things for the exhibition."

"That sounds exciting. I can't wait to see it."

His shoulders lift in a shrug. "That's if I can get it all together on time."

Does a flash of nerves cross his face? He's always so confident—sometimes conceited, just not in an 'I'm better than you' kind of way. He just knows what he's good at.

"I'm sure you'll get it done."

After taking a quick shower, I dress in simple beige pants with a white blouse and head to the kitchen for a bite to eat. As much as I'm craving a cream cheese bagel with chocolate sauce I don't have time to call down to the restaurant, so I opt for toast with peanut butter and a cup of coffee.

Lucas is already dressed for work and finishing his coffee. Although his clothing is nothing like the suits his brothers wear. He's in faded jeans, a black t-shirt, and a khaki-colored jacket. My heart always skips a beat at how handsome he is. Will I ever get used to that feeling?

Lucas flicks out his wrist to glance at his watch. "I better run."

I walk him to the door, cup his face, and give him a quick goodbye kiss on the lips. "Have a great day," I say. Just like a girlfriend or wife would do when their partner leaves for work. But I'm neither of those things. Realizing what I'd done, I drop my hand from his face and start to step back. Lucas clasps my wrist and tugs me forward so I bump into his chest.

"I need something to last me throughout the day." His mouth catches mine in a long, deep kiss. As he tunnels his fingers through my hair and parts my lips with his tongue, my toes curl and my body tingles.

This isn't pretend anymore. Not for me. Surely not for Lucas. We've crossed that line. Lucas must feel it too. When he comes home from work tonight, I need to talk to him. Tell him how I feel. If he can't give me more, as much as it will tear my heart out, I'll have to say goodbye. I can't be in this limbo kind of relationship. It's too much for my heart to take.

When we break apart, we take a moment to hold each other and get our breath back. "See you this afternoon." He pecks my nose and seems reluctant to leave. If Claudia and my mother weren't arriving at any moment, I'd convince him to stay home.

"Bye," I say.

He turns to leave, stops, then spins back around. Hoping he's changed his mind, I'm ready to call my mother and cancel our meeting. Instead he says, "I forgot to tell you I'm invited to a film and photography awards ceremony tonight."

I deflate with disappointment. I really wanted to talk to him. "Sounds fun."

He pulls a face. "More like long and boring. What will make it tolerable is if you come with me. Please don't make me go on my own." He puts his hands together and holds them under his chin like he's praying.

"I would love to go with you. Except it's such short notice. I don't have an appropriate dress." The clothes Lucas provided had everything except something suitable for an awards ceremony. "I'd need to make appointments to get my hair and makeup done, and I doubt I can get anything scheduled last minute."

"Leave it to me. I'll send our glam team over later. And I know Juliette will have something suitable for you to wear. I'll send her over too." With that, he gives me a quick kiss then rushes out of the apartment.

Wait... Does he mean Juliette Monet? Their head designer who creates some of the world's most beautiful gowns? Surely I heard wrong.

I place my fingertips on my lips. My mouth is tingling from his kiss. This time there was no mention of pretending to be a couple. Turning it on for the people watching. This feels like a real date. Or did he forget to say so because he needed to rush to work?

A few minutes later, there's a knock at the door and I let Claudia and my mother in. I lead them into the living room, and we get comfortable on the couches.

Claudia barely glances my way. Her nose is buried in her phone. Lines are creasing her forehead. I inwardly sigh. What more crap about me is she reading? I twist the ring on my finger, waiting for her to hit me with it.

When she doesn't take her eyes off her phone and taps away at her screen, I can't wait any longer. "What's being said about me now?"

Claudia's head snaps up. "Oh, nothing. All is quiet for now."

That is more ominous than reassuring. Like more bad news is about to drop. However, there's no point stressing over something that hasn't happened. And I need to focus on the work my mother has booked for me. "So, Mom, what job do you have for me?"

"I've booked a baby shower for you to plan next month."

"Who is it for?" I try to remember what celebrities are currently pregnant.

My mother bites her bottom lip as her fingers tap the arm of the couch. "It's for a couple who live in my apartment building." You remember Tao Yang and her wife Virginia who live below me? Tao only has two months until her due date and needs a party planner urgently. I know it doesn't seem like much—not compared to what you're used to—but she has a few high society friends who will be attending. It's a good way of networking and getting your name out there again in a more positive light," she explains with a flicker of concern on her face. Like she thinks I'll be worried this job isn't good enough.

For a moment, I wait for the disappointment to hit. I've planned parties for musicians, actors, supermodels, and politicians, all at the top of their field. This is a huge drop in my career. But when the disappointment doesn't rear up, I realize I'm more than okay with it. I don't need huge celebrity names to enjoy what I do. I love planning parties. Whether big or small, it has always given me joy to create a space someone loves.

"Of course, the money isn't close to what you usually charge," she says with regret.

"I've got enough money to live comfortably for the rest of my life. I'm not worried about that. I don't need a luxurious lifestyle to be happy."

Claudia makes a scoffing sound, and I turn to look at her. "You say that now. I bet you'll change your mind when the money dries up and you're living in a dump."

Something is wrong with Claudia. She's never so cynical and mean. I guess this affects her too. "If you're worried about getting paid, or your job, don't be. I'm positive things will pick up again."

She gives me a stiff smile. I've been so caught up with my life and falling in love with Lucas have I missed a problem with her?

"In more good news," my mother says, "the publisher has agreed to publish your book. Like we discussed, they're slicing your royalties, but it will be in stores. That's the main thing. I'll set up a meeting with them next week to sign the contract."

"This is all so great. Thanks, Mom. I couldn't have done this without you."

Claudia's phone beeps with a text. As she reads the message, her shoulders slump. Once she's finished reading, she tosses the phone next to her on the couch. "Who have you talked to about your fake relationship with Lucas? Seriously, Pen, you're making it difficult to work for you. The hole you keep digging yourself in is getting deeper and deeper. I can't save you anymore."

The comment is like a slap to the face. Why is Claudia so harsh?

"What's happened? Who knows their relationship is fake?" my mother thankfully asks, because at the moment I'm too drained from all this drama that keeps coming up to speak.

Claudia blows out a frustrated breath. "According to the latest stories, Lucas and Penny are faking their relationship for a publicity stunt. Their reputations are tanking, and this is their way of building it back up. Actually, for the first time, the media has gotten a story right. Might as well let them run with it. There's no coming back from this."

"So that's it? You're giving up?" my mother asks.

Claudia rubs her fingertips up and down her forehead. "What more can I do? Every time I try to fix things Penny does something to ruin it."

She's got blow after blow coming for me today. "How is this my fault?"

Rolling her eyes, she says, "You told someone about fake dating Lucas."

I'm not liking Claudia's attitude toward me. It's something I've never seen before. "I told no one except the two of you."

"What about Lucas? Would he tell anyone?" my mother asks.

"Only his family, and no one would leak it. They're a tight group. They stick together. It was actually his brother's idea."

"Then you must have told someone else," Claudia accuses.

"No. I didn't," I grind out with frustration.

"Did you say anything to Darren when you visited him?" she asks.

A cold shiver runs through my body. "He was suspicious about our relationship. Didn't think I could get anyone like Lucas unless it was fake. He even suspected we were doing it for good publicity. I thought I'd convinced him he was wrong." Did I though? I played it off as him having a silly thought and he could believe what he wanted. I obviously didn't convince him. Once again, I'm paying the price for the fifteen minutes of fame he'll get from this.

Throwing her hands in the air, Claudia says, "Congratulations. Looks like you'll be planning random women's baby showers for the rest of your life. Because your reputation is completely ruined."

I propel from the chair and dig my hands on my hips. "What is your problem? I thought you'd be more sympathetic about what's happening to me. Instead of acting so cold, giving up, and telling me my reputation is ruined, maybe try to offer some solutions. If there's no *Penelope Aldin*, there is no company, and that will include all staff, even the ones in this room." Not in all the years we've been best friends and colleagues have I ever gotten mad at Claudia before. Nausea rolls in my stomach that it's happened.

Claudia's face drops with remorse. "I'm sorry. This is so stressful. I hate what people are saying about you. It's all lies, and you don't deserve it. You especially don't deserve me getting bitchy about it. I've taken my frustrations out on you. I feel terrible speaking to you the way I did."

Sagging onto the couch next to her, I pull her in for a hug. "I'm sorry you're under so much pressure." While she's trying to fix my reputation I'm having the time of my life living with Lucas. I'd forgotten what stress she'd be under. "Let's ignore what they're saying. You're right. There's nothing we can do to fix it. Let's focus on the things we can control, like planning the best baby shower New York City has ever seen."

Claudia smiles. "Sounds like a great idea."

My mother glances between us. "You're really not going to do anything about what they're saying?"

"What's the point? Nothing's working. They'll only find something else to post about me. The less I say, the better."

"Here's an idea. If you really want your reputation to skyrocket again, you can always 'leak' your forest photos. Sex tapes have done wonders for many celebrities. Maybe this will help you too," my mother suggests.

My jaw drops open. "What the hell, Mom? That's disgusting."

"Elizabeth, you can't be serious," Claudia says, looking as shocked as I feel.

My mother laughs. "I was kidding. Sheesh, can't you take a joke?"

"That wasn't funny." Even the thought of those photos being leaked freezes the blood in my veins.

"Sorry, sweetheart, I thought I was lightening the mood."

Claudia turns to me. "Just keep on the down-low. We'll ignore what's being said, and hopefully, it will die down soon."

Sounds like a good plan, if I wasn't going to an event with Lucas tonight. Where we'll be in the spotlight again. Can we pass as a couple if the media is questioning whether it's real? Will they see past the lies proving it's fake?

Well, it's not fake for me. I'm in love with Lucas. If I get a chance to talk to him after the event, I'll find out if he feels the same way too.

Before my mother and Claudia left, they tried convincing me not to go to the awards ceremony. Telling me it will be a disaster and nothing good will come of it. That the media will hound us with questions about our relationship. How they'll scrutinize us to get the scoop on the truth.

They're right. That will happen. But I promised Lucas I'd go with him. And after calling him with my concerns, he told me we shouldn't worry about what's going to happen. Just ignore whatever they throw at us.

Easier said than done when you have cameras pointed at your face and questions you have to lie to.

Soon after, a team of Alessi staff and glam squad turn up, rolling racks of dresses and accessories into the living room. Dozens of boxes of shoes, trays of jewelry, and clutches are put on every flat surface.

For a moment I'm stunned by the flurry of activity around me. You'd think I was attending the Oscars.

What amazes me even more—even though Lucas told me she was coming, but I didn't know whether to believe him—is when Juliette Monet floats into the room on a rainbow of color. She's wearing an off-the-shoulder dress layered in multicolored ruffles with purple chandelier earrings. Her bright red hair is slicked back and braided, which hangs over her shoulder. A yellow and red flower is pinned next to her ear. She looks like a flamenco dancer on acid and is absolutely stunning. I've admired her gowns for years. Now she's dressing me. That's what you get when you're dating—*fake* dating—one of the owners of Alessi Fashion.

"Hello, darling." She waltzes over to me, waving a yellow folding fan in front of her face with blackbirds etched on it. With a flick of the wrist, she closes the fan then kisses me on each cheek. "Lovely to see you again. We are going to have a lot of fun dressing you up today."

"Thank you so much for doing this. You must be so busy. I appreciate you taking the time."

She lightly taps her fan on my shoulder. "It's my pleasure. I love dressing the Alessi men's women."

"Oh...I'm not...we're..." Then I stop myself. I can't tell her we're fake dating. I'm not sure what Lucas has told her.

She smiles at me. There's a knowing look in her eyes. "I know what's going on. I know more than you might think."

I frown. What does she mean by that? Before I get the chance to ask, she taps her fan on her chin and scans me from head to toe.

Turning to a woman who is taking a garment out of a bag, she says, "Siobhan, please get me the red."

For the next couple of hours I play dress-up in the most stunning Alessi Fashion gowns I've ever seen. Juliette is taking in my hair coloring, skin tone, and the shape of my body. I've tried every color and every style, and each gown fits like a glove. How did Juliette know what would fit?

Back in the red dress I tried on first, I stand in front of a full-length mirror. I turn from side to side to take in all angles. The soft fabric twists to the side to sit on one shoulder, leaving the other one exposed. It hugs my body, showcasing my curves and cinching in the waist, giving me an hourglass figure. This creation is gorgeous. I've never felt more beautiful.

"Which gown will you choose?" Juliette asks.

"It has to be this one," I say. "But I bet you already knew that."

"I knew it was perfect for you the moment you put it on."

"Why did you let me try on all the rest? I've wasted so much of your time."

She waves the folding fan in front of her face. "Darling, it's my pleasure. I don't get to do stuff like this very often."

"Thank you. I appreciate it." I run my hands down the length of me. "Do you think Lucas will like the dress?"

"That boy will swallow his tongue when he sees you." She grins.

Next, I'm thrown into hair and makeup. Juliette leaves me in the trusted hands of the glam squad. They pluck and comb and tease and brush, and two hours later, I hardly recognize myself in the mirror. Large curls hang down my back with one side pinned behind my ear. The makeup is soft and emphasizes my blue eyes. It's been such a fun few hours. One I'll never forget.

Soon after the team packs up their things and leaves, Lucas arrives home. He's already dressed in a tuxedo, and my stomach does a back-flip at how gorgeous he looks. I've only seen him in jeans and a t-shirt. Lucas in a suit is mouthwatering.

He gives me a huge, appreciative grin as he scans me from head to toe. "You look stunning."

"I've had a lot of help to look this good."

Taking my hand, he pulls me closer. "Strip this all away and you are the most beautiful woman I've ever seen."

I dip my head at the compliment. "Thank you. You're looking beautiful yourself." His hair is combed back. The suit is tailored to fit across his broad shoulders. He looks like a super-sexy James Bond. "Oh, and I can't believe you actually sent Juliette Monet here to style me."

"Only the best for you, Pixie. You know, as much as I love looking at you in this dress, I'm going to love it more when I take it off and it's lying on my bedroom floor."

I gasp with mock horror. "You can *not* toss this gown on the floor. That's blasphemy!"

He chuckles. "Okay, while we are in the throes of passion, I'll stop, carefully remove it from your body, place it on a hanger, put it in a garment bag, and hang it up."

Laughing, I gently poke him in the chest. "That's what you better do."

My thoughts drift to what I want to talk to him about. After I tell him I've fallen in love with him, will he want to remove my dress, or will he pull away and run screaming from the room?

Chapter Twenty

❖

LUCAS

Arriving at the award show, we wait in the limo for our turn to reach the red carpet. Penny's leg is bouncing and she's twisting the chain of her purse in her hands. Taking her hand, I bring it to my lips and kiss her knuckles. "Everything will be okay," I assure her.

"You know what they're going to ask."

"There are too many celebrities here tonight for them to worry about us. Maybe they won't even care that we're here."

She gives me a dubious look.

"We don't have to do this if you don't want to. I'll have the limo take us home."

She shakes her head and pulls her shoulders back. "No. They're not making me hide."

"That's my girl. Good for you." There are those words again. *My girl*. That's exactly what she is to me; my girl.

When it's our turn, the limo pulls up to the carpet. I get out of the car, move around to Penny's side, and help her out. As soon as our feet hit the red carpet, cameras are pointing our way.

I lean my head to her ear and whisper, "We'll pause for a couple of photos and then take off inside, okay?"

She nods. Her hand trembles in mine, and I give it a gentle squeeze to let her know I'm in this with her all the way. I'll never let her go.

After the photos are taken and we're about to step off the carpet, a journalist calls out, "Lucas, why are you here with Penelope Aldin if your relationship is fake? Why the act?"

My body stiffens. Even though I was prepared for these questions, I still want to punch the guy in the face for asking. I turn toward Penny; her face is stricken with embarrassment. Who the hell do these people think they are causing someone so much pain?

"Penelope, why would you lie to your fans?" another man calls out.

Sliding my arm around her lower back, I pull her close. Like somehow I can use my body to shield her from their fucked-up words. Normally I'd ignore the assholes, but I need to say something for Penny. "Whatever bullshit that's going around now is just that...bullshit. Nothing about our relationship is fake. Penny is the smartest, funniest, most beautiful woman I've ever known." Turning toward her, I smile down at her. "I love Penny. She is who I want to spend the rest of my life with."

Giving a surprised gasp, she searches my face, and I see a questioning look in her eyes, like she's wondering if there is any truth in my words.

Holy hell. The declaration just flew out of my mouth, and yet, I meant every word. And it doesn't scare the crap out of me. Giving her a soft kiss, I turn to the journalists and say, "Now move on to something more interesting. There's no story here."

Taking Penny's hand, I guide her inside and away from the press to a quiet corner of the room.

"Lucas, you shouldn't have done that. That is way more than we agreed to. Be seen together, share a kiss or two in public—that's all. I'm sorry you felt you had to tell them you love me. Now it will only be harder to end this when it comes time to."

Taking her hands, I rest them over my heart. It's beating hard against my chest. "I told them I love you because it's the truth. I only wish I told you first and hadn't done it so publicly."

Her eyes widen. "Wh-what are you saying?"

"Every time I look at you I can't imagine you walking out of my life. I want to wake up with you every morning. Kiss you at the end of a long day. Spend every moment loving you. For the first time ever, I know what it's like to love someone so much it feels like my heart is going to explode. Penny, you're the love of my life."

She covers her mouth with her hand. Tears slide down her face. Praying they are good ones, I brush them away with my thumbs and cup her face.

"What about your beliefs? You think you're like your father."

"There is no way my dad loved my mom like he said he did. Because if he felt half as much about her as I do you, he could never have cheated. Could never have even looked at another woman. My love for you wipes away any beliefs I had. You are it for me. Always will be, whether or not you want me."

Penny's bottom lip trembles, and her eyes well with tears. Instead of responding, she drops her face in her hands and sobs. My heart sinks to my stomach. Oh fuck. Does she not feel the same way? The next few seconds that pass are the longest of my life.

Then she lifts her face and gives me a watery smile. "I love you, Lucas. I love you so much."

My heartrate kicks up. "You do?"

She nods. "I wanted to tell you after the award ceremony. Gosh, I was so scared you didn't feel the same way. The thought of having to walk away from you was heartbreaking. I couldn't breathe just thinking about it."

Cupping her face with both hands, I plant a firm kiss on her lips. I rest my forehead on hers and say, "Pixie, I've loved you since the moment you sat next to me in math class. When you came back into my life, I was too screwed up to recognize it. I'm sorry it took so long to tell you."

"All that matters is that we are here now, loving each other. Everything else doesn't matter."

I hook my arm around her waist and pull her close. "I want to take you home so we can *love* each other more." I wiggle my eyebrows so she understands my meaning.

She looks over her shoulder. "But we just got here? The press are still out there. If we leave now, what will they think? I can't deal with any more questions. This night is magical. I don't want them ruining it."

Taking a moment to ponder the situation, I come up with a plan. I pull my phone from the inside pocket of my suit jacket and send a text to the limo driver. Then I reach my hand out and say, "Follow me. I'll get us out of here."

Without hesitation, she takes my hand. I guide her through the guests gathered around waiting to be seated, not stopping for anyone who tries to grab our attention for a chat. We zigzag through tables decorated with flowers and candles to a side door that the staff are using. Slipping inside, we run hand in hand, laughing, through the corridor. I've never had as much fun as I do when I'm with Penny.

We make it to the kitchen, and I snatch two bread rolls out of a basket and toss one to Penny.

"Hey, the kitchen isn't for guests!" a man standing at the stove, who I'm assuming is the chef, yells at us.

"Sorry, it's an emergency," I call back. "Thanks for the bread."

Finding another door, I crack it open and peek out. Thankfully, it leads outside into an alley with no one in sight. Running to the road, I look up and down the street and see the limo parked a few yards away. Through the cooling night air, we make our way to the car. Out of breath, we fall inside in a fit of giggles.

"I think we gave the poor chef a heart attack." She lifts her hand holding the bread roll. "Thanks for the snack." She laughs before taking a bite.

"I thought you might need some sustenance for the night I have planned for you," I say in a warning tone, giving her no doubt as to what's on my mind.

She swallows hard. "Oh, what do you have planned?"

The limo pulls out onto the street, and I press a button on the control panel. A dark block-out partition screen separates us from the driver. "Let me show you."

Chapter Twenty-One

PENNY

Lying in bed with our arms and legs entwined, my body heavy and sated after our lovemaking, I can't think of a better place to be. Or a better man to be with. Lucas Alessi loves me. Those words fill my heart with so much happiness it's going to burst. It's what I wanted. Dreamed about.

Now he is mine. For real. No more pretending.

When we're in public we don't have to act like we're in love. Because this is the real deal. I can't wait to share my life with him.

Lucas' fingers ghost over my shoulder and down my arm. "What's on your mind?"

I shift my position so I can lean my arm on his chest and prop my chin on my fist. "You. Us. How we don't have to pretend anymore."

"Pixie, I stopped pretending the first time I kissed you."

I pull my head back. "What? You were the one who suggested the plan. Why didn't you tell me how you were feeling?" I was so scared to tell him how I felt in case the feelings weren't reciprocated.

"For a time, my head ruled my heart. I was too fucked up about my beliefs to trust what I knew deep down to be true."

I lightly pluck at his chest hairs. "And what was that?" Yes, I'm fishing to hear it again.

He stares deeply into my eyes. "I love you, Penny. Always have. Always will."

A quiver rakes through my body. Never will I tire of hearing those words. "I love you too."

Dipping his head, he kisses me. A kiss that tells me I'm his. And I know he'll always be mine.

When we break apart, he says, "Stay with me."

"I've been staying with you every night for days. I'm not leaving this bed."

He shakes his head. "No, I mean don't go to a hotel. Live here with me permanently." Clearing his throat, he says, "Arrhh…well, that's if you want to." Being in a relationship is new to him. His vulnerability squeezes my heart.

"Living here with you has always felt like home. I'd love to move in. As soon as Darren is out of my apartment I'll have my things sent over. You might change your mind when you see all my stuff. I'm a bit of a hoarder." I giggle.

Not laughing at my joke, he sits up and leans against the headboard. He pulls me up next to him. "I never want to talk about that asshole again. The sooner he's gone, the better."

"I agree. He should be out of the apartment tomorrow. That part of my life is over. I'm putting it behind me. You're my future," I say, snuggling into his side.

He holds me tight. "I'll be by your side every moment I can get. You're gonna get sick of me."

"Never."

He plants a kiss at my temple. After a couple of minutes resting in each other's arms, Lucas says, "I never got a chance to ask how the meeting with your mom and Claudia went."

I blow out a breath. "It's a good thing I'm moving in with you because I might end up being homeless," I joke.

"Things are that bad?"

"No, not really. The book deal is still happening, which is great. Although they've slashed my royalties. And Mom has lined up a baby shower for me to plan, so that's exciting." I really am looking forward to it.

His hand brushes up and down my arm. "That's awesome. Who is the shower for?"

"A couple who lives in my mom's apartment building."

Lucas twists around to face me. "Not a celebrity?"

"No. But it's work and I'm grateful."

"You've planned parties and events for the most famous people in America. How do you feel about this?"

For a moment I wait for the surge of disappointment. For the feeling of failure to flood through me. Except relief washes over me and excitement takes over. "I actually feel great about it. It's like a weight is lifting from my shoulders. It's not like I need the money. I have enough put away to live comfortably. But I like being busy, and this is perfect."

"This is your career that you built, and now because of the asshole it's getting stripped away. That must hurt."

"At first it did because I thought it was what I wanted."

"You don't anymore?"

"No." Being honest and admitting what's been a slither of a thought is freeing.

"Why?"

"Most of my life I was either invisible or seen as not good enough. Then my YouTube videos started getting views and suddenly *I* was seen. My work was being noticed. I was *good* at something. People wanted to interact with me. I was someone."

Lucas picks up my hand and links his fingers with mine. "I always saw you. You were *someone* to me."

My heart fills with love. I smile. "I've achieved everything I've ever dreamed of and more. After what's happened, I've learned that I don't need recognition to feel powerful or worthy. In fact, being in the spotlight is more trouble than it's worth. I'm happy to step away. Do smaller things and get back to basics. Do things because I want to, not because I'm being pulled in every direction to keep a bunch of people I don't know happy. A lot of the A-list celebrities I've worked for are demanding, spoiled, and at times ungrateful. I don't need the stress anymore."

"If that's what you truly want, then I'm happy for you."

"It is."

His lips tilt into a crooked grin. "You know, if you ever get sick of planning parties, you can always model for me again. I know lots of beautiful spots in the woods by the cabin you can pose in."

I playfully slap his arm. "Never in a million years."

Lucas laughs. "You're such a spoilsport. I have the most beautiful woman in the world in my bed and I can't take advantage of her."

Laying my palms on his pecs, I push him onto his back and hover above him. "You can take advantage of me as much as you like."

He curves his arm around my waist and flips me onto my back. I squeal with laughter. His gaze drops to my lips. "That's exactly what I'm going to do."

The next two days were a busy hive of activity. Thankfully, the move out of my apartment was drama-free. Darren had done what I'd asked and left, taking all his crap with him. I decided all I wanted was my personal items. Darren has tainted everything else, and so I donated the rest to goodwill.

After Lucas' declaration of love on the red carpet at the award ceremony, my mother has called multiple times with offers of work. Celebrities are wanting me to plan events, organize their houses, attend their parties. When the media portrayed me as a cheater, they'd turned their backs on me. Now my love story has captured everyone's hearts, and I'm receiving more invitations than ever before. To my mother's disappointment, I turned them all down.

I've shut the door on that time of my life, and I'm stepping into a future I'm thrilled about. I'm living with a man I love and who loves me. I'm happy with where my career is at. I have family and friends. That's all I need.

There is nothing more that the media can do to bring me down. No one can hurt me now. I won't let them.

Chapter Twenty-Two

···◈···

PENNY

Over a breakfast of pancakes, strawberries, and coffee, Lucas is reading something on his phone, his brow creasing.

"Is everything alright?" I ask.

His head snaps up to look my way. "Sorry, what?"

"You're frowning at your phone. Is something wrong? You look a little distracted."

He sets the phone on the table and picks up a fork. "Sorry. Just last-minute adjustments Antonne is insisting I make to the exhibition tonight."

"What kind of adjustments?"

Taking a bite of the pancakes and then a sip of coffee, he says, "Just a couple of photos he wants me to add. I'm not sure if it's the right thing to do."

"Go with your gut. You'll know if it's right or not."

He stabs at the pancakes. "I've never done this before. What if I bomb?"

"I've seen your photographs. Amazing doesn't come close to describing them. People are going to love them."

He smiles but it doesn't reach his eyes. He must really be worried. "Thanks. Although, I'm not sure many people want to come see the photographs of a fashion model photographer. They'll probably think the room will be filled with beautiful women wearing Alessi gowns. I want people to see it's not an Alessi Fashion photoshoot."

"Your photos tell a story. You've captured the heart and soul of your subjects. I have no doubt they'll see that."

"I hope so."

I reach across the table and place my hand over his. "I know so," I say enthusiastically to try and get him out of his melancholy mood. I know firsthand what it's like to present your work for others to criticize. It can be paralyzing.

Rising from the chair, he collects his plate and coffee mug and stacks them in the dishwasher. He walks to me and kisses me on the forehead. "Are you coming tonight?"

What a strange question. Why would he ask that? We've been talking about it for days.

I stand, wrap my arms around his neck, and kiss his lips. "Of course I am. I wouldn't miss it. I'll meet you there. I have to drop off sample invitations to Tao for her baby shower on my way. It's the only time she has available."

"It's okay if you're busy and can't make it."

Is he so nervous about the exhibit he doesn't want me there?

"I'll be there," I assure him.

His shoulders rise and fall on a heavy breath. "Great. Good. I'll see you tonight. I'll be at the gallery most of the day. Call me if you need me for anything."

"I'll be fine. Good luck." I give him a quick kiss. "I love you."

He smiles, and for a second, all the worry etched on his face disappears. "Love you too." With that, he walks out of the kitchen.

⬥

Later that morning, I'm going over color samples for Tao and Virginia's decorations when the apartment phone rings. It's Samuel informing me that Claudia is wanting to visit. I tell him to send her up. While I wait, I tidy up the table and place everything into neat piles. After a few minutes, there is a knock at the door.

When I let her in, I immediately know by her expression she has bad news. My shoulders sag. Every time I see her there seems to be more drama. What's going on now?

"What's wrong?" I ask.

Claudia sets her purse on the coffee table and rubs her fingertips along her eyebrows. "It's going to be bad."

Chilly prickles pinch my spine. "What is?"

She takes a deep breath. "Maybe you should sit down for this."

My insides turn to ice. Suddenly I want to cover my ears and not listen to what she has to say. "I'll stand." My legs are too frozen to move.

"I have a friend at Express Media, and sometimes, over drinks he leaks stories about what's going to hit the press. Last night we were out, and after he had one too many cosmopolitans, he told me photos of...of..."

"Of what?" I encourage when she doesn't continue.

She gnaws at her bottom lip. "Are you sure you don't want to sit down?"

My hands ball into fists by my side. "Spit it out."

"He told me photos of you are going to be published."

"What do you mean? What photos? I haven't been in public in days or had any interaction with Darren. What photos could the media possibly have taken?"

"They didn't take them. Someone else did."

I scratch my fingers through my hair. "Claudia, you're not making any sense. What photos?"

She clears her throat. "The ones in the forest. Express Media has them."

For a moment, I'm confused, then it hits me. The breath gets knocked from my lungs. "My *naked* photos in the forest?" Of course those photos; they're the only ones I've taken.

Claudia nods, her eyes shimmering with tears.

Now my legs no longer feel like they can hold me up and I sink onto the nearest chair.

"I know how this is going to make you feel. Especially after what happened to you senior year. It's going to dredge up old, painful memories." Claudia doesn't need to point that out. It already has.

I drop my face in the palms of my hands. This can't be happening. How am I going to live through the humiliation again? This time on a larger scale.

I mentally shake away the initial paralyzing fear and try to think clearly. "This isn't possible. Lucas said he deleted the photos. It must be a mistake. Could they somehow be the photos from high school?"

Claudia sits next to me. "He described a forest. The rain. No mention of a beach. They are the photos Lucas took of you."

My head snaps up. "When will they be live?"

"In the morning."

"Can we stop them before they're published?"

"I've been on the phone all morning with our lawyer. There's nothing she can do."

"They're being published without my permission. There must be something she can do? And how did Express Media get hold of them?"

Claudia shakes her head with regret. "Unfortunately, they have the owner's permission."

"That's ridiculous. I would never give them permission."

"Not you...Lucas." Claudia's tone is filled with accusation.

My heart sinks to my stomach. "He wouldn't."

But what other explanation can there be? He's the only one who has access to his camera. No, I can't believe he'd do something like that after everything we've been through. After he told me he loved me.

Claudia puts a comforting hand on my shoulder. "He's done it before. Now he's done it again. Probably still blames you for Garrett's death, and this is his revenge."

Too agitated to sit, I jump to my feet. "No... It was Travis who took the photos on the beach. Lucas knows how much it hurt me. He would never do that to me. Because he loves me." He told me he doesn't blame me for the accident. Did he not mean it?

Rising from her seat, Claudia stands next to me, a sympathetic expression on her face. "Then explain how they've gotten leaked. I know there's no way you'd do it."

I pace the floor. "Why? What would he get out of it?"

Why would he want to break my heart in such a humiliating way? Earlier this morning he said he was worried no one would show up at his exhibition. Is this his way of attracting attention? Nausea rolls in my stomach.

This can't be happening. Lucas loves me. "There must be a mistake. Lucas deleted the photos," I say to remind her, or am I just in denial?

"There's one way to find out if he really did. Is his camera in his office?"

I nod.

"Let's find out."

She starts to leave, and when I don't follow because my feet are glued to the floor in fear, she turns back, takes my hand, and pulls me along behind her.

"Better to get this over with," she says. "Then you can deal with the low-life, lying jerk."

Walking into Lucas' office, even though I've come in here many times, now feels like I'm violating his privacy. By looking through his things, I'm guilty of being suspicious. Doubting his love for me and wondering how the hell I've found myself in this position again.

"Is this it?" Claudia drops my hand, picks up the camera on his desk, and hands it to me. My hands shake so violently I almost drop it.

"Yes," my voice croaks.

Turning it on, I click through the many photos. Some I recognize as pieces he's adding to the exhibition. Just as I'm about to give up and breathe a sigh of relief because Claudia is wrong, the next photo stops my heart. In it I'm lying naked on the forest floor on a bed of leaves and moss. Weak light filters through the canopy, cascading over my pale skin.

The blood drains from my face.

He didn't delete them.

He lied.

"From your expression, I can tell you're holding the proof that he's not to be trusted," Claudia says. There is an air of smugness in her tone, like she's enjoying being right. "What are you going to do?"

I set the camera on the desk and hug my arms around my waist, trying to keep myself from falling apart. "I don't know." I can barely breathe. How am I supposed to know how I take the next step?

"Would you like me to call Lucas and tell him what a piece of shit he is? He's worse than Darren."

"No. I'll deal with it." Like a zombie, I walk from the office and into my bedroom. Sitting on the edge of the bed, I stare sightlessly at the floor.

"I always knew he couldn't be trusted," Claudia says from the doorway. "He spun you a story, and you fell for it. This was his plan all along. Get you to fall in love with him to then stab you in the back. I tried warning you."

I rub my hands up and down my thighs. "Yes, you did." From the first day I showed interest in Lucas—back in high school—Claudia continuously let me know that he was no good and he'd never return my feelings. He was a jock. I was invisible.

"I'll keep trying to stop the photos being published. Don't hold your breath though. Express Media is holding onto a goldmine."

Lying on my side, I tuck my knees to my chest. Tears threaten to spill. I've cried enough to last a lifetime. I'll be damned if I let them go.

Claudia rushes to my side and kneels next to the bed. "Oh, Pen. I'm so sorry this is happening. You're the strongest person I know. You'll get through this again. I know you will. Let's order pizza and ice cream, and we'll binge-watch crime shows so we can plot revenge on Lucas Alessi."

"I just want to be alone," I say, my voice barely above a whisper. I'm too drained to speak. To move.

"Are you sure?" Her eyes fill with concern.

I nod.

"I'll call you later to make sure you're okay."

"Thanks."

She gets to her feet and looks down at me. "I hate leaving you like this."

"I'll be fine." I give her a small smile, the gesture a huge effort.

"Love you," she says, and I watch as she leaves the room.

Left alone, I lay still on the bed. My trust is broken. Everything I believed to be true is destroyed. How can someone I love, someone who says they love me, do something so brutal? For what? To bring me down? What did I ever do to deserve this?

Lifting myself up, I swing my legs over the side of the bed and brace my hands on the edge of the mattress. I can't waste another minute here. There are things I need to do.

Deal with someone who can't get away with this again.

I call a cab and make my way to the lobby.

This is the last time they get to humiliate me.

Chapter Twenty-Three

◆

PENNY

Four hours later, filled with a lot of anxiety and stress, I'm at the art gallery, hiding behind a black curtain, separated from the crowd. A crowd Lucas wasn't sure would show. Well, they did. Hundreds of people gather around, admiring his works of art, highlighted with lights adjusted at just the right angle. Judging by the expressions on their faces and the buzzing chatter, they're a hit.

Soon they'll be in for a huge surprise. Or shock. I'm not sure how they'll react. The thought of what I'm about to do sends waves of nerves through my body. My hands are shaking. My mouth dry. I'm at this point because I trusted someone I loved, and they betrayed me.

Never again will I give anyone power over me. I'm in control of my life, and I'll be damned if I let anyone bring me down. With a little bit of steel in my spine, the nerves simmer. Taking a deep breath, I peek through the crack in the curtain, careful so no one sees me. If I'm spotted, it will ruin everything I've planned.

People fill the room. Waiters are passing around glasses of champagne and hors d'oeuvres to guests admiring the photography. Then my gaze lands on Lucas. He's dressed in a black suit jacket and trousers. The top three buttons of his white shirt are undone, showing a slither of his tanned chest. With his hair neatly brushed back, he is the standout of the event. He's smiling and looking happy as he accepts compliments, handshakes, and air-kisses from his guests.

Finn, Harper, Hayden, and Alyssa are gathered around him. My nerves are bubbling to the surface again, and I splay my hand over my stomach. Can I do this with his family here? I take deep breaths to settle my racing heart. I can't think of them now or I'll never get through what I'm about to do.

A minute later, I see my mother and Claudia make their way through the crowd. I need them both here to see this through. It took some convincing to get Claudia here. She couldn't understand why I would want to be at Lucas' exhibition after what he did. Without giving my plan away, I made it clear that when I'm done Lucas' reputation would get the hit he deserves. She smiled like the Cheshire cat. She didn't want to miss his humiliation.

My gaze once again falls on Lucas. He flicks out his wrist to check the time on his watch and then searches the crowd and looks toward the entrance like he's waiting for me.

Good.

Everything is going according to plan.

Now that everyone is here, I can start. I send a text, and within seconds, Antonne pushes through the curtain. I couldn't have done this without him. It took a lot of effort for him to help me. Yet he made me feel like it was no bother. I know how much work it is to put a show together. It's not easy to arrange and add things at the last minute. I'm grateful for his time and patience.

"Sweetie, are you ready?" Antonne is dressed in a white suit with an orange shirt which emphasizes his brown skin. Towering over me in white platform shoes, he has gold and diamond rings on every finger. They flash before me as he waves his hands around as he speaks. "This will be absolutely fabulous."

I shake my arms by my sides and roll my shoulders like I'm about to get into the ring for a fight. Well, I guess I am. I'm fighting for my future. "Yes, I'm ready."

I've often been on a stage and addressed an audience. Doing cooking demonstrations and making Christmas decorations is a lot different than what I'm about to do. This is personal. I'm putting everything I have out there for everyone to see.

Antonne takes my shoulders and kisses both of my cheeks. "You've got this, sweetie. See you in a minute."

He ducks back around the curtain and into the gallery. I hear him clap to get everyone's attention.

Then he says, "Ladies and gentlemen, can I have your attention please?" When the murmur of the crowd quietens, he continues, "We have one more treat for you this evening. I'd like to introduce you to Penelope Aldin."

I step out from the curtain, and all eyes are glued on me. People are clapping at Antonne's introduction with a mix of confusion and surprise.

I clear my throat and address the audience. "Hello, everyone. As you might be aware, I've had a lot of publicity lately, and not of the good kind. I've had strangers shove cameras in my face, follow me, interrupt private moments, and spread lies about me. Now I'm faced with something else. Something more obtrusive than anything I've had to deal with before. Private photos of me are set to be published in the morning. Photos that I thought were deleted and would never see the light of day. Once again, I'm facing humiliation. When I learned what was about to happen, I was shocked and mortified. I wanted to hide alone in a darkened room and not show my face again. This is what the person who leaked the photos wanted—to bring me down. Cause another scandal, and damage my reputation even more than it already is.

"I believe they hoped people would see these photos as something dirty and salacious. But they are far from that. More like a work of art. Beautiful. Captured by a man with a tremendous amount of talent. Someone who not only sees beauty in models wearing Alessi Fashion, but also in things that inspire him, as you can see from the photographs on the walls.

"One stormy day, I was his inspiration. He made me feel like the most beautiful woman in the world. And for that reason, I want to share the amazing photographs he took of me before some sleazy tabloid does. The media won't taint this for me. Once something like this would have broken me." I glance at Lucas; pride is shining from his face. "But like someone I love said to me, I'm unbreakable."

I nod at Antonne, and he whisks back the curtain, revealing the enlarged photographs hanging on the wall. The audience gasps in surprise then break out with enthusiastic rounds of applause. They're smiling and cheering, and by the expressions on their faces, they're loving what they see.

There is one person I'm focused on—Claudia. All color has drained from her face. Her betrayal sliced through me. Years of what I thought was friendship gone. Why? What did I ever do to her to cause such hatred? When she starts to leave, Lucas, his family, and my mother block her path. Lucas leans down and whispers something into her ear. Her jaw tightens, but she doesn't move.

Reaching my hand out toward Lucas, he comes to me, takes it, and kisses my knuckles before placing a kiss on my lips. Then he turns to his guests. "If anyone wants to doubt our love, or try to sell stories about it being fake, just take a look at these photographs. In case you're still wondering, I love this fucking woman."

He cups my face and kisses me deeply to the amusement and cheers of the crowd.

Lucas pulls back. For my ears only, he whispers, "You are amazing. Do you know that?"

"I feel amazing when I'm with you. Thank you for doing this for me. This is supposed to be your exhibition's big debut, and I've made it about me."

Brushing my hair back from my face, his fingertips are feather-light when he touches my cheek. "This is about us and how much we love each other. We are in this together. Always."

"As much as I'd love to bask in this with you, there's something I have to take care of."

I glance over at Claudia, who is still surrounded by the most important people in my life. She must have worked fast to find the photos when left alone in the apartment. Why did she go to so much trouble?

When Lucas sees who I'm looking at, he says, "I'll come with you."

I shake my head. "I need to do this myself."

He places his hands on my shoulders. "Are you sure?"

"Yes."

"I'm here if you need me."

Gosh, I love this man. He is my rock. My heart. My everything.

Leaving him, I walk over to Claudia. "Follow me." Not waiting for her to answer, I turn and walk toward an office at the back of the gallery Antonne told me I could use. When we're inside, I close the door behind us.

Claudia crosses her arms over her chest and gives me a haughty expression, like she doesn't care what's to come. Yet her gaze is flicking around the room, looking at everything but me, giving away her fear.

"Why?" I thought our friendship was solid. Never in a million years did I think she'd stab me in the back so viciously. I did not see this coming.

With a shrug of a shoulder, she says, "Why what?"

"Now's not the time to play dumb. The paparazzi always finding me, the photos getting leaked. Why did you want to destroy me? You were someone I trusted. Loved. The only person who knew what my life was like."

Making a scoffing sound, she rolls her eyes. "Oh please. You always played the victim. Always using the 'my life was so difficult' card. You've always gotten everything you wanted handed to you."

Her comment is like a slap to the face. The person standing in front of me is a stranger. How was I so blind to this hatred?

"Why would you say that?" I ask. "I've always worked hard for what I have."

She points a finger at me. "Did you work hard to get Lucas' attention at school? Did you work hard when your stupid YouTube videos went viral? Oh, and let's not forget, you even bagged a top football player. So when you say you worked hard, what a joke."

"So, this is all about jealousy? You're jealous of what I have?" Everything I've done I always made Claudia a part of. Even included her in the business.

Her gaze travels from my head to my toes and back again. Her nose screws up in disgust, and I know she's trying to make me feel insecure. I will not let people's opinions of my body affect me anymore. "There's nothing to be jealous of," she says.

"I don't believe you. Lucas rejected you in high school because he wanted me, so with the help of Travis you planned to get me to skinny-dip and leaked the photos. Then came Darren. Did you want him too? When you learned he was cheating on me, you wanted me to find out in the most humiliating way so I'd never take him back and then you could have him?" This is so twisted.

She gives a mirthless laugh. "I already had him. He was fucking me long before you. What you didn't see in that video with him and Karen was me joining them. I cut that out."

Nausea rises to my throat. How was I so blind?

"You were Darren's ticket to stardom, and he rode it hard—along with some other people." She smirks like she thinks sleeping with him hurts me. Anything to do with Darren no longer affects me.

"You think you're hurting me." I open my arms out wide. "Yet here I am standing taller than ever. Your plans have constantly backfired. With everything you've thrown at me, I've only gotten stronger."

The smugness drops from her face. "Your career is over. Just because you've showed some nudes doesn't mean it will take off again. You are old news. No one wants you."

"Except for Lucas. He wants me. He *loves* me. Would do anything to make me happy." Now it's my turn to look smug. "You must *hate* that. As for my career, I've come to terms with it never being the same again, because I'm choosing for things to be different. I'm happier than I have ever been. All your scheming and backstabbing has given me more than I could ever have dreamed possible. So, I should thank you for giving me something valuable—Lucas."

Claudia's mouth opens and closes, then her lips slam into a thin line. My happiness and her failure to bring me down must be killing her.

I can't stand to be in the same room with her a moment longer. I've gotten my answer. It all came down to jealousy and Claudia being a wicked person. Instead of working for the things she wanted, she had to drag me down to try and steal them from me.

"I never want to see you again. If you so much as post a single thing about me online, sell any more photos, or breathe a word about me to anyone, I will hit you so hard with a lawsuit your head will spin. Understand?"

Claudia gives me a baleful glare and doesn't answer.

"It's not a threat. I will do as I say. You're lucky I didn't get the police involved with the little stunt you tried to pull with my photos. So do you understand?"

With a tight jaw, she nods her head and scurries from the room.

When she's gone, the strength in my legs give out, and I collapse into the nearest chair. With shaking hands, I cup my face. I can't believe I held it together the way I did. I must have been running on adrenaline. As it fades away, my body trembles.

A few moments later, Lucas barrels into the room and drops to his knees in front of me. He takes my hands in his. They are so big and strong, and I immediately stop shaking. He's got me. Always will.

"Are you okay?" he asks. "I saw Claudia storming out of the gallery."

"I'm fine." Although it will take a while to mourn the loss of a friendship I thought I had.

"This must be such a shock."

I brush back a lock of hair that has fallen over his brow. "She hurt me like nothing I've ever experienced before. But with you by my side, I know I'll get through it." The love shining for me from his eyes is enough to tell me I'll be okay.

Smiling, he kisses my lips. "I'll never leave your side. I'm yours forever. Never forget that."

I return the smile and kiss. "You have me forever too." He pulls me in for a hug. "I thanked Claudia for the things she did to me."

Lucas pulls back. Creases form between his eyebrows. "Why would you do that?"

"If she hadn't done all those things, you would never have helped me at the hotel. Never taken me to your cabin, and we would never have fallen in love."

"If she hadn't started the whole thing in high school, something could have happened between us then."

"We were so young. What were the chances of it lasting?"

"True. I only wish she didn't hurt you so bad in the process. Did she tell you why she did it?"

"Jealousy, and I think there's something seriously wrong with her. No one in their right mind would behave like that. Anyway," I say, tapping my hands on his chest. "Let's forget about Claudia for now. Tonight's about your exhibition. Your guests are loving it. Congratulations. I'm so proud of you."

He dips his head at the compliment. "It's gone better than I expected. Your photographs are a hit too. Although, you didn't need to expose yourself so much."

"They are beautiful. I wanted them all to be seen, and not in some trashy way. Have they sold? I can't imagine having my pictures hanging in someone's place."

He shakes his head.

My shoulders slump with disappointment for him and a little relief that no one will have the photos up in their homes. "I'm sorry."

"No one bought them because they're not for sale."

I frown. "Why not?"

"Because they belong to me. They are getting pulled down as we speak. Everyone has seen and praised them. Seeing you as the goddess that you are. Now, they'll get hung in my apartment for my eyes only."

I laugh. "Sounds good to me." As liberating as it felt to show such wonderful art to a room full of people, I'm happy to know it was only for a short time.

"You know what else sounds good?"

"What?"

"Leaving and getting you home." A hint of heat is in his eyes.

"What about the exhibition?"

"Antonne can wrap it up." Lucas gets to his feet, takes my hand, and pulls me up to meet him. "Follow me."

My heart swells with love. "I'll follow you anywhere."

Chapter Twenty-Four

LUCAS

As I sit on the bed, propped up with pillows, I'm grateful I get to hold Penny in my arms every night for the rest of our lives. After finding out her photos had been leaked, things could have turned out a lot differently.

A heaviness weighs on my chest. "I didn't get to apologize for not deleting your photos off my camera. I promised you I would. Every time I tried, I couldn't do it. They were so special to me. Never did I think anyone would steal them. I'm so sorry. I hope you can forgive me."

Penny tilts her face up and smiles. "Nothing to forgive. I'm glad you didn't delete them."

"Are you sure about that? A lot of people have seen them. The New York Post photographed them. They're all over the internet."

"It's been a long time since something positive has been posted about me—about us. I have no regrets." She splays her hand on my chest. "I can't believe how quickly we got everything set up for the exhibition. Antonne performed a miracle." After Penny figured out what Claudia had done, she called me to set up the plan. A plan that went perfectly.

"He sure knows how to put a show together. Didn't even break a sweat when he had to rearrange the whole exhibition in a matter of hours right before the guests were due to arrive."

"I'll have to send him a gift basket." Penny smiles.

"Make sure you add a bottle of vodka. He'll need it." I comb my fingers through her hair. "With everything going on, and the rush to get the photos ready, I never got to ask you how you knew it was Claudia and not me who leaked the photographs."

She gives me a surprised look. "I can't believe you'd think I'd accuse you."

"It looked like I was holding the smoking gun. I wouldn't blame you if you did."

"There were only four people who knew about the photos. You, me, my mother, and Claudia. As much as my mom wants to boost my career, she'd never stoop so low. The only one left was Claudia. She immediately pointed the finger at you. Wanted me to believe you leaked them. What she didn't know was how much you love me. I had faith in that. Our 'fake' relationship was more real than anything I've ever experienced before. When you love someone, you don't hurt them. You'd never hurt me. It only took a moment for everything to make sense. All the things that had happened in my life—the naked high school photos, Darren's video, the paparazzi always finding me when no one should know where I was, leaked stories—was all her doing. I made Claudia think I believed you did it so I could make a plan."

"What a sensational plan it was. You were amazing. I'm so proud of you," I say. She gives me a shy smile. I kiss her forehead. "I'm sorry for what she put you through. Will you be okay?"

Her eyes turn sad. "If I'm honest, I'm going to miss the friendship I thought we had. Even though it was all a lie, I feel like I've lost a friend. I know it sounds silly."

Holding her tighter in my arms, I say, "It's not silly. It will take time to heal from the loss. Just know I love you more than anything. I'm always here for you."

"I love you too."

As I lean over to kiss Penny, a loud knocking comes from the front door.

"Who could that be?" Penny asks.

I blow out a frustrated breath. I have a pretty good idea. My family are the only people Samuel lets up to my apartment without warning me first. "We better get dressed. My brothers are here."

Penny's eyes widen. "Now? It's late."

"They don't care." I get up and grab sweatpants and a t-shirt from the closet. Penny quickly gets dressed in jeans and a pale blue shirt.

Hand in hand, we make our way to the living room, knowing the knock on the door was a warning that they'd arrived. Hayden, Alyssa, Finn, Harper, and Elizabeth now have made themselves comfortable in the living room.

"What the hell are you doing here?" I aim the question at my grinning brothers.

"We thought since you left the party, we'd bring the party to you," Finn explains.

"Plus, we've paid for a babysitter for another two hours, so we're making the most of it," Harper adds.

"Did you ever think you were intruding?" I already know what their answer will be. They don't give a fuck.

Hayden shrugs. "Nope. By the way, we've ordered pizza."

I shake my head with mock disgust. Beside me, Penny giggles.

Finn goes to the bar and pours drinks.

"Help yourself," I grumble.

Finn lifts his glass in a toast. "We will. Now, what can I get for the ladies?"

They give him their orders, and he gets busy making cocktails like he's in some swanky bar.

Elizabeth pulls Penny aside but not out of earshot. "Sweetheart. Are you okay?"

"I am," she says with confidence.

That's my girl. She won't let anything break her.

"I can't believe what that witch did to you," Elizabeth says. "I'm shocked and disgusted. How did I not see who she really is?"

Penny places her hand on Elizabeth's shoulder. "You're not the only one. I spent nearly every day with her, and I never saw the snake she really is."

"Well, good riddance to her." She holds onto Penny's hands. "Sweetheart, the photos were beautiful. You looked stunning. You *are* stunning." Tears shimmer in Penny's eyes. Elizabeth pulls her in for a hug. "I'm so proud of you."

When they break away, both women are wiping the corners of their eyes. "Thanks, Mom."

Elizabeth joins the party, and I put my arm over Penny's shoulder, pulling her close. She places a hand on my chest. My heart beats with so much love for her surely she can feel it against her palm.

Penny is my life.

I never knew what happiness was until she came back into it.

"Are you ready for this, Pixie?"

She tilts her face up to me. "Ready for what?"

I nod toward my brothers and sisters-in-law. "Them. Us. You're a part of it now. You're my family, and they come with it."

A tear slides down her cheek, and I swipe it away with my thumb, leaving my hand to cup her face.

She smiles brightly. "I couldn't think of a better place to be."

Epilogue

Two months later

PENNY

"I now pronounce you husband and wife. You may kiss your bride," the celebrant announces just as the sun kisses the tops of the mountains, throwing the sky into an array of pink, orange, and violet.

The fairy lights strung from the tree branches reflect in Lucas' eyes as he curves his arm around my waist, dips me, and places a long kiss on my lips. Our family and friends all cheer. My heart soars.

This man is mine, and I am his.

Forever.

He places a quick peck on the tip of my nose. "My wife."

The words cause goosebumps to explode over my skin. I've never been so happy. "My husband."

Soon we're surrounded by our guests, congratulating us with kisses and hugs. The band starts playing the song for the first dance, and Lucas takes me by the hand and leads me to the makeshift dance floor in a clearing by the cabin. We sway to the beat of the music, chest to chest, with my arms hooked around his neck.

"This is the best wedding you've ever planned." Lucas smiles down at me.

"Of course it is. Because it's ours. I only wish you'd given me longer than two months to organize everything. I could have done more."

After the night of Lucas' exhibition and my photos being displayed, my reputation skyrocketed. Once again I was talked about in a good light. Job offers were pouring in from the most famous and prestigious people. Talk show hosts wanted me on their show. Book deals were being thrown my way. None of it was important anymore. I turned them all down. It's the small weddings, baby showers, and other more personal events that have my juices flowing. Moments like the one I'm having with Lucas is what I want to create for people.

We decided to marry in the woods by the cabin. It's the perfect location. This is where our love started. I couldn't think of a better place.

Lucas pulls me close. "You're lucky I gave you two months. If it were up to me, I would have whisked you away to marry you the day I proposed. Now you're going to make it up to me for making me waiting so long." He grins at me with a sparkle in his eyes.

"Oh, how might I do that?"

"Let me show you." Taking my hand, he leads me off the dance floor.

Over my shoulder, I glance at the people on the dance floor. "Where are you taking me? We have guests. We can't just leave them."

"We won't be long. Everyone is busy dancing and drinking. They won't miss us."

Now that the sun has set completely, we follow the pale moonlight deeper into the woods until Lucas stops and pushes me up against a tree.

Leaning into me, he nuzzles his face in my neck. "I couldn't wait a moment longer to touch you."

"We have plenty of time after the reception, and for the rest of our lives," I weakly protest. In fact, I'm thrilled he's pulled me away, because seeing him in his tuxedo has made me weak at the knees. When he hooks my leg around his waist and grinds his erection against me, I swallow hard.

"I want to start our married life off with a bang." Lucas cups my breast, and there's no mistaking what he means, and I arch into him.

My body quivers with wanting. Thankfully, my wedding dress is loose enough to bunch at my waist, allowing him to glide his hand up my thigh and between my legs. When he gets to my panties, he pulls them aside and pushes a finger inside me. My head falls back on the rough surface of the tree. I squeeze my eyes shut, my hips rocking back and forth.

Needing more of him, I unbuckle his belt with frantic fingers, then unbutton and unzip his trousers. Sliding my hand behind his underwear, I take hold of his erection and stroke him from root to tip.

His head falls onto my shoulder as he pumps into my hand. "Oh God, Pixie. I can't wait a second longer. I need to be inside you now," he moans.

"I need you too."

He doesn't bother removing my panties; they're light and lacey, and he rips them off. With one hard push, he's buried deep inside me. My breath catches as our eyes lock.

"I love you, Penny."

"I love you. I always will." My eyes mist with tears.

As he drives into me, I don't feel the bark against my back and what it's doing to my dress and hair. I'm too caught up in the moment to care.

All I feel is Lucas.

As the tension builds between us, he presses a finger against my clit, and I go soaring, crying my release into the night. "Lucas!" The pleasure rips through me. A second later he's joining me as our bodies quiver and shake from our orgasm.

He drops my leg to the ground, and we hold each other as we get our breaths back. When we pull away, Lucas takes in my appearance and chuckles. "You have something stuck in your hair." He plucks out a few twigs.

The carefully placed up-style has come tumbling down around my shoulders. The back of my dress is snagged to the tree. I'm sure there is a lot of damage to the delicate fabric. None of that matters. Only this moment does.

"You know, I have another exhibition in six months. I can run and get my camera from the cabin. If you remove your dress, I can take more photos of you. They'd make the perfect addition to my collection." Lucas' exhibition did so well, he's exploring his photography outside of Alessi Fashion and putting on more shows. I'm so proud of the work he's creating.

I playfully punch him on the arm. "Not a chance. That was a one-time deal. Just like this marriage."

Lucas brushes the hair back from my face and kisses me. When we break apart he gives me the sexiest grin. "You're stuck with me forever."

My heart fills with so much love for this man. My man. "Forever isn't long enough."

Acknowledgements

Firstly, I'd like to thank my loving family, Tom, Jaime, Ryan and Leah. They continually show me love and support and they are my number one fans. A huge thank you to TL Swan and the Cygnet Inkers. The ladies in this group are amazing and always have an answer to my many questions. To my wonderful beta readers thank you for taking the time to read Unbreakable. I'm so grateful for your feedback and praise.

Finally to my wonderful readers. I'm so thrilled and grateful you read my books. Thank you from the bottom of my heart. xx

About Sonia Stanizzo

Sonia Stanizzo is a contemporary romance author living in the beautiful south coast of New South Wales, Australia with her husband and three children. When she's not dreaming up stories about couples and their road to finding love, sometimes bumpy but always a lot of fun, she can be found taking pole dancing lessons, reading and writing.

Thank you so much for reading Unbreakable. I hope you enjoyed meeting Lucas and Penny and loved them as much as I loved writing them.

Say Hello!

Want to follow me on social media? Follow me here:

Facebook: facebook.com/soniastanizzowriter

Instagram: instagram.com/soniastanizzowriter

Ticktock: ticktok.com/@soniastanizzowriter

Sonia's Website: soniastanizzo

Sonia's email: soniastanizzo@gmail.com

Join my newsletter for free books, new releases and giveaways:

Newsletter

www.ingramcontent.com/pod-product-compliance
Lightning Source LLC
Chambersburg PA
CBHW030606120726
47904CB00006B/1787